Night Without Time

Kieran York

Scarlet Clover Publishers

Littleton

Cover and interior design: Beth Mitchum
Editor: Rogena Mitchell-Jone
Front cover photo: Kieran York
Back cover photo: Brenda Starr

Published by Scarlet Clover Publishers
www.kieranyork.com
P.O. Box 621002
Littleton, Colorado 80162

Printed and bound in the United States of America, UK, and
Europe
ISBN-13: 978-0692287668
ISBN-10: 0692287663

Night Without Time

Kieran York

Books also written by Kieran York:

Earthen Trinkets
Careful Flowers
Appointment with a Smile
Crystal Mountain Veils (A Royce Madison Mystery)
Timber City Masks (A Royce Madison Mystery)
Sugar With Spice (Short Fiction)
Blushing Aspen (Poetry)

Touring Kelly's Poem (forthcoming fiction)

Dedicated with Love to Clover York
– The Princess Among Us

Time, like money, is measured by our needs.
- George Eliot, *Middlemarch* (1871)

ACKNOWLEDGEMENTS

How can I not *always* acknowledge Beth Mitchum? My friend and mentor – I thank her for her encouragement, collaboration, and for keeping me stabilized. She is incredible.

I thank my editor, Rogena Mitchell-Jones. Professional, a gifted grammarian, and fun. Rogena is also a wonderful friend.

I thank my friend, Shawn Marie Bryan, for building my amazing new website. I'm fortunate she's my friend. Shawn Marie is terrific – whatever she's doing. We invite you to check out the Scarlet Clover website at:
www.scarletcloverpublishers.com

I thank all of my friends and my family – ever-supportive – and I am indebted to each of you for kindness and love.

Chapter 1

The quest for accuracy brings about complexity.

How would the unexpected, and *sudden*, fortune be divvied up?

My family was a knot that always resisted being untied. We were a family of women, and our ingredients rarely blended. Before my grandmother died, she called my sisters and me a trilogy of sisters amiss. One might ask about the goodwill of the feminine heart, but we had enough sibling rivalry to go around the world – often and quickly. The goodwill deal took a backseat.

Determining how the fortune was to be shared wouldn't be easy in my family. Nothing had ever been easy. Expected or otherwise. No one was comfortable. Unexpected or otherwise. That was the Brent family reality.

My family of three sisters and a mother was way too discordant. I was in the center of my siblings. My sisters and I have a tangled throwback set of genes. Our mom is a spunky, irascible mother. We had no idea how similarly we'd been authored by our DNA.

Our roles as culprits and accomplices were constantly changing and rearranging. If there was really familial love – were we too busy or too disinterested to notice? Difficult to determine, I considered.

I knew we would all need to take time to sort – to ponder – how we felt. We were now tied together by a fortune. This was a life-changing day! My grandmother would have said that a bombshell had been dropped.

Well, actually, Grandma had two favorite sayings. Don't play *puppies* with an old dog. And be like a butterfly – go where you please and please where you go. Although they had very little to do with whatever point Grandma was trying to make – she fit them in as if they were tailor-made for the topic at hand.

Reflecting on the days – well, actually, years – leading up to this one day was difficult. There were patchworks of discomfort. From the time I was a very small girl, grasping at memories was difficult for me. The household was volatile. Not frighteningly so, but in an unsettling way.

I recalled wishing to be saved from harshness – all the jealously of sibling rivalry. TV ads had filled my childhood brain with happy endings, gleeful events, and sharing familial joy. We three sisters had become women threaded together within the weave of time. We each smuggled our own dreams.

Now, a dream larger than any of us ever expected had come true. What happens when an unforeseen treasure suddenly appears? How, I wondered, would it change us? We would each be drawing our histories from different databases. That meant I would need to be resigned to the intrigue of quarrels.

This sudden fortune would most probably be the cause of our fighting like a trio of tigresses. Not that we needed another dumpling in the soup – we already fought at a regular clip. When we would, our mother would say our brains were never finished – and she held little hope that the completion of those brains would ever pull us into civility.

I looked down at Littleton, Colorado earth. Lifting my foot, I saw the scuff on my sports shoe that was caused by hitting a clod of dirt beneath. "Aw, damn!" I howled with an accompanying grumble.

"Language, Vicky!" Isabel Sullivan exclaimed. My elder sister, Isabel – the eldest of the three Brent daughters, constantly corrected my younger sister's and my language. She thought our mouths needed emissions licenses. "As I was saying before your outburst, Leandra is a heartless bitch!"

"My language!" I commented as I looked around the neatly groomed backyard. I'd spent much of my childhood and adolescence in the garden of our family home. The ground beneath the thirty by thirty square garden was darker with each year's additive of nutrients. Buckling up from the soil were rows of mid-summer produce.

Maybe the reason I enjoyed Colorado winters was that I disliked the garden area.

It was near the 1930s home's backyard garden where the accident had happened when I was a child. I've never passed by the path where my life changed without having great remorse. My guilt was a guilt so overwhelming that it often squeezed my heart until breathing became difficult. When I caught my breath, it was with a huge gulp and an enormous pang. There was a void inside my ribcage.

For years, my culpable emotion was hidden – internalized. I knew I was to blame for all the family's turmoil and unhappiness. Even now, as a grown woman approaching thirty-eight years of age, it weighed me down.

I squinted back at my older sister. I wished I'd been born an only child. Or not at all.

Isabel's glare was fired up. Mid-afternoon made both of us tired and irritable. We'd had a very productive, busy morning. Now Isabel leaned nearer to me in a conspiratorial motion.

"Vicky, Lea will have her paws out begging when she finds out about Momma's little windfall. Well, not such a *little* windfall."

Ours was a paycheck to paycheck family. Paper money was never a small deal.

And now this! When a shocker comes up, my mind becomes crowded. I experienced a percolating group of thoughts.

I answered, "But the money is Momma's to do with what she will."

"That kind of money is too much for her to even begin to know what to do with! I read in women's magazines what purchasing power is. Why, it's a queen's ransom. All for an old trinket we assumed was a piece of junk."

"Yep, it is truly a wad of money."

Isabel's words rushed, more so now than when she was a child, and they clipped right along then. Even in her early adult years, she spoke faster than most everyone else in the family heard. "My house is tidy, but aged. It's getting a little shabby. It could use remodeling. With Tad graduating from high school, we definitely need extra money. We've been saving in his college fund for years now. But it is meager. Adequate finances would give him a chance for a better life."

"Let him work for college the way I did," I said with an accompanying grimace. "And maybe Momma won't tell Leandra about the money – the treasure."

"That's right. Momma knows that Lea would be the first of us with hands out. Paws, then claws out," she said with a certain tip to her head. Isabel gave a mischievous snort. "Lea's fingernails are certainly claws."

Momentarily, I frowned before uttering, "Sure, Lea wants money. But we all wouldn't mind a little infusion of cash." Pausing, I bit my lip. "Okay, suppose Lea doesn't find out about the money? Momma isn't stupid. She knows what Lea is capable of doing, so she might want us to keep a lid on information about the windfall."

Isabel's eyes shifted, darting back to the kitchen's backdoor in search of our mother, Willa. Isabel and I were both aware that Willa Brent usually snuck up on us for the expressed purpose of information gathering. In a shushed voice, Isabel said, "Momma has never kept her mouth shut about anything having to do with good news." Her phrasing teamed with disapproval. "Mind you, she's never had many good times."

"Isabel, there are things you couldn't get out of Momma for the world. And you know what I'm referring to." I knew Isabel would chastise my statement.

"Vicky!" Isabel's short, stocky frame leaned back. Her hands clamped to hefty hips as she rocked. "Momma keeps quiet on some family secrets. But maybe she doesn't consider this a family secret or any other kind of secret."

"Look, don't sweat it. We'll tell Momma that it would be best to keep it between the three of us until things settle down and decisions are made. Then tell Lea."

Isabel again nearly whispered in her best collusive utterance. "When the TV program airs, how do you expect to keep it from her?"

"Lea's never watched a PBS program in her life. What makes you think she's going to be channel surfing and see Momma's ten minutes of fame with her old sundial on *Antiques Roadshow?*"

"Someone is sure to tell her. A neighbor. A church member. Momma's church friends always watch the show. And by now, she's probably called the entire congregation. Even if she hasn't, someone she knows will call to say they saw it. It's going to come out when the show airs." Isabel gave a greatly tormented sigh.

"Like I said, we can convince Momma to wait until after her decision. Unless the newspapers hear of it and do a feature." I frowned. "Shit, I hadn't thought about that."

"Vicky Brent, please, please, watch that garbage mouth. Talk that way in front of your friend, but not me. Even Charlene doesn't approve."

A chuckle escaped. "You gonna sic the cuss cops on me?" I crossed my arms. "And Charlene and I are *friends*. But we are also in a committed relationship. Partners, significant others, lesbian lovers, and Sapphics – are all words to name us. Besides, we're going to marry."

Disgust covered Isabel's face. She spit out the words, "Same-kind marrying! The less said about that, the better. Tad shouldn't be hearing such talk. And Tad doesn't want the fact that his aunt has a female lesbian lover getting out all over town."

"Isabel, lesbians are female. You're being redundant." I smirked. "And besides, Tad can make my expletives sound like Sunday school." I genuinely loved my eighteen-year old nephew, Tad. The quiet young man was nothing like his mother. He had is father's easy going way. Isabel harbored grudges and reeked of pious intolerance.

Mostly, she resented anything positive that came her younger sisters' way. Yet, I considered, there was some good-heartedness in Isabel when she was winning. It seemed a dichotomy. When either Lea or I've been in trouble, she's tried to stand by us. It was only when life elevated either of us younger siblings that Isabel began her sniping campaign.

"My son should not have to apologize for his aunt's immorality. Living such a life with a…"

"Lesbian? Sapphic? A *woman* lesbian? A lesbian is a woman." It amused me to think of how difficult the word was for Isabel to say. "Lesbian. Let the words roll over your tongue, Isabel."

"You know Sully and I don't approve of you, but we've come to accept."

With joviality, I answered, "Sure! You say the word 'lesbian' and it looks like you're spewing out a mouthful of vinegar and pickles. You hate that I'm Sapphic. But Sully has always accepted. From the day I came out."

"My husband is one of the finest men the good Lord placed down on this earth. We love the sinner and hate the sin. That's what we do." She wrung her hands tightly as if massaging them.

Isabel, like so many of her ilk, knew how to separate sins and sinners.

Covering my eyes, I let out a huge groan. "Sully isn't as pretentious when it comes to sin." I considered Sully to be both brother-in-law and friend. Sully, the poor devil.

I was aware that when I was at my happiest after having found a woman who became my soul mate, my sister resented the fact my lover was hugely successful. Considering her own husband had barely eked out a living, Isabel complained about placing too much importance on the almighty dollar.

Isabel and Patrick 'Sully' Sullivan had begun dating when Isabel was seventeen and Sully a year older. It was convenient that they'd been raised in the neighborhood. Both families considered it a pleasant match. Luckily, Lea and I both felt as if Sully was our brother.

Suddenly, from the side of the fence, we heard a ruckus. "Derwin!" The pitch was agitated and the voice alarmed. It was Dottie Wake's squealing scream of anger. "Where is that little fucker?"

We recognized Dottie's inebriated call for her nine-year old son, Derwin. Watching as she attempted to open the gate, Isabel and I shook our heads. "We're back here," I greeted Dottie.

"Is your mom around?" Dottie's bullhorn voice questioned – demanded. She scoured the backyard. She was in her early-forties. Her huge body and face had once been fit and desired. She was nearly six-feet tall. She'd packed on enough pounds to make her look huskier than many male wrestlers. I guessed that she'd had a testosterone overload – a filled hypo-injection – somewhere along the line. Her gladiator sandals didn't help refute that. Now her dyed black hair hung like fringe over her shoulder. Her scrolled face was smudged with makeup that had needed to be removed days ago. In a decade, she'd gone from femme fatale to monster.

After not seeing Dottie for nearly the past five years, my sister Lea described her as lowdown and tacky.

"She's inside," I answered Dottie. "Derwin is probably following after some of the neighborhood kids."

"I tell him to stay home," she defended herself. "There are rotten kids out there. I tell Derwin if you park yourself under an asshole, you get nothing but shit."

She was clearly loaded up on booze. She was in her chatterbox stage of drunkenness.

"What in the world is all this shouting?" Willa Brent asked as she burst through the backdoor. She had been changing into one of her gardening outfits. A floppy hat covered her head, and very long shorts and baggy shirts dressed her body. Her gardening attire was completed with an old pair of heavy-duty hiking boots. The screen door swung away from her as if it were punched backward. Momma repeated, "Dottie, what're you going on about?"

"Damn kid, always missing." Dottie glared. "You Brent women encourage him."

"Stop your caterwauling this moment," Momma's voice yelled. "Your kid comes over here hungry. We give him a meal and a little chat. You're drunk, so just back off."

Momma didn't mind screaming back at Dottie, especially when Dottie was out of her brain drunk.

Dottie tottered a moment. "My kid went missing."

Willa Brent's small stature, thinly designed, was no match for the gargantuan-sized frame of Dorothea Wake. Momma was used to interceding in school fights. She had worked for the grade school's cafeteria for nearly thirty-five years. Hands combed through her brown, greying hair. Her usually pale complexion had tanned some. Her brown eyes snapped. "My daughters are getting ready to leave now, and they'll look for him."

Placated for the moment, Dottie asked, "All three of 'em gonna be looking?"

"These two. I don't know where Lea is."

"Better keep track of her or she's gonna be back in the slammer."

"Go home. Sober up. And leave my family to me," Momma clamored. Her scowl was poised to turn into a battle.

Dottie recognized it and left quietly. As soon as she'd turned to go home, Isabel approached our mother. "Momma, Vicky and I were thinking about Lea."

Momma's mouth contorted a moment. "I just told Derwin's Momma you two would look for him. So go. There's plenty of time to talk later." She wiggled her fingers, scooting us on our way. "Go. See if you can find him. I hate when Derwin goes missing."

After Isabel obediently exited the gate, I hung back. "I just need to talk with you a couple minutes."

"Victoria Lee, march!" Momma's shrug staunchly-lifted into the shoulders of a general. "Move, Vicky. You know Isabel will have a little moan if you aren't right behind her."

Dejectedly, I turned. I figured I would first check at Arlen's Pump 'n Pop Shop. It was where Derwin usually went. The twenty-four hour gas and convenience store was on the corner of a nearby, somewhat dingy, strip mall.

Between the house and my vehicle, I muttered, "Rats!" I looked up at the rope of pewter-colored clouds that seemed to be lurching across the sky. There were always a couple summer weeks in Colorado that provided afternoons with high-power thunderstorms. We seemed to be entering their power surge – or so predicted the clumping clouds.

If that wasn't apropos for the goings-on, I considered. I could sense that there would be trouble when it came to asking Momma to leave Lea out of the information loop.

My drive toward Arlen's was pensive. I hated going anywhere without a reason. But my petrol tank was filled, and there wasn't anything I needed from the small convenience store. Other than the fact that I might locate the oft-missing kid. Derwin might be hanging out hoping that Arlen would pop for a soft drink. Arlen often did just that. He felt sorry for Derwin, too.

Derwin was called a *special needs* kid. I just referred to him as a special kid. One that I had to help round up once in a while. I hoped I'd find him safe with Arlen – getting a free soft drink.

I might even find Lea there.

Chapter 2

Slamming my vehicle's door, I looked up to see Leandra's sultry walk toward the convenience store. For several moments, I watched. If anyone does – I know most of my younger sister's thoughts. When we were growing up, we shared not only a bedroom, but we shared nighttime stories – dreams of what we might become. Every dream was whispered to one another and to the night.

Leandra Brent was a part of my story. Part of why my soul was never tranquil. Not since the accident. It was as if Lea existed within me.

Lea was a guileless Venus in denim, who believed that the core of her own heart might become a sunburst. For years, she had been told as much by invisible lovers. Years of breath burning away like magic vapors, quivers that dialed her heart, along with whispered promises, had directed her toward the small chunks of confidence she had left within.

But love, Lea considered, was very much like she was. She was life's lost luggage. There was precious little appreciation for missing suitcases unless you're the matching traveler. Where romance was concerned, she never seemed to correspond to anyone. Where living was concerned – she never appeared to coordinate with anything.

Lea was currently looking for a job. She'd reported back to me. She confided that she might never find work. Lea carried index cards in her oversized handbag. Most of the cards had huge slashes of ink crossing over the writing. She'd heard all the reasons why she couldn't be given a job. Don't let the door hit you where the good Lord split you, one woman had cackled. No room at the inn, Lea had replied as she slammed the employment office's door behind her.

There weren't many jobs for a felon – especially a woman finding it difficult to believe there might be a position available.

Low self-esteem was a Brent family byproduct. It had been carefully passed down from generation to generation. *Self-praise doesn't go far.* That was the Brent mantra. The crisis of self-forgiveness was rampant in our background. Magazine articles talked about the loss of dignity. My family never encouraged thoughts about dignity – or other behaviorally reassurances.

However, Lea had argued, too much modesty and self-deprecation got her nowhere. That was the place she currently resided – emotionally. Physically, her place was at our mother's home in Littleton, Colorado. Littleton, a suburb southwest of Denver, was as complicated as Leandra's family.

Littleton began with an older, central area. This core community was where the Brent family lived and had lived for all three of our lives – as well as our mother's life.

Just as the Brent family had expanded – so had Littleton, Colorado, USA. There were now great areas of elegant, expensive houses in new developments that had continued to crop up week after week. These additions were added to the quaint and charming older Western-styled interior of the town.

Imbedded within Littleton – also within the Brent family – was an almost apologetic symbol of new mingling with old. Both shouted mea culpa for the rustic, as well as the newly developed areas. The Brent family's progress was somewhere between stagnant and minuscule. No one named Brent had ever made a fortune, or progressed – until now.

Lea and I couldn't be certain if the lack of confidence came from our family never exerting an effort to complement one another. Yet, both Isabel and I had seemed to make our way in the world. Of the three female siblings, Lea was at the tail end of the brood and of the goodwill. Instead of the traditional 'babying' thrust upon many youngest children, she was perceived as little more than a troublesome afterthought in everyone's mind. At least this remained her perception for the last three and a half decades.

Lea had told me that she couldn't help wondering what kind of dismal future she had carved for herself from her yesterdays. That remained to be seen, I mused while crossing the parking lot. Lea's concerns were not reflected by her gait. Her tall shapely form dictated a certain elegant carriage.

I studied my younger sister. Leandra got the looks. Her features seemed to have been drawn from an eighteenth-century cameo. She formed her long, sun-streaked curls around her face with flourish and style. Her face was exquisite in silhouette showing its right side. Along one side was a high cheekbone with a lightly creamy complexion. When she turned, her classic loveliness was interrupted by a scar along the length from beneath her hazel eyes to her jaw line.

Although she deftly applied cosmetics to improve the gashed left side of her face, there was no hiding it from view. Her earliest recollections were of adults whispering the word 'hideous' behind her back. And the children she encountered were usually transfixed at first. Then it formed into a *shocked* stare – rather blank and yet filled with both curiosity and repugnance. However, she mostly despised their pity when viewing the horrendous caving web of lacerations on her cheek.

Lea had promised herself she would have reconstructive surgery done before reaching thirty-five. But she had also made that promise to herself when she was approaching twenty-five and thirty. Thirty – that was the promise that had cost her dearly. It had definitely not worked out. It was the cause of her incarceration.
I believed I was to blame for her accident, which meant I was also to blame for her being imprisoned.

Although Lea had rationalized that her older sisters had all the advantages, she knew it wasn't an excuse for her actions. So she was weighted down with guilt, too. Lea had firmly believed that her two elder sisters were her mother's little darlings.

Our father had skipped immediately after Lea's birth. He was never to be seen again. Isabel and I didn't allow Lea to forget that he'd vanished so quickly after her birth. It must have had something to do with Lea. We'd all suspected a reason as to why he'd bolted so rapidly. We knew early on that *circumstance* causes errors in life.

Our mother, Willa Brent, never disputed that there might have been justification. She did not reject, nor contest, the possibility of

Kieran York

indiscretion on either parent's part. She remained staunch. It had not been her daughter's fault that her husband hightailed it.

Willa Brent never again mentioned our father to us after his exit. When questioned, a shrug of her shoulders was her answer. Her husband, Simon Brent, had booked. That was that.

With her three small daughters, Willa moved in with her widowed mother. Grandma Isabella Victoria Donnell took my family in with great relish and delight. That old home in an older neighborhood became the home of three generations.

It was a den of women, they'd joked. Lea felt strangely that the joke was on her. If not for her being born, perhaps there would be a father figure. That provider would have cared for his wife and two daughters. One thing was for certain. Lea was different enough from us to be excluded. She looked nothing like any of our family. She experienced childhood exclusion. Yet it was a lid that carefully was clamped when the conversation skirted the issue.

I recognized that Leandra's inclination was definitely pacifistic in nature. She had been the victim. She wore the scars.

"Job hunting?" I quizzed as she strutted toward Arlen's store.

"Checking up on me?" Lea gave a toss of her head.

"Momma sent me looking for Derwin. Dottie came over screaming about him being lost."

"Dottie doesn't give a flip about him. She gets a little extra from the state because Derwin is slow. Too bad they don't give extra for being gay."

My lips tightened like a pulled-apart rubber band. "First, being gay and lesbian isn't a special needs thing. Second, the kid is only nine. I'm not certain if he understands the concept. Maybe he never will. He's probably not gay."

"You'd know." As we entered, Lea pointed toward the candy aisle. "Problem solved." She nodded to Derwin. "How are you, honey?"

Derwin smiled shyly as his bronze eyes examined her. Slightly slim – in a weakly way, and uncoordinated, he drifted from foot to foot. A wooden motion was part of his stance and his gait. The handsome biracial youth was short for his age, and his angular face had an immature child-like quality.

19

His dress was standard – shorts covered his stick-like legs, a brightly colored yellow tee-shirt, and tennis shoes. His well-worn outfits were often smudged and torn. Dottie always called his second-hand store clothing his play clothes. Momma often supplemented his wardrobe with things she found at the discount stores – her favorite shopping experiences.

"I'm fine. Do you like it outta jail?" he stammered.

We both laughed. Lea answered, "Just sprung last month, so I'm getting used to it. I like anywhere better than jail."

I knew Leandra well enough to know the thought produced an addendum. Leandra thought she even liked living in the basement bedroom of her mother's house better than being incarcerated.

Derwin's trembling smile broke into a laugh. Although he was only turning five-years of age when Lea was incarcerated, both Derwin and Lea realized their closeness was a bond from some strange element of human fascination.

People stared at him because of his effeminate ways, as well as the somewhat obvious disability of slowed, staggering words. They stared at Lea because of the scar on her cheek. Both were aware people felt pity for them. What a lovely girl – but too bad about the side of her face. What a handsome youngster – but too bad he's mentally challenged.

Lea and Derwin understood one another's unique qualities. Before prison, when the boy Derwin visited the Brent household, he was drawn to Lea. They would joke that he followed her like a puppy. Their mirror reflection was birthed of anguish, or perhaps torment.

There was recognition about how both Derwin and Lea reined in their tempers. It was evident that they wanted to shout into the faces that stared at them. They wanted to defend themselves. Derwin wanted to scream that he couldn't help being *behind.* And Lea wanted to scream that her face was the result of an accident. A terrible accident that she'd never fully understood. She'd only been two-years old, and unable to even recall brief bits of the day of wild emotions. There was nothing definite, other than what she'd been told about it.

Both Lea and Derwin shared the pain of uninvited experience. They were spectacles of sympathy, and perhaps that hurt most of all.

"You gotta go back to jail?" he questioned with halting speech.

"No, Derwin. Prison is in my past. I'll never go back." Her jaw set with stalwart determination. "Never," she repeated.

"We got us lotsa changes around here."

"You've grown up, kid." Lea gave his chin a tap. "That's a big change."

Derwin grinned before saying, "Your grandma wasn't the only one who died last year."

"She wasn't?" Lea questioned.

"Naw," Derwin reported. "Mr. Tanovich died, too."

A pronounced grief washed over Lea's face. With sadness reflected in her voice, she uttered, "I used to love going into his music shop. He was always so sweet. When he played those guitars, the world seemed to stop to listen." Her words were immersed in sadness. In his late seventies, Eli Tanovich would take a guitar from the wall of his tiny music store and play classical music, and then finish with a mini pop rock concert.

"He died of heart," Derwin explained

"Heart attack," I entered into the conversation. "We haven't had much time to give you all the news of the past few years. Momma might not have mentioned it."

"She probably never even knew I liked old Mr. Tanovich," Lea said sullenly. The probable reason Lea hadn't made an attempt to visit him was her own shame. She hadn't wanted to go out much at all since returning home from prison. "It doesn't matter. I know now."

Derwin continued, "He wasn't so sick acting. One day he just slumped over. Anyway, now his son is come back from California. He was gonna sell stuff off, but then he decided to stay."

"I never knew his son," Lea said. Tanovich had moved his shop from downtown Denver – down on Broadway – about a decade ago. After experiencing a robbery, he'd decided to relocate to Littleton. He'd lived in a second-story apartment above his business. "He always said that his son was a musician on the West

Coast. He went to visit his kid a couple times, but his kid never showed up here. That I knew about."

Derwin sniffed a moment. "His son isn't nearly as nice as old Mr. Tanovich was."

Lea asked, "Why do you say that?"

"He runs us kids out of there like we're in the way. Not like his daddy."

"People aren't always as nice as their parents – or sometimes nicer." Lea's allowed her thoughts to drift a moment. Derwin had not only been cheated by his learning disability, but his single mother was a holy terror. "Well, I better get home. I've been job hunting all day long."

"What you gonna do?" Derwin inquired.

"I can do nails. Fix hair a little – that kind of thing. I'll take any legitimate job I can get."

I asked, "Have you checked with Gypsy yet? Momma has gone to Angelo's Beauty Salon for years."

I also knew Momma was reticent about her felon daughter working in the area.

"She told me not to bother Gypsy. She isn't hiring."

"She said Gypsy isn't hiring? She said that because she thinks you'll misbehave and embarrass her." My assumption held truth, and Lea knew it. "What the hell, Lea. The salon is nearby. And maybe Gypsy would actually take a chance on you." I encouraged, "Give it a try."

Leandra frowned briefly, contemplating the possibility. "She can always tell me no way." She paused. "Don't you think…" her question stopped as if the words died before they reached her lips.

"Go see Gypsy." I gave her shoulder a playful swat. "Get out there. There's a job with your name written on it." My voice was as enthusiastic as I could make it. "I need to deliver this little runaway back to his mother – so I'll see you back at the house. Good luck."

On our return ride home, Derwin's sing-song voice threaded through the radio songs. I parked in the driveway between the Brent and Wake homes. "Thanks for the ride," Derwin glumly spoke. "My mom is probably gonna scream at me."

"You can't be running off, Derwin. It's not good," I chastised. "Grown-ups need to know where kids are."

His nod was tucked in between defeat and acceptance. As I watched him, I wondered what would become of the shy kid. And I wondered what would become of my ex-con sister.

My lover, Charlene, had once mentioned that sometimes a ravaged soul couldn't come back. It was an uphill climb for a woman who had a felony. But Char also was encouraging by saying that the job market was beginning to look better. Outlook, I repeated her oft-stated word for grabbing fate by the balls.

The job market was tight enough. Times were never good for a woman with Lea's kind of past, but something good would come along.

For Leandra, it seemed like keeping her off the devil's payroll might be a tug of war.

But Leandra needed to be on some payroll.

Chapter 3

After watching Derwin's slouching walk up to the front entrance of his tattered home, I heard a whoosh and the slam of the door. Remaining was the sound of a shovel slamming into the back garden ground. As I approached the gate, I spotted Momma.

"Hi, Momma," I said, grabbing a pitchfork. I began to help her weed and aerate the garden. "Quite a day, huh?"

Momma stopped. She leaned against the shovel's handle. "It's a day I'll never forget, for a fact."

The image quickly cast over my mind.

The antique sundial had been haphazardly wrapped in the morning's newspaper and stuffed into a worn, tan cotton shopping tote. It had been presented in that way at the *Antiques Roadshow* appraiser's stall. Momma, Isabel, and I thought it strange when the appraiser called several others over to have a peek. They'd bunched around, whispering excitedly, and then began questioning Momma. The three of us knew relatively little about the heirloom. Other than, it was approximately fourteen inches high, brass colored, and seemed uninteresting to family members – me included. In fact, we thought it was one of the most unattractive possessions belonging to our grandmother – and now, our mother owned it.

For years, it sat on the top shelf of the curio cabinet without notice or concern. Correction, Lea was intrigued by it. She loved it. When she was a small girl, she was fascinated by the description of its ability to tell time by the setting of the sun.

Both Isabel and I were far more interested in laying claim to the seven Hummels than the tarnished old sundial.

Before we knew what was happening, Willa Brent of Littleton, Colorado, was under the bright lighting being taped with one of the appraisers. She sat across from the appraiser at a small table.

Strategically between them was the object of *interest*. It had never interested Momma before.

When questioned, Momma could tell only family history about the well-aged sundial. The earlier origin of the heavy chrome-colored disc was a mystery. Its later history was intact. It had been passed down from at least Momma's great-grandmother's time. Most of the family had come from Cornwall, England. Coal miners relocated to the hills of Colorado searching out silver and gold. The other side of her family had migrated through the Yorkshire area.

Upon arriving in the United States, her great-grandmother's family had settled in New York for a generation before her grandmother followed her grandfather to a homestead on the plains of Eastern Colorado. They'd had kin in the area. When grown, Momma's mother found her way to Denver, Colorado. There, Grandma Isabelle married, settled, and had a daughter.

The words used by the appraisers were dramatically emphasized and whirled in my mind. Bits of the conversation lifted – *the most extraordinary...never seen one as precise and elegantly engraved. Earliest seen. Astrolabe of Gothic type. Quatrefoil inscribed in rete. Gold.* Momma inhaled deeply as her dark eyes widened. Her light-medium complexion became rosier than usual. Her fingers combed through her thick, medium-trimmed hair, and she felt a tremble as he continued his discourse. *Circa mid-thirteen-hundreds – perhaps earlier or earliest. English. Museum quality. Amazing, simply amazing. Do you have any idea what it might be worth?* Momma's head rocked as she motioned that she had no earthly idea what the value might be.

Her small frame shook when its value was announced. She repeated, "Four-hundred thousand to five-hundred thousand at auction. On a good day, maybe upward of that sum. For insurance purposes, at least half a million dollars!" She could barely breathe. "You said *hundred thousand? Half million?*" The appraiser's grandiose smile gleamed as he replied affirmatively.

Still trembling, she clutched Isabel's hand and squeezed my waist. I was certain my mother had never felt such a lift of spirit. Of course, there was joy when we three were born. But she'd expected our arrival. This was tantamount to earth-shaking. For a moment, it was as though the planet had been jolted to its core.

It was even surreal when we drove home from the convention hall. I'd suggested that Momma securely tuck the sundial in a bank's safety deposit box. There it would be safely inserted into the mini-vault.

Our community bank was on the way home, so it was a wise idea to make certain it was secured. It was now the family's prized possession. As she placed her treasure inside the vault, Momma confessed to us that she was having one of the first selfish daydreams of her life. She was on a beach. It was sunny and wonderfully calm. Her heart was serene. Then the thought pinched. It was not the selfless treasure. The sunny beach was not solving world hunger, nor was it assisting with church matters.

Momma was into church – and selflessness. She may very well have dreamed about the ravages of blistering ole hell.

The vault door closed and she firmly locked it. The treasure was sheltered.

Now, as we looked into one another's faces, I wondered which of her daydreams she might be tending. I never knew, but then I wondered if we ever *understood* our parents. Was that possible?

Understanding is a form of loving. Certainly, I felt I understood Charlene. She had taken up permanent residence of my mind. It was her own place – sort of a grotto to her. I had granted her access to my brain's paths. I would always admit that the first part of our relationship – those dozen years ago – had been lust-driven. But we had laughter and the magnificence of never wanting to let go of one another's warmth.

Understanding Momma was different and always had been.

Momma looked over the rims of her sunglasses. "Glad you found Derwin. Not that Dottie will notice if he's back. At least I tried keeping track of you three. And when I was working, you had Grandma. Your grandmother would be so pleased about this sundial miracle."

I nodded, having witnessed my mother's momentary joy. Her face beamed across the garden at me. She appeared happy, yet haggard. Her life had been a rough edge. Although she had always attempted to bring civility to her family, it often seemed hopeless.

Adjudicating the problems of the three daughters had fallen exclusively into her lap now that her mother had died. Before, with her mother, she'd shared responsibility and had a fighting chance.

Before dying, Grandma Donnell had taken on much of the parental burden for all those many years. From the time we were young, Grandma took care of us. Momma worked to make ends meet. Grandma was the disciplinarian and the dispenser of approving pats on the head. When she died last year – in her mid-eighties – a great gap was generated. Grandma Donnell often said that if God hadn't gotten through to her granddaughters, what hope had she?

I suddenly summarized my last thought. "Momma, Grandma would be smiling."

"Yes, earlier I was thinking about your grandmother and what she'd think of all this," Momma spoke serenely – nearly piously, "and there's not an iota of doubt. She'd be approving."

"Grandma would be thrilled," I replied. I thought about that expression of my grandmother – when she was pleased – hers was an antique wax doll's glowing face.

"Finally, she'd have something to be happy about."

After sucking in a large breath, I stated, "Well, Grandma didn't seem unhappy."

"She had to have been, because none of us turned out the way she wanted us to."

"Momma, you've done fine. You've provided for us. Our father left, but that wasn't your fault." Momma's glance skittered to a vacant area of the yard.

"Well, none of us is how Grandma wanted. Simon left us. Sometimes our spirits build their own nests. And our bodies build different nests than our souls."

Mommy was a great mixer of metaphors – so I was lost on the *nest* thing. I skipped to my generation. "Lea had her troubles. My being lesbian didn't suit Grandma, but all in all, it went okay."

"She didn't want the family's dirty laundry flagging. She used to say keep the dirty linens at home in a private hamper. But Leandra made front-page news. And you didn't hide what you are."

"Why should I *hide* what I am?" My words were said with an edge.

Momma struck the shovel into the ground, taking a huge chunk out of the soil. "I recall her talk with you. She said she didn't like how you lived."

"She could be fussy," I mused. "Her favorite saying was 'always something and never nothing good.' Remember?"

Momma grinned with amusement and embarrassment. "All the time, yes."

"We always laughed at her grumpiness. But we loved her," I confessed.

"It's too late for regret." Momma glanced up at the sky. "The three of you are already baked into the cake. I don't see any of you becoming what your grandmother wanted you to be. We all disappointed her in some way or another."

Obstreperously, I'd proclaimed to my grandmother that being lesbian was not dirty laundry. Grandma gave an indignant grunt, and then told me she would love me no matter what. But that she took no pride in her granddaughter's decision to take up with a bunch of lesbians.

Five years ago, when Leandra was sentenced to eight years in the women's house of corrections, Grandma's heart was broken. Not only because her grandchild had failed, but she, herself, had in some way failed in Leandra's upbringing. It was a terrible blow. Grandma had always preached about keeping one's hands off other people's property.

She hadn't lived to see Lea get out after serving five years – the other three years were time off for good behavior. That might have made Grandma somewhat happy – but hardly deliriously so.

When Isabel accused her youngest sister, Lea, of tainting the family's name, and had announced that she felt like withdrawing from the family, Grandma insisted she remain. Hold the family together no matter what transpired, she demanded.

I looked up when I heard my older sister's voice 'yoo-hooing.'

The gate flapped open, and Isabel rushed through. She obviously hadn't wanted to miss anything. "I'm glad Derwin was found, but maybe he needs to be in foster care."

"That might not be better," I commented.

As if remembering something, Momma slapped her leg. "Did you two stop by just to reminisce?"

"Isabel and I were talking about maybe not saying anything to Lea right away."

"Why would I not say anything to Lea?" Momma questioned.

"It might be better not to mention the appraisal of the sundial," Isabel chimed in. We always attempted to tread carefully so we wouldn't upset Momma. She was easily *mortified*.

Momma had plenty to be mortified about. Her husband ran out on her. When I came out to her – it was a mortification over-spill. And when Lea's little upset with the law happened – well, Momma was off-the-charts mortified. The two things we never encouraged was Momma becoming livid or mortified.

Momma's heartfelt sigh was one of objection mixed with a sturdy pouncing of anger. She thought of what her own mother would say now. "Let me get this straight. You want me to lie to Lea? You want me to deceive my own daughter?" Her exhalation was an explosion. "I knew when you two were huddled together earlier that you were up to no good. You want Lea to be excluded all together. We'd have us a lie on our conscience."

"No, Momma, not lie," Isabel rushed her words. She lacked the poise of a debutante. "Just don't go out of your way to tell her."

"And you," she said pointing in my direction, "buy into this scheme?" The question was rhetorical – but I felt the need to answer. Momma didn't give me time to think up an answer. "Well?"

"Until there's a definite plan...." My throat went dry as cornflakes. *Rats!*

"There isn't going to be a plan," Momma argued. "It's going to be my decision. As far as I can tell, you're a trio of broom riders. And the two worst of the lot aren't the one who spent time in the penitentiary."

"Of course," Isabel conceded. "I just want you to have time to think things over. It's just an idea – until your arrangements are made."

"Idea!" Momma challenged with her glower in full bloom. "For a fact, that idea is not only a dog that won't hunt, it's a dog that won't gnaw on a T-bone!" Caviling was not going to be tolerated when it came to the best break her family ever had. "I have three daughters. If we're on the gravy train, we're on together. If we're headed for a train wreck, we're also on the same danged track." Pain permeated the moment. It was invisible at first – it hid under the guise of anger. "You two little skulking rats are snots out of hell's nose!"

Isabel's head lowered. I looked away as I murmured, "Sorry, Momma."

Momma had no love of deceit wherever it selected to park itself. "Now I'm going out back to my lovely summer gardening. And both of you, remember this – it's hard to get one over on me. I know what you're up to. Don't try to keep up with a gazelle. You two can check out the CIA. Find out if they need a couple of covert, devious, little sneaks."

Isabel and I went back to the gate. I then turned and waved. "I'll call you tomorrow, Momma."

Under her breath Isabel said, "Well, that puts us in our place!"

"Did you catch that string of descriptions? Momma must be reading mysteries again."

"She buys whatever she finds at garage sales," Isabel corrected. "But she *loves* mysteries and garden books."

I glanced back at Momma. I heard her mutter, "Pipsqueaks."

She continued jabbing at stringy bindweed with a hearty slice of the well-worn hoe. She moved through the mounds of greenery with her dreams. She hadn't even realized she'd forgotten to put on her tattered gloves. For the first time in her life, my mother must not have cared if her hands were clean.

Chapter 4

I'm not Renaissance woman material. I'm just not. Rather than say how 'goodness' wins out, I insist that every dog has its day. And bitches usually get an extra few days thrown in for good measure.

I'm optimistic, yes, but I realize the Sisyphean way of life. Living in the rough and tumble – rugged pioneer state of Colorado shows a person very large stones and very high mountains. Of course, I'm not fully aware of eternity's map, but once in a while, when observing my family, I get the entry-level humor of it all. Yet part of the joke is that life and altitude is as rocky as the mountains.

Charlene Webster and I have the common denominator of humor. Her special name for those who rankled her is *jockstrap*. Difficult situations or people would usually bring out her little song – here a jockstrap, there a jockstrap, everywhere a jockstrap. She would put up her skank fortification. Her stance was daunting. She disliked the jocks that hit on her. She disliked those dispensing bull.

Although Charlene could be 'particular' about people, she was the woman I loved more than anything. Her touch has always been real. I always yearn for her – for the feel of her. The elegance of her was always alluring. I cherished her so.

I was just entering my vehicle, and about to phone Charlene, when my cellphone chimed. Immediately, as if dialed by some premonition's force, I knew it was Isabel. Isabel instructed me to come to her home for a confab. When I began my excuse, my regrets, she just told me to shake a leg. Although it would make me late in getting back to my own apartment – and perhaps upset my sweet woman, I agreed.

Calling Charlene to tell her I would be an hour late getting home was always unpleasant. I reconsidered – she'd always call later anyway, so I delayed my call. I planned to hold off telling her of the day's news. Unless humor was attached, she was rarely interested in the Brent family's happenings. No matter what the drama, Charlene attempted to ignore it.

I unhappily drove to Isabel's small bungalow-style home.

Financially, Isabel and Patrick Sullivan had done marginally well in life. They'd successfully maintained their home, raised their son, and kept their marriage intact. From the beginning, Patrick, known as Sully, had been an exemplar husband with a difficult, demanding wife. He'd finally moved into lower management with the factory where he'd worked since graduating from high school. When he was elevated to a managerial job a few years ago, he never failed to make sure everyone knew it was *lower management.* Isabel wasn't crazy about that. She wanted everyone to know it was a very important promotion.

His own dreams had been pressed into the background, and he gave up on his hopes of becoming an auto mechanic. There were few motors he couldn't tame, but Isabel was his priority. His plight was a paycheck. His joy was his son, the car engines he was able to save, and stopping by to sip beer with his pals at the corner tavern. There was also the camaraderie of shooting pool and a bowling league to excite his mediocre competitiveness. His wife allowed him out of the house two nights a week.

Isabel considered her husband adequate. She knew that he had fallen in love with her thick, dark brown hair – which was now beginning to be salt and pepper, her somber sable-bronze eyes – which were now beginning to dull and were surrounded by soft crinkles of middle age, and her once petite figure, which was now becoming broad from what she for years had called her 'post-birth' syndrome weight gain.

Isabel had fallen in love with Sully's wavy red hair – which was now lighter and thinning, his piercing blue eyes – which were now tired and spectacled, and his tall, lanky body – which was now stooped and slightly potbellied. Although their union had changed, it had remained together. To both, marriage seemed tiring. Yet both were resigned to hang in there until death did them in.

Or whatever it was death did to break them up. I've never been one to hit the biblical quotes perfectly, but it never phased me. Either Momma or Isabel would be there to correct me. And if they weren't there – there was no reason to be all that precise.

Sully wasn't a *quoter* either. Often I thought Sully fantasized to cope. There were times when I could see a haze of longing in his tired eyes. Usually, however, that was when he was leaning over a car fender and was absorbed in fumbling with a rickety carburetor. So admittedly, he probably wasn't getting any sexual gratification – or sensual satisfaction. His dreams would never be expressed. They were hidden behind his metal-framed bifocals.

"You took your sweet time getting here," Isabel complained as she led me through the house to the kitchen.

I had little time to construct an airtight alibi, so silence was my answer. The assault would start. I knew she would rant about her superiority of biblical rulings at least once during the conversation. "I needed to get home. Charlene's waiting for me."

"A few minutes isn't going to hurt." Isabel batted her eyes as she walked to the sink. "You always linger behind at Momma's. What else did Momma say?"

"She called me back to talk with her. I wasn't lingering. I think she's going to tell Lea."

"You couldn't talk her out of it?"

My answer sounded like a grumble. "She's not buying a silence conspiracy." My light brown, oh-so-expressive eyes questioned, "Well?"

"We need to get Momma sorted. She'll see it's only prudent. You've got to admit with Leandra's criminal record, she isn't trustworthy."

"Isabel, she did her time. She pulled nearly five years."

"For thieving." Isabel's eyes shifted with embarrassment in even saying the word, much less having a felon in the family. She was like that with words.

The word *thieving* was only one step below the word *lesbian* in Isabel's vocabulary. Both words were spoken as if they were the most sinister, malevolent tags ever constructed by language.

As she spat them out, it was as if she might have just tasted poison and filthy dishwater.

"She only embezzled to have the money to fix her face."

"And look what it ended up costing her. And us." There was a moment's pause before Isabel huffed, "Imagine if she finds out that the old sundial is worth at least three or four times as much as Momma's old bungalow row house. And Momma's family hearthside is nearing dilapidation."

"Hearthside?" I repeated with bemusement.

"A word I picked up out of a book. It means house."

"I know." I grinned. "Isabel, Grandma's ... I mean, Momma's house – hearthside, is just like yours only a little bigger. Only a few blocks away – it's even in the same subdivision. For God's sake! Both houses are modest – not the slums and not castles." I crossed my arms. "Hearthside!"

"Stop blathering, Vicky. It wouldn't do you any harm to improve your mind with a good woman's magazine or two. Your garbled, hit-and-miss vocabulary could use a good dose of female magazines." Tumbling phrases weren't of interest to Isabel.

"I read plenty of lesbian books and magazines. They are aimed at a female market. And I blog a column, too. People like it. They think it's funny and good natured." I loved my garbled, hit-and-miss words. One day I would write a book of my own. Something inside of me wouldn't allow it yet. My forte was articles – blogs. Get in, make your Z, and get out. Finish up in a couple sittings. "I do read," I said combatively.

Isabel's sound was a partial growl and a weird humph. "Dirty books about women."

"Some romance," I said with a laugh. I ruffled my short, caramel-colored, semi-curly, thick hair.

"A book on fashion wouldn't go amiss."

"If you don't stop haranguing me about my androgynous wardrobe, I'm going to my hearthside. Or do you consider apartments to be hearthsides?"

Isabel shifted feet. With an uncomfortable shrug, she instructed, "Let's get straight what we are going to say to Momma to convince her."

"Are we going to march in and tell her to fork over the damned sundial? And, by the way, don't mention it to baby long-fingers." I chortled. "Loosen up, Isabel. We just keep telling Momma that in her own best interest, it wouldn't be a good idea to allow Lea to get too involved in it."

Disgruntled, Isabel nodded. "Maybe it's best that way. Momma will see that the sundial can either be passed down or sold with the proceeds divided between mother and daughters."

"She doesn't need to give any of us anything. When Grandma died, the entire house and contents went to Momma."

"But Momma knows I'm the only daughter who provided the family with a direct descendent. My son is the natural heir." Her voice was smug, as was the lift of her eyebrows.

"Char and I could adopt. And Lea isn't past childbearing age. She could have a dozen little embezzlers. We could call them Leandra's bandits." My laugh glided to a stop. At times, I had to remind myself that Isabel's comedic appreciation was very, very weak.

"She's never indicated intentions or any desire to be a mother. Besides, the men she selects are always losers. Improbable she would plan matrimony, much less motherhood. She's not domestication material."

"Just because you're the only traditional mommy, doesn't mean you should walk away with the sundial." My frown of concentration was deepening. Isabel wanted to walk with the entire treasure in her coffers. In the name of her son, she would petition for the entire deal.

"Tad is the sole – the rightful, legitimate heir. But the decision will be made by Momma," Isabel murmured. "It's still like a dream. Today's events are possibly the most amazing that ever happened in my lifetime."

With amused sarcasm, I spoke, "I find that statement not only possible, but highly probable."

Isabel heard the muffler's howl from Sully's car. She looked out the window and across the backyard. "Sully's home. You know how Momma likes Sully. Maybe she'll listen to him about not letting Lea become too involved."

With large, hurried steps, Isabel led the way through the backyard. I nodded as we approached Sully. He'd had time to lift the car's hood and stab a dipstick into the auto's oil line.

"How did the *Roadshow* go?" he quizzed as Isabel entered his workshop garage. It was a place he considered his sanctuary. Filled with auto parts, an old VW bus, and assortment of mechanical tools, the old shop seemed cluttered. But Sully knew where every tool could be instantly located. It was a relatively small garage that adjoined a narrow alleyway. Since it was far too difficult to maneuver autos in and out on a daily basis – his argument for a workshop area went unchallenged.

"I tried to call you earlier. You won't believe!" Isabel exclaimed.

"Her Hummels are actually worth something?" he questioned Isabel. He wiped his oil-smudged hands on a rag and threw it onto the side shelving.

"No. Now listen. The sundial…"

"Sundial? You took that old thing?"

"Yes, and Sully, it's worth a fortune." Isabel's hands dramatically flew to her chest. "A half million dollars!"

Sully scratched his head. His grin indicated doubt. "You're trying this out on me? Right?"

"Damn it all, Sully, I'm telling you it is worth maybe half a million."

He pressed his eyeglasses back. His eyes widened as he checked my face for agreement. He sat back against the tall stool. Bewildered, his body slumped. "You're serious." He recognized his wife would have never used that language if she hadn't been.

"Yes. Momma took it to the bank. Put it in a safety deposit box. I just got back. Vicky and I discussed the fact that it might not be a good idea to tell Leandra, but Momma wouldn't listen to us."

"Why wouldn't you tell Lea?" he asked. He immediately turned his gaunt face toward the wall. "I get it. She's a felon. You were afraid having a felon amongst us might endanger the sundial." He paused searching for the words. "It might not be safe."

36

"Sully, my own sister stole money from the bank where she worked."

"But not from her mother. Lea would never do that."

"It was a concern to both Vicky and me. That's all. Who knows what bad habits she picked up while she was in prison. She's only been out a month."

"You know my opinion on that." Sully's voice held an edge. "The judge made an example out of her. She should never have gotten that much time."

"That's not the point. She stole thirty-thousand dollars."

"And it was retrieved. And she served her sentence."

"You sound like Momma now."

Sully examined his wife's face. Isabel had not visited, nor allowed her child to visit Lea while she was in prison. She had written and accepted all phone calls, but never once had she visited. Sully had driven his in-laws to the prison many times. He had seen the pain and pallor in his youngest sister-in-law's face. Lea always asked about Isabel and Tad. Excuses were made on Isabel's behalf.

"What exactly did your mother say?" he asked.

"Said we were sneaky little snots for trying to exclude Lea," I blurted.

His mouth creased into a half-hidden grin. "Well?"

"Whose side are you on?" Isabel's voice became brittle.

"Isabel, I've found it unwise to pick sides when it comes to you and your family. But right now, I'd say being on my mother-in-law's side is the smartest thing. And besides," he broke with a laugh. "And besides, she's rich now, so I'm backing her to the hilt."

Isabel tossed the new replacement oil filter that had been on his workbench counter. It missed him. That increased her anger. "After I divorce you, you'll need a handout from my mother!"

They were both aware it was a hollow threat. Isabel turned, slamming into the door on her way out. She returned to the house. She would leave him in his primal retreat until dinner was served. Then she would continue her argument. Although she was devoted to her husband, she'd never really considered the complexity of their love. It seemed to her to be an emotion of futility.

I gave Sully one of those small tip of the fingers wave goodbye.

Following after Isabel, I wondered how her little legs could move at such a clip. She was clearly allowing anger to do her sprint.

I said, "That's that. I'm leaving. See you tomorrow." I nearly sprinted to my SUV, hoping not to hear Isabel calling me back. There really wasn't anything left to say, although I knew Isabel was gnawing on an argument.

Chapter 5

Laughter is an amazing event.

Charlene Webster threw back her head and howled her unique, sublime laugh. She began sorting through the kitchen cabinets in our deluxe three-bedroom apartment. "You could have told me earlier that you wouldn't be fixing dinner. I would have picked something up." She paused as she pulled out a bottle of wine from the wine stand.

"Isabel insisted I stop by. I told her I needed to leave. She just continued to pound. You know how she is. Blah, blah, blah."

"Okay, so Isabel was being her sanctimonious, pompous self. She thinks Lea and you aren't the procreation types. Also, she's saying that your mother should give her the sundial because she needs to pass it on to her son?" After nearly doubling over laughing, Charlene glanced back at me. "Did your Momma whoop her good?"

"Called us a couple little shits – well, snots, to be precise." I watched as Charlene pulled a variety of vegetables from the refrigerator. Because of the massive amounts of produce from Momma's garden, the fridge usually looked as if a produce truck had tipped over and exploded inside.

"Why you?" Charlene chuckled. "Oh, no. You didn't throw in with Isabel?"

"You know how overbearing she can be." Embarrassed, I glanced down at the floor. Then, quickly, I began sorting vegetables for a salad. "I'll use some of the shrimp from last night on the salads. And maybe garlic bread, cheese, and wine." Continuing to work on the salad, I didn't even look up to check if the menu sounded good.

Charlene opened the wine. She kissed my neck on the way to get wine glasses. "Babe, it will all settle down." I inhaled the faint scent of her expensive perfume. It was flowery with the hint of wilderness chemistry.

Continuing on, I muttered, "Hon, I'm just in shock about this."

"Which part? No supper, the half-million, or the attempt to screw over your own sister? Which fucked up part?"

Grimacing, I inserted, "Isabel thinks you don't cuss."

"Not around her or your family."

"I didn't curse until I got into softball."

"And don't change the subject. I can't believe you would consider keeping something from one of your sisters. Plotting, like an evil twin against your baby sister. Vickie, use that search engine between your ears. Remember, Isabel usually gets you into trouble and then waltzes away – leaving you to deal with your mother on your own. She bails while you get left with the scrub-up."

"But I understand that maybe we ought to keep an eye on Lea. I mean, she could have learned bad ways in prison. And she's such a drama queen." I glanced back into her face. "Char, I wouldn't want to see her out of the money pool. I just don't want her to have a chance to dip into the pool before the money is divided up."

"Lea was in the slammer because she'd already succumbed to evil ways. She has baggage with debris hanging out of it, but come on." Charlene chained her laughter through the next few moments. "Hiding the news from Lea! Really!"

"You know how I get when I'm around Isabel. She's always had some mystical control over me. There's probably a psychology term to cover it. I think it's called 'older-sib-is-a-bitch' syndrome."

"You're marching in her footsteps. She intimidates you. She intimidates everyone. Even me. Like you said, I'd choke on a curse word before saying it in front of Isabel. Even when she's going on with her Bible babble – I want to toss in a couple *fucks*."

"I'm not in Isabel's footsteps. I'm not wired that way. I just don't want Lea messing with Momma's money."

"The three of you are sibling rivalry poster women. You all need to realize that it's your mom's bucks. I hope she sells the sundial and spends every last nickel on cruises and fun. Your mother has worked her entire lifetime. Never a break. She deserves a good time."

"A half a million bucks would be considered a really great time."

Charlene roared. "It can be called half a million great times if it's coming out of your mother's purse. Her spending habits are definitely a nickel at a time."

"Yep, she can be tight as a tick. I've gone to garage sales with her."

I recalled the Saturday mornings when Grandma was alive, and the three of us would drive around the community in search of garage sales. Grandma's maxim was whatever the seller asked for an item – offer them half.

"Your mother's swag could end up being half a million treasures. A buck a pop."

"I finally had to stop going on her treasure hunts with her and Grandma. I was being chastised for giving the asking price. I'm not a prime garage-saler." I nodded. "In fact, I can remember when Momma thought the charges were too high. She would start singing, 'So high I can't get over it.' Well, she and Grandma would laugh as if they were co-conspirators. They embarrassed the hell out of me."

Charlene poured the wine and sipped. "Good wine. It would be better with a steak. Oh, well"

"Oh, and another thing that made me late was Derwin. He'd skipped out from his home – another runaway session. Dottie came dashing over and was in one of her fits. That was when Isabel and I were talking with Momma."

Char took another sip, and then chuckled. "God, Dottie and her fits. With that drunken brain of hers, I'm amazed that she even knows she's got a son. Well, one thing about your mother. She's willing to tolerate crazy living next door."

"Momma sent Isabel and me after him. She loves to offer our detective services to look for Derwin."

"That little plot intermission probably irritated Isabel. She doesn't like being interrupted when she's trying to rearrange your mother's mind."

"I was glad Momma insisted. Derwin shouldn't be roaming around on his own."

Charlene shook her head. "Derwin is a truly sad case."

"I worry about him. He's always running off. And he's a cute kid. What if some pervert grabbed him? Pervs would take a handsome kid like Derwin in a minute. It happened to the little girl in Aurora – snatched. Derwin needs supervision."

"Your grandma always said the good Lord looks after kids like Derwin. She was crazy about him from the time he was a baby."

"Yes. I remember back a decade ago when his grandfather died and Dottie inherited the house. She was pregnant – or soon became pregnant. Momma said there were so many male visitors over there that Dottie was either looking for a 'father figure' replacement or she was whoring."

Tittering, Charlene added, "I remember that. Your grandmother would look out the window. She called it her peep show."

A decade ago, Dottie wasn't a bad looking woman, I considered. Before she'd attempted to drink the city dry and live the party life, she'd seemed nice enough. Then after her pregnancy, all seemed lost. She had never accepted motherhood. Although I no longer lived at Momma's, I watched her demise.

"Grandma minded Derwin from the very beginning. With Dottie's parents no longer there to give her pointers on how to raise a kid, she needed help."

"Although your mom and grandmother tried – Dottie didn't care."

"Grandma loved Derwin. We all do. But Grandma was charmed by his innocence. One time when he was about four, he said he liked the way Grandma's face was decorated. He was tracing the wrinkles on her face at the time. Grandma got a big kick out of that."

"Too bad Dottie didn't pick up some tips from your grandmother."

I never liked to say it's too late for someone, but I wondered if Dottie had a chance at rehabilitation. "Derwin deserves her love."

"Dottie's no mother to him. She never has been. It's as simple as that."

"Char, I believe the poor kid is mishandled. Is that a word? Mishandled? Well, I think he's being physically abused. Probably not sexually, but abused. Certainly neglected."

"Maybe Dottie is assaulting him. That's way different than mishandling a child. Someday your mother is going to slap the shit out of Dottie."

Nodding my head in agreement, I offered, "Someone should, that's for damned sure. The Brent family cares more about his welfare than Dottie does."

I watched my lover of the last dozen years. Charlene Webster had just turned forty-four. Our relationship had started when I was in my mid-twenties and she was thirty-two. Charlene was the elegantly dressed beauty that most people at the public relations firm had a crush on. As the firm's Sapphic – a wild-worded copywriter, I was no exception.

There was no doubt of my sexuality. I was always dressed haphazardly, in clothing that simulated men's clothing. I chose to call my androgynous fashion – comfort clothing.

Charlene met with clients, and as vice-president of the company. She was always coifed and confident. Her blonde hair draped down around her shoulders. Green eyes snapped with authority. However, those eyes could draw you into a kiss. With a medium build, she was shapely and sensual – rather than sexy. But sensual made her extraordinarily sexy to me. Certainly, some terrific goddess had sculpted her body.

Although I was only a low-rung copywriter, I found her to be the woman of my dreams. One of the other lesbians had called her a tasty-looking chick. I took umbrage with that evaluation. It was then I knew I was falling for Char.

Soon after I was hired, my glances and I followed Charlene around like a besotted, lovesick fan. Putting my career down the dumpster's flush for making a pass at a straight vice-president of marketing was not appealing to me. So I worked a clandestine endeavor. I continued watching carefully. I finally found my suspicions about Charlene being Sapphic were correct. I figured out that those loose-leaf smiles from Charlene's lovely face were indeed flirty. Eyebeam exchanges – they were for real. We began taking coffee breaks together. Next were our intimate lunches – yet never anything other than enjoying one another's company.

At the time, it seemed like forever, but it was only a matter of a few weeks when we got together. We were in her office. She had a chunk of copy in her hands. She waved it in my direction and told me she loved the treatment I'd done with one of the ads. Then she pulled it up on her computer. As she scrolled through it, I saw something in her eyes that made me want for our souls to kiss.

They must have because she then leaned near to me until our lips met. I called it gate-crasher love. We hadn't anticipated it. This is not to say we hadn't desired it.

From the very moment of that kiss, Charlene and I both – simultaneously assumed our relationship. The assumption was without additional words, or the need of additional words about the immediacy of the bond. We just were bonded. We both absolutely knew we'd be together. There wasn't any talk about belonging. We just belonged.

I'd waited another couple of weeks before announcing my relationship to the family. They'd been aware that I'd roamed and darted in a single Sapphic life.

The family had obviously expected me to come to my senses and get over my crush. They always expected their prayers to be answered.

But I considered Charlene a perfect mate, lover, house spouse, significant other, or whatever the tag might be. She was worth all the condemnation the Brent family could pitch at me. When I made my announcement to the family about moving to Charlene's apartment, my family reacted as if they guessed it was coming, but didn't really want to know details.

Charlene was ideal, but I didn't know if the family would accept her. She was kind, decent, and successful. She was also highly organized and diligent, as well as one of the most moral people I'd ever met. Charlene knew the company regulations about no fraternization. She called a friend in a nearby word-smith office and saw to it that I, her younger lover, was fitted up with a position of lead copywriter with a public relations firm that interfaced with hers.

For me, it was a promotion, pay raise, and I would still see Charlene during luncheons. Thankfully, her conscience wouldn't allow sneaking around, trivializing both our relationship and her firm's policy of fraternization with those of us who were considered underlings.

It seemed a perfect arrangement for everyone except my family.

Momma was at first livid, then that converted slowly to mortified. Although she tried to tamp it down – I knew she was visually releasing my soul to the devil.

Isabel was merely livid. I was embarrassing her. She sniped at family get-togethers. Yet, for all the turmoil Isabel caused, there was often a wedge of goodness she would drag out to display. When Charlene's mother was critically ill several years before, Isabel gave her condolences, had Masses said, and sent cookies. In her own way, she was there when Lea was sent to prison. She sent small gifts and baked goods, yet could never force herself to visit.

Still, it was difficult for the family not to approve of Charlene. They soon realized withholding approval was not helping. My woman was reliable, financially stable, personable, and made me happy. Isabel retained her superior attitude and biblical censure.

"Do you really think Dottie is physically abusive to Derwin?" Charlene inquired, breaking into my thoughts.

"I'm not sure. I know she calls him names no kid should be called. I've noticed that when she calls for him, he sometimes hunches back – cowering. I've asked Derwin about bruises. He says kids pick on him. Playground tumbles and fights."

"Kids with problems get picked on. He could be being picked on for a list of reasons. He's a bi-racial kid living in a predominately Anglo community."

"He's never mentioned that might be a problem. He's very light skinned. I've heard that sometimes that creates a problem on both sides. I can't imagine why? I keep wishing we could dispense with all the ignorant bigotry." I added, "Thankfully, most people accept him. Let's face it, all people should be accepted."

"Most, but not all are. I've always hated bigotry. The same bullies grow up bullying minorities. They are the hate-mongers."

"Grandma used to claim that there's enough stuff to dislike people about without color. There are the cruel people, the dishonest people, and all kinds of qualities to hate a person about. Grandma believed in hating for those qualities – the rude, obnoxious, and evil people. Why should it have anything to do with color? Well, that's my theory, too."

Charlene's jaw clamped tightly. "Some kids might even be picking on him because he acts slightly effeminate."

"He's a kid with gentleness – and sensitivity. He doesn't exactly flaunt any kind of sexuality. I'm thinking, even if it's true about Dottie physically abusing him, he probably wouldn't tell anyone. Kids don't want to tell on their parents."

"If he's got gay tendencies, maybe he feels guilt."

My eyebrow shot up. "Meaning everyone has guilt when they think they might be gay?"

"Maybe, but what I'm really saying is that we don't know what he is. He's a good-hearted kid. That's all that matters." I slipped a piece of shrimp between Char's lips. "Delicious," she teased.

"Speaking of kind-hearted – I think Momma's kind-heartedness has stretched all it can. She was pissed off at us, I mean completely pissed."

"You can't blame her. Vics, I'm usually not on your mother's side. But in this case, I am."

"I can see both sides. But yes, I agree. Lea should be told." I considered her feelings might be because of my own guilt. Long ago, guilt seemed to have bucked me and broken me with years of pain. "If it weren't for her background – her injury," I paused. "Well, maybe I want to believe she's okay. Is that feeling sorry for her or truly trusting her? Maybe she isn't trustworthy. She might try to talk Momma out of the money."

"Isn't that what you and Isabel are doing? Not trusting without justification?"

"How was work today?" I abruptly asked, changing the subject as I went.

"You're so flipping transparent." She took me in her arms. "Can we relax and keep your family problems at bay until tomorrow. It will be a brand new drama then."

"I'm going to tell Isabel that we were wrong. Momma is right."

"Being wrong will be a new concept for Isabel. She can be such a smug, intolerant jockstrap. "

"Like you say, a new drama will be there tomorrow. There is always something."

"Vicky, if you get shut out of the money, so be it. We're doing fine without them." She paused, reading my expression. "It would be nice to have a little extra so that you could reduce your work hours and begin writing. That's what you want. But you could do that now. My salary certainly would cover all our expenses." She held up her hand to silence me. "I know. Your own stupid pride won't allow that. But we could do it."

"A sweet offer, but again, no. It isn't even about Momma's money and thinking I might be left out. I've always felt left out. I've always had to contend with bossy Isabel. And then with the baby of the family. I've never felt a belonging."

"Maybe none of you feel as if you belong. Isabel might have felt alone – being responsible. And with Lea, she always elicited pity because of her scar. Have you ever considered that everyone over-compensates for not having a father on premise when you were growing up? I think you all still do over-compensate."

"Let's drop it." I felt a terrible rush of sorrow. Guilt was nearly suffocating me again.

Of course, there would be new drama tomorrow. Each of us brought our own conflict to the table. The dynamics were jammed together like war stories that chased themselves through history.

I wasn't certain that Charlene could understand. She was an only child. She was always in full agreement with her family. Her family genuinely accepted us. It was my family that made us both uncomfortable. There was religion. There was also the constant disagreement about Charlene and me getting married.

A headache happened each time these conversations came up. Loving both family and my sweet woman provided extra doses of drama. Momma would jab and then tell my sisters not to say another word. She would warn that the wheels were about to come off the wagon. Confront, charge, and then she would retreat. Just like Charlene was doing. Was it true that you pick spouses who are like your parents?

"Being wrong is a new concept for most people. Particularly Isabel," I spoke precisely. "I agree. My family's elastic is very tightly pulled."

Charlene chuckled. "Life is random events mixed with gobbledygook." She topped up our glasses. "I'm starving."

Carefully placing the two platters of salad on our small table, I mumbled agreement, "Me, too."

She reached across the table to squeeze my hand. Romance is mostly made up as it goes along. Char knew how to reach for me when I was down.

Chapter 6

The telephone was ringing loudly – nearly shouting into the morning. My eyes opened slowly. "Victoria Brent, where are you?" Momma's impatient voice asked.

"Just climbing out of bed." I turned into the sweet embrace of Charlene. My lover stirred, and then returned to her normal deep sleep. She often slept with a smile on her face. I'd noticed that the first morning we'd awakened together. Seeing that smile had stored so much love into my heart, I knew I would never get over it. Waking with her softness and warmth encouraged me to cuddle tighter into her clasp. Her arms wound around me always felt like my soft landing.

"Momma, I'm going to miss Mass this morning."

"God blesses us with this wonderful treasure, and you aren't going to give thanks?" Momma quizzed with her usual brusque agitation.

Squinting at the alarm clock, I acquiesced. "I'll make it to ten o'clock Mass, Momma."

I pulled myself to a seated position. Charlene's arms were around my hips with a tight grip. As I slid away, Charlene leaned up on her elbows. "Don't leave. Please, Babe."

"Go back to sleep, Beautiful. I've got to get ready for Mass."

"I thought you were going to tell your family you won't be attending church from here on?" Charlene's eyes were only half open, and they batted in an attempt at focusing.

"Char, I can't tell Momma I won't attend. Not when she's just had a huge blessing."

"Come on, Vicky, you know you don't want to go. It doesn't uplift you – or console you. You return from your Jesus visit with a sadness that lasts all day. Even if the Broncos win, your face is hanging, your teats are hanging, and no matter what I say, it's

wrong. The only thing that lifts your spirits is our mattress frolic."
She fluffed her morning hairdo – which was always adorable.

Aware of my own somberness after church, I nodded. "Char,
I'm sorry. It means so much to Momma. She wants the family
together for one hour a week. That's not much to ask." But I
admitted that the solitude of church and all the holiness might not
have been the problem. It might have been the time it gave me to
think about my own guilt.

"But it isn't one hour with your family. It's a flipping fulltime
job."

"There's no disputing that." My admission was a slap to both
of us. "Look, Charlene, I wish it could be different, but –"

Charlene rolled back over. "If we split, it won't be anything
about our love that breaks us up. It will be your damned family.
They're always involved with our lives and expect us to always be
at their beck and call." She suddenly sat up. "I guess it really is
your fault. You could stop being a twenty-four-hour, seven-day-a-
week daughter slash sister."

Frowning, I backed away from her assessment. "I've got to get
ready." Charlene rarely awakens upset. This was the exception to
the rule. She was as cheerful as a rattlesnake, so I was going to
leave it at that.

Charlene muttered, "That's right. I'm out of the mix. Isabel is
a ditch-water bitch. Yet, you're kiss-ass attentive to her every
whim. And Lea is a conniver. And your mother is like a flipping
dominatrix."

Suddenly, I twirled around. "And if I do inherit a hundred
thousand from the family treasury – are you still going to be
pissing and moaning about my family?"

Her laugh was mildly obnoxious. "You'll probably never see a
nickel. Your mom will feel sorry for poor Lea's face and get it
fixed. Then she'll realize poor Isabel has a child to put through
college – and a home refurbishing. Isabel is the perfect daughter
because she has a real family. It is made up of a man, woman, and
a begotten brat. Your mom will throw what's left into the Church
coffers. It will help fight the perils of homosexuality and women's
rights."

"I agree, Char. But it's how I was raised." Before more could be said, I slammed the bathroom door shut. Swiftly – with vehemence, I unwrapped the over-sized tee-shirt and pajama bottoms from my medium shaped body. When I was small, my grandmother used to say I was built like a brick shithouse. She cursed more than Momma did. Maybe I took after her. However, I cursed mostly when playing softball. Back in my softball years, my body was called husky. Now it had become a slightly overweight body. But solid.

With a fit of temper, I kicked my night clothes across the bathroom floor. Clamping my hand on the shower's handles, I twisted hard, purposefully.

Although angry, I had to admit the exact same thought had crossed my mind before I went to sleep last night.

Both my older sister and my younger sister had sob stories. I didn't have any backstory with tragedy. Nor did I have the impending problem of a child to put through college. I was set up in a solid relationship, a classy apartment, and my ride was a new SUV – everything I needed.

But my family wasn't aware I wanted something else. I wanted to make words iridescent on the page. I wanted to one day allow my creativity free reign. It was word wanderlust. My crazy dream suspended me with promise. It had been with me most of my life. Up until now, most of what I did was to make creative bare-bones passes through the skies of advertising agency propaganda. My blog was where my Muse connected. Although I wanted to get serious about writing, I used the goofball's procedural of excuses. Char attempted to confine me to our home office. I was always interrupted by an emergency call from either my family or employer. That squelched the deal. I'd delete those words – the ones inside me that begged to escape.

Of course, according to my mother, all I needed was the Lord. And that was free for the taking. If I could just give up the sin of wanting to devour another woman, I'd be accepted. If I could just stop having an overwhelming desire to be a lesbian, I could be added to the church roster of membership.

I drove to church with my mind whirling.

I considered that Charlene's statement about never seeing a nickel was probably more likely than not. I squinted into the morning's hyped-up sunshine.

The old stone church savored Sunday mornings. For without the parishioners – it wouldn't be an aged relic all carved upon to greet the devoted. It gazed out at the world of today. With all the passing short-short skirts and wrong-doing presented – that church must have thought it resided at the base of hell.

I slid into the familiar pew beside Momma, Lea, and Isabel. Momma always landed in that pew. She'd been a member of the Ladies' Altar Society for years. Those ladies took dibs on where they would roost, so most of the congregation knew where one another perched. They expected her to snag that pew every Sunday. It had also been where Grandma had knelt, stood, sat, sang, and prayed. Not at all ostentatiously staged in the front of the pack, the pew was a polite distance. It was in the first third and off to the right side.

Grandma once stated that the front row was where the gauche showoffs parked their asses.

As I prayed, listened, and watched, my mind wandered. Thoughts were raining through the ritual, the bells, the choir, and the damned incense smoker. That thing drove my allergies wacky. Charlene was correct. I was technically a practicing Catholic. For all practical purposes, I could mostly do as I was told. But there were portions I just couldn't believe. I wasn't a sinner. I was a Sapphic. I was a cafeteria Catholic. That was the best I could do.

I wanted to believe in the tranquility of an hour a week where my family was pleased. Together as we could be, we were silent. It may have been a ruse, but when we clasped one another – greeting and welcoming – it seemed pleasant. I liked that message of us.

I remembered back when Lea was imprisoned. I'd look at the space where she usually sat. Sometimes a tear would spill when the priest talked about sins. Sins are weights dragging the soul away. Yet when I thought of being responsible for my sister's massive facial scar and her incarceration – I already experience a blob of hell on earth.

Lea smiled over at me just at the moment my thoughts were culminating. Looking away, my eyes filled to their rims.

After service, Lea caught a ride with me to the pancake house where we normally stopped for lunch after Mass. Isabel had suggested we ride together – and I knew the reason behind it. It wasn't to give Lea and me a chance to talk as Isabel had stated. It was an opportunity for Isabel to cajole, encourage, and work on Momma. Separate cars were a way of gathering support and separating opinions.

The other reason for the two-car deal was that the pancake house was nearer my apartment. I wouldn't need to double back.

Momma obviously hadn't told Lea. Lea would have been gushing about it into my ear throughout Mass. But the obvious social place for making the announcement was our stop-off at the pancake house.

Driving the dozen blocks to the restaurant was a short journey, so Lea got right to it.

"What the hell's going on?" Lea asked. She perceived something amiss. "Momma and Isabel were side-glancing. Don't tell me they're plotting to kick me out on the street."

I chided. "Nobody will kick you out. It's your imagination. Don't be paranoid." Leandra Brent was astute about emotions even before her stint in the slammer. Being around criminals far worse than she could only have imagined might have enhanced her abilities to discern plots.

"Isabel would love to see the back of me. I'm an embarrassment to her. And to Momma. I don't understand why you bother with any of us."

"You're all the family I have." I parked, got out of the car, and was halfway inside before I heard Lea's crazy-assed stilt high-heels clicking on the parking lot pavement.

Depending on what transpired between Momma and Isabel, I figured it was about to get interesting – from a human interaction point of view. Either there would be the same tension or my mother would be making a startling announcement. Either way, Lea was on to it. She definitely knew something had been happening.

Before we unfolded the menus, Momma and Isabel arrived and were seated. After a deep breath, Momma announced, "I have something to tell you, Lea."

Lea's back went straight as a steel rod. "Me?"

Isabel quickly spoke, "Tad will be home from his mountain camping trip on Friday."

If she thought that was throwing a blockade up and shifting topics – she couldn't have been more mistaken.

"We got good news," Momma said. "At the *Roadshow* we got some really good news."

"The Hummels?" Lea guessed.

"No, it was that old sundial," Momma announced. Her voice was filled to the brim with swagger.

Side-glancing in Isabel's direction, I watched the bright tomato-color intensify over her complexion. "That's right, Sister," Isabel announced as if it were her idea to tell Lea. "It's worth a fortune."

"Why didn't you tell me yesterday?" Lea asked.

"I was saving up the good news for having this little lunch party," Momma inserted. "For this kind of good fortune announcement, we need a festive atmosphere."

An automatic choke came up from my throat. I wondered when the waitress would bring the candelabras around to be lit and get the 50-piece orchestra going. "Yes," I mumbled my agreement.

Lea's lower lip began flapping like a sparrow wing in the wind. She was *so* on to it. "I see. My guess is you didn't want to even tell me about it. You three know – and maybe you thought it wasn't secure if I knew about it. Or more than likely, you three remembered when Grandma was alive and promised me I could have that sundial. I was the only one who wanted it."

She looked around suspiciously. Momma was deep in thought trying to recall that time. Suddenly, it struck me. I recalled Grandma and Lea talking about it. "Lea, I remember when you and Grandma talked. I remember she said you could have it."

Momma looked at me dubiously. "Vicky?"

Isabel had gulped a huge mouthful of water and had begun to choke. Before Isabel had her chance at changing my story, I piped up, "Lea did want the sundial. And Grandma said yes."

I was glad the waitress gave us a reprieve from our conversation. As we ordered, the room took on its own silence. It went from blocks of background conversation to a drone.

Immediately after we'd ordered, Lea refreshed everyone's memory. "It was when we were talking about the Hummels. You two claimed them, and I said to Grandma that I wanted the old sun clock. I called it a *sun clock*. The sundial. She said if no one else wanted it – it was mine. And the two of you sat there at the table and didn't object. Everyone nodded. You said that would be fine. Isabel said it would be more Hummels for both of you."

Momma's voice was riddled with a resolute timbre of pride. "I have a fine memory, and I don't recall anything like that. Besides, the house and everything in it belongs to me according to Grandma's will. She probably gave everything she owned away a dozen times when her gout was playing up. But she put her will together, and I am the heir."

"That's not fair," Lea's words moaned.

Isabel jumped in with both sandals. "It's legal." She glared at me, defying me to open my mouth. "I think both you and Vicky got your wires crossed. Even if you didn't, Grandma's will stands."

"What is *my* sundial worth?" Lea stubbornly quizzed.

I glanced down at the shirred eggs that were set in front of me. I enjoyed that first sniff of bacon and hash-brown potatoes. I hoped that I would be able to swallow them. The toast would be even a more difficult time getting down my esophagus.

"Half a million," Momma answered with a soft snorting breath.

Lea dropped the spoonful of jam she was whittling out of a little plastic container. Isabel's energy was all tied up trying to remain calm as she attempted to stop her eyelids from batting. Momma folded her napkin daintily across her chest.

Momma stressed, "It is my sundial. And you wisenheimers just sit back and keep your powder dry. We Brent's don't fight in public. Your grandmother always told me to be a lady in public. And she told all of you that, too."

When she said the word 'lady' – all three of their glances drifted toward me. I was wearing women's clothing, but I'm sure Isabel was thinking it was more appropriate for safari wear.

"Half a million," Lea crooned as if she might be getting ready to spend it. The shoe stores and fashion boutiques of Littleton would be pleased to see her coming.

Momma's unintelligible grumble was nearly muted with a mouthful of pancake. Isabel hadn't even looked at her platter of breakfast.

Momma was probably praying for all she was worth. She was ever-faithful. Yes, in the hierarchy of things, I would say Momma was a couple rungs up from devout. She was an 'all in' Catholic. Or very nearly so.

Now, her faith would be tested by her three daughters.

This was going to get really good very soon.

Chapter 7

"And?" Charlene's inquisition began as I burst into our apartment. Her brow went upward. Her eyebrows were delicate. They became scant half-moons as they lifted into a question. "Your mother told Lea?"

"Yes. As you predicted Isabel acted as if she'd insisted on Lea knowing." I inhaled deeply. "She acted as if it were a magnanimous gesture that she'd wanted told – maybe she'd even begged Momma to deliver that message."

Char shook her head. "She's such a reptile."

"I agree."

"Isabel is a reptilian jockstrap. That's all there is to it." Char's comments were always delivered deadpan. I enjoyed that.

"Yes. She kept quiet at first. Then she whittled her way in. The real debate started to convert to a moment of peril when we were still in the restaurant. Momma slammed her silverware down as she told us to stop the bickering. She was also tired of being a mediator. She just wanted to gobble her bacon and eggs in peace. We scarfed down our food and then agreed to reconvene at the house. Another hour of shouting was in store."

"How did you leave it?"

"Holy blazing crap," I exclaimed. I plunged down into the easy chair opposite of hers. "It's a mess. No one is talking to anyone."

"Your family is so rudderless. Their visual perception is askew." She gazed at me a moment, then her eyes closed. "And I suppose you stuck by every word Isabel uttered?"

"No. Actually, I recalled something of importance on Lea's side. Isabel nearly levitated."

"If it was something on Lea's side, Isabel probably did punch out the sky."

"Lea had once asked Grandma if she could have the old sundial and Grandma said yes. I remembered the conversation. I said I'd remembered and Isabel went off on me."

"How did your mother react?"

"Momma reaffirmed her belief that the will stated everything was hers. The rest of us could pound sand if we didn't like it. I think she said we were selfish, petulant turds."

"Your mother said that?"

"Charlene, Momma reads all kinds of things in all kinds of books. Anything might come popping out of her mouth at any time. Usually, it's sweet and non-toxic. When she says something toxic, she usually turns hemp-colored."

"You inherited her lack of a filter, Sport."

"Meaning?" I leaned forward and into my question. My hands stretched outward as if I were asking for her to drop her question into my arms. "You're inferring I have no filter?"

"Not much. You say exactly what you want – how you feel. Like telling Lea you remembered the deal she had with your grandmother. If you'd thought about it a moment, you might have realized that was tantamount to throwing in with Lea. If you're in cahoots with Lea – well, the other side will be infuriated. Your mother will get a case of the old *livids*." Charlene chuckled as she slipped into her white sports shoes. "Let's take a walk."

"Rats! I'm exhausted. I feel like I've been through a freakin' war."

"Strenuous exercise will do us both good. It will help empty the stress this is causing you. It's either a walk or maybe saying a few rosaries. That sometimes settles you down."

I hadn't realized that Charlene was aware that sometimes I found something comforting about saying prayers. There was no explanation, other than the years of having taken shelter in prayer. However it might be handled, I was grateful for any decrease in strain.

Grinning, I invited, "How about a balm-like, healing sexual experience?"

"Or a walk in the park."

"Okay, we could play YumBerry the Muffin." I opened my eyes as widely as I could. "Otherwise known as Wine, Cunnilingus, and Us?"

She snickered. "Let's save that for tonight."

I shook my head in agreement.

As we walked through the small park adjacent to our upscale apartment, my mind was whirling. I would have been much happier if it were my libido whirling.

However, I had to admit my lover woman had selected a walk that was like harvesting tranquility. It was isolated enough to allow my thoughts to feel as if they'd segued to a pasture's quiet. Yet there were flowers and hedges, along with huge trees. Usually, the open spaces were filled with people playing with balls or Frisbees. Today, they were probably all screwing their socks off or watching porn – or both.

The air was the softness of mild sunshine – barely recognizable. All the problems began to recede. Yet the overwhelming pressure only hid out for a few minutes at a time. Char and I had similar strides. We looked ahead, giving one another permission to identify our own projects. Although there was always communication – our walks were only designed to be with one another. Not rummage one another's thoughts.

We trekked nearly half an hour before an utterance slipped through my lips. "Remarkable."

"What's remarkable now?"

"How a couple hours with my family can marinate my brain?"

"Maybe you'll be able to stay away from them next week. Let them boil over," she suggested. After a moment's hesitation, she noted, "You're being quiet, so they must have filled your agenda with plans."

"Momma has it in her mind that she should have photos for insurance. Isabel volunteered Tad's services to photograph it. Tad will be back from his camping trip at the end of the week. So on Friday, we're all supposed to convene, go to the bank, and get the sundial. Take it to Momma's house. Shoot the photos to her specifications. She wants all the important, pertinent shots. Tad is an excellent photographer."

"Who isn't with digital cameras? Delete mistakes."

"Well, he does have a flair for it," I praised. "Anyway, he's doing the photo shoot. Then we'll return the sundial to the safety deposit box later."

"No armed guards?" she asked, tickled that my family was so dysfunctional.

"With only my mother and sisters guarding – I think we can get through without a sundial heist. Besides, we haven't told anyone, and vowed to keep it secret."

Char threw back her head and laughed her throaty laugh. I loved seeing her magnificent neck. I loved the sound of her laughter. She indicted, "Secrets. And security. With your money-grubbing nephew, Tad, and his devious mother – and with your sister, Felon Fingers, present?"

"You said yourself that Lea is probably okay. She's laying claim to it, so she'll protect it. Isabel isn't into Commandment smashing. And Tad isn't smart enough to pull off a condom, much less a heist."

"He's got some of Sully's genes, so there's hope for him yet."

"Also, between the four of us, he knows it would mean blunt-force trauma if he touched the damned sundial." My eyebrows bobbed upward.

A rolling laugh from each of us filled half a city block. I figured our humor would neutralize Charlene's inquiry. "Glad I'm working, so they won't expect me to be there."

"I don't think anyone mentioned you being invited to the little soirée. I plan to tell my boss that I'm working from home. I can catch up on the work later. Or maybe I'll use up one of my free days. I never call in sick."

"See, my being withdrawn helps. You complain when I'm wearing my 'bored-with-the-misfits' expression, but it works. They don't want me there. Do you?"

"I knew you were working. Besides, Momma isn't upset when Sully doesn't accompany Isabel every time she comes over."

"Early on, Sully warned me. He said to stay out of the internal goings on of the Brent women. Isabel really trained Sully. The poor guy commiserated with me when I was first having problems with being accepted. He said he'd gone through it to a degree." She stopped walking. "Do you think they really love each other?"

Frowning, I considered it. "I'm not sure. She treats him badly, but I think there's some reason they've stayed together. Other than Tad."

"Maybe they just wore one another out. When I first met them, I figured she married him as a sperm donor with a weekly paycheck attached."

"Do you really think people eventually tire of one another?" I asked.

"Maybe sometimes. But we'll always be in love, Vicky."

"I know. If you can take a dozen years of the Brent women, you definitely have staying power." I slipped my hand into hers. "I'm just glad that you're happy about being detached from my family. Especially when they get boisterous."

I hoped the lapse in conversation would continue.

Suddenly she snapped, "Especially then."

Feeling somewhat exonerated from any arguments beyond that, I was thrilled to get back to the apartment and begin dinner. Pot roast, potatoes, carrots, onions, seasonings, and tonight's feast would keep us busily eating. It would also provide a couple days of leftovers. Momma had sent over a pecan pie last evening. We hadn't even touched it but would certainly get to it after dinner. Char claimed pecan pie was an aphrodisiac. Not that we needed one. We appreciated homemade pie for its delicious self.

After dinner, there would be time designated for just the two of us – that was my territorial idea of heaven.

I'd had it with bristling conversation. I always preferred backpacking in the wilderness, away from my family's persistent woes. Silence, along with a corridor of nature – was perfect. Well, that and Charlene's orgasm. And mine matching. I never failed to take Charlene with me on my fantasies – or meet up with her along the path.

Even the thought of Char is a song from the voice of love. Char's loveliness is music.

Chapter 8

Monday was a day of designated rebooting. I completed my work tasks as quickly and concisely as possible. The day began with perkiness – not just my breasts, but I was perky all over. Throughout the day, all the *blah, blah, blah* prattle just rolled off me.

Morning sex brightens the day. It sort of reinforces all the soft instructions you've had about romance. Euphoria reawakening – that would be the title of a blog about morning sex.

By mid-afternoon, I was debating if I should leave my office and return home or chance dropping by to see if Momma was okay.

Having worked at the school cafeteria so many years, she was used to the early hours. By mid-afternoon, she was off work, and usually puttering around in her garden, or baking luscious deserts and flavored breads to dispense throughout the family. Knowing that she would be calling me and inviting me over, I preempted. I phoned her.

"Momma, I just got off work. If you're in the garden, I can come by and help."

"For a fact, I am in the garden. But I'd rather you drop by Angelo's and pick up Lea. Gypsy called saying she'd try her out as a nail gal. Lea will be working three afternoons a week doing nails. Gypsy said she'd pay Lea half the charge. And there would be tips."

"Great," I was genuinely happy for my wayward sister finding gainful employment. "Having anything on her resume is a good thing. Even better, Angelo's is within walking distance. So why does she need a ride?"

"She wore her high platform shoes and said her feet hurt. You know Lea and her wild outfits and shoes. Anyway, I said I'd ask you to pick her up. Then maybe you'll still have time to give me a hand in the garden."

Charlene and I always had fresh produce from Momma's garden, and usually ate a salad every night throughout the summer. So I felt a duty to the garden. "Any pastry?" I asked optimistically.

"I just put a couple pans of herbal bread in."

"Okay, I'll stop by Angelo's and pick up Lea, then see you."

Lea and her damned three-story high pumps, my thoughts complained. She was freakin' tall enough. I was mid-tall and mid-short. I liked that because Char and I match heights. You might say we're middle women. Family wise, I'm in between – a few inches taller than Isabel. Momma must have started pumping us through the birth canal from short, then medium, and finally long Lea.

Lea not only used it to her advantage, she hovered when she put those weird shoes on. It did give me a source of laughter when she got a pair that made her tip slightly. She sometimes looked like a marionette. I'd take my flat-on the-floor sports shoes.

Walking inside Angelo's was always a treat. When I'd take Grandma in for her hairdo, she would pick which magazines I should read. Handing them to me, she would tell me to start out with the several she'd selected.

I pretended to read about the current household tips and fashion sensibility. I also intently listened in on the conversations. Sarcastic comments must have been selling at ten cents a dozen. Grandma would get the thumbnail report on the ride home. She lived for that gossip.

She would lean close to me to report what she'd heard. Some stories would ignite a hundred hidden thoughts. Grandma's thoughts were probably going a thousand a minute.

As I entered, I was well-aware that Gypsy and her gossip squad were going at it hot and heavy.

Gypsy was a former stripper and had just turned fifty. With her big blond hair and her humongous large boobs, she still fancied herself parading down the runway. She once told Momma that the wiggle never goes away. I always liked her style and devotion to motion. I wouldn't have wanted to rub my face in between her boobs, but when I was an early teenager, I did wonder what it might have been like.

"Come on in, Vicky," she invited. "We were just talking about unfaithful men. Some of those chasers would hump a donkey even if they were Republican." Her laugh not only filled the small shop, but when the door was opened, it filled half of Littleton. "Cheaters blame it on booze, their frigid wives, and being tempted. Do you girls cheat?"

A little jolt of surprise put me off guard. I stammered, "I personally don't."

"And your what's-ya-call-her, partner?"

"I call her Charlene. We're both faithful." I was amused at Gypsy's attempt at being politically correct. "Neither of us would dare." I thought of this morning's passion. And last night's erotic sensations. "We're happy."

"Well, that's good. I've kicked a lot of men's ass outta my bed for betraying me." Her glance penetrated. She was assessing my hair, I hoped. With hands on her hips, her head cocked. "I was gonna suggest a hairstyle. Your hair is just too short for curlers. But drop by for a trim anytime."

"I may do that," I lied through my teeth.

"Shelly over there, she does as good as a barber on men's styling," Gypsy bragged.

I swallowed. Of course, my cheeks were flushed, but I maintained my smile. I didn't want to tell her I frequented a little shop not far from where I worked. My stylist at the unisex shop was a hot kid of maybe twenty. She crooned songs in my ear as she trimmed my hair. I wasn't going to change her off for Shelly the Telly. I'd heard Shelly go to town on some of her patrons. No secret was safe. Chatter was Shelly's game. Crooning versus chatter? I'll go with crooning.

I nodded to Shelly. Then I asked Gypsy where Lea was.

After Gypsy told me that Lea had gone next door to the Tanovich Music Shop, I left. This was when Gypsy and the *gals* would be evaluating my short hairdo and lack of makeup. I could do a little evaluation myself. Shelly looked like someone had delivered a rhino's rump and placed it on her head like a wig.

Even Gypsy's 'do' looked like a tray of croissants fell on her hair and formed a circle.

That's probably why they never unloaded on me. Surely, they'd looked in the mirror and said to themselves, 'Hair just doesn't naturally grow in this shape.' And they would be correct.

I entered the quaint music shop. It was small, but adequately stocked with musical instruments, sheet music, and all the accruements. While weathered, and certainly not crispy new, it had a definite charm about it. The music stores in the mall had no charm and had only a couple of marginal musicians hawking instruments.

Aristotle 'Ari' Tanovich leaned his stringy, tall frame against the counter. His features were handsome, dark, and mystically profound. I could see his father's resemblances. Eli Tanovich was also thin and tall, and with interesting, rugged features. I'd often witnessed Eli's dramatic, yet humble motion. I thought about his later years. He seemed stooped and sullen as he walked through the streets of Littleton. Yet inside his shop, his smile would lift and make the entire place brand new.

His son Ari's shoulders were lifted with the youth of mid-thirties. Although Ari had been a California musician, he certainly didn't act hip-hoppy, nor rock star. I kept waiting for swagger and crotch grabs. But he left the bulge in his faded denims alone. His dark, curly hair wasn't heavy metal. It was trimmed nicely, probably not by Shelly the Telly. His hands were clean, and he'd kept the store tidy. Fairly normal looking, I thought as my head turned toward my younger sister.

Lea, in her elevated shoes, began a gushing campaign immediately. "Ari is a star."

Embarrassed, Ari stuck his hand out for a shake.

"Nice to meet you, Ari." I took his clean hand and felt his warm handshake.

With a sincere gulp, he uttered, "And I'm not a star. I was a studio musician most of the time I was in L.A. I did work with a couple of bands, but our band members never seemed interesting enough. We left the stage, and hotel rooms standing." His smile was issued with what I thought might be overt humility.

Some decisions just come from out of the blue. Lea needed supervision, so it might as well begin early so I could get it over with. It would begin with a mistruth. "Lea, Gypsy wanted to see you a minute."

She scurried out, and I gave him a polite half smile. "Ari, my sister is a wonderful woman, but she needs to keep herself out of trouble."

His laugh was a burst. "She told me she was just released from prison. So now, you're here to find out if I'm clean. Because if I'm not, she would be in trouble for associating with me – right?"

"On point so far." An elderly lab-shepherd mix dog waddled across the floor and stuck his snout out for some scratches from Ari, and then from me.

"My father's dog. Mine now. Dad found him roaming the streets a few years ago and took him in." I detected somberness in Ari's eyes. "Dad named him Gershwin."

"Because he was the *pianist* dog on the block," I giggled out the old joke.

"No," Ari found me sadly comical and my aged joke plain sad. "It was because Gershwin was my father's favorite musician and composer."

"Back to the interrogation," I said with a more mellow voice than I'd used before. "It's important – my sister is important to me."

"Funny thing, I just met your sister, so I know she's important. She has a quality of bringing joy into a room. My dad used to tell me how she'd drop into the store and make his day." His eyes seemed to dim. "She dispenses happiness." He insinuated, "You dispense questions."

"So we both understand – I would be very upset if she had a problem because of you." I tipped forward so he would know I was serious. One of my softball coaches said leaning forward indicates determination.

Ari must have played baseball because his laugh burst through clenched teeth. He reached in his back pocket to pull out his wallet. Fingers adroitly excavated a driver's license from a mound of other cards. He handed it to me. Amused, he asked, "Have you ever done a search on the net?"

"Yes." I memorized the details on his license and handed it back to him. "Well, sort of."

"Okay, look me up. No arrest record. I was detained at a concert when I was nineteen. I've smoked marijuana, but that was years ago, and I was never charged. It's legal now anyway, but I don't indulge in blazing up some weed."

"Me neither. And Lea doesn't either."

"Well, that's one family quality you share."

I frowned for an explanation.

"You sure don't have your sister's personality. She's sweet and glowing."

Maybe I should have smiled a tad. "We can't all be Sunshine Suzy," I dryly, and coolly, replied.

Bursting into the shop like a pissed off SWAT team, Lea stormed. She chastised me. "Vicky, Gypsy didn't know what you were talking about. She didn't want to see me."

"My mistake," I said with a quick wave. "Nice to meet you, Ari and Gershwin."

Grabbing Lea's elbow, I made a break for the door.

"Vicky, you were a little rude. Ari seems very nice. I went over to give him my condolences about his father. I really liked talking with Eli. He was so smart. And nice."

Sometimes I see what's ahead. Not clairvoyance – just plain old vision. Before hoisting my tired limbs into my vehicle, I looked up. There was a fluffy set of clouds overhead. Then I glanced back at Lea. She was riding an entire bank of clouds.

Romance and all the attached rigmarole was probably not far behind Ari and Lea. Everyone in the family would be wondering how that might play out.

They were absolutely sweet on one another and Momma was going to be livid. I hated it when anyone was livid. And when Momma was livid – well, *livid* went into overdrive.

Chapter 9

Lea posed with elegance and immeasurable lift to her spirit throughout the trip back to the house. It was her monologue that concerned me. Ari was *such* a nice man. Her words continued to propel her everlasting admiration of this guy she'd just met.

Pulling into Momma's driveway, I realized I hadn't said much at all. I'm not the gushy, flirty type, so I wasn't going to promote her lust.

When she shut the car door, she added, "And I know his father said that his son was unmarried." The ride had assisted in pulling her skirt up, and so she tried to unrumpled it as she stood. Between her frothy outfits and her flounce, she came off as a decorative chorus girl.

"Lea, he may be a scoundrel." I was secretly hoping he wasn't a miserable jockstrap. "You always begin relationships with thinking the guy is heaven-sent. Look, I'm not trying to rain on your flipping parade. I just want you to be realistic. You aren't always sensible when it comes to choosing men."

Grandma, Momma, Isabel, and I always thought she was encouraged to bilk the bank by one of her lazy, no-good boyfriends. He had vanished the minute she was taken into custody. Grandma was so mad she called the miserable slack a *fucktard*. But I figured from the way she pronounced it, she'd just heard it somewhere and had no idea what it was. She did that one time when she'd said *mo-fo*. Not a clue. But Grandma knew both mo-fo and fucktard were derogatory.

"I have a good feeling about Ari," she argued. "He's sensitive."

"Maybe he's gay." I headed for the backyard gate. "Look, I need to get back there and help Momma. Exercise. Charlene says I'm getting a sagging jawline."

"He *is not* gay."

"Incredible. You can tell, huh?" I felt argumentative.

"I have straight gaydar."

Sighing, I delivered Momma's message. "Oh, Momma said to tell you your room needs a cleaning."

"My maid is blind to dust."

I rolled my eyes. Bemused, I asked, "You don't expect Momma to clean your bedroom?"

"Of course not. I'll do it later."

"Momma also said you're cooking supper tonight, so you might want to get a head start."

Obediently, she entered the enclosed back porch slash mudroom. I skimmed my mind for residue from the meeting of Aristotle Tanovich. Ideas spewed – but forming an evaluation was more difficult. Thoughts of listing pro and con flailed.

Granted, con people can *con*vince us of anything. Ari might have come close to putting one over on me. Certainly, I'd intended to hate him at first sight, but I had a mellow feeling about him. Maybe some criminals perfectly hone their craft of gaining people's trust.

"Holy blazing fuck!" I exclaimed as my foot slid into an imploding sinkhole – well, more of a rut in the garden. I knew the moment those words blazed out that Momma would be expecting me to pull out my rosary and burn those beads with prayer. "Sorry, Momma."

"You'd better make sure you confess those words and that outburst," Momma warned with a snarl. "And you might wanna keep your rosary close at hand." She eased her hoe against the shed. Nearing me as I hopped, she helped me sit down at the edge of the sidewalk. "It's gonna be just fine, Vicky. You're the most athletic one of the bunch – and you're not exactly agile."

"Sorry I cussed." I hadn't been to confession in years and years. "I'll make sure to tell God how I cussed because I'm a clumsy klutz." In my defense, I always thought confession was weird.

So, if God is almighty and all-knowing – why are we reminding him how egregiously we'd sinned? Erring is a happening – it goes on all the time. A creator wouldn't have time for my sniveling sins. I used another moment of silence to pitch a 'Hail Mary' skyward. That was always comforting to me. I don't know why – but it was. Then I returned to my spiritual tug of war. Is our earthly purpose to remind God about what bad things we've done? Like we're little memory banks? I think not.

There were just so many things to bring out my worst cynicism.

Hobbling up and around, I twisted away from Momma's attempt to hold me up. "I'm fine, Momma. Just fine." I felt a smarting in my ankle. Pressing on, I took a shovel and began attacking weeds. It had to be documented somewhere that weeds grow a hundred times faster than flowers and vegetables.

"Now, you tell me about this Ari fella. I chatted with Gypsy, and she said that was all Lea could talk about. She was bubbling over about going next door after she got off work to talk to Mr. Tanovich's son."

"I talked with Ari and he seems okay."

"Vicky, Derwin says he's unfriendly. He shoos the kids out of his store." Momma's eyes were seriously concerned. She leaned against the hoe. "And he's in a rock band. Well, we all know that Lea can be a bit of a playgirl – but a fella like that could get in there and..."

I interrupted. "Momma, I'm going to check him out. On the internet, I'll investigate to see if he has priors. I did asked him about his background when Lea went over to talk to Gypsy." I gave Momma the rest of the information I knew.

"Is that all?"

"It was only a ten minute chat. I got a tat count – two small tattoos on his upper arm. A guitar and his initials. And I didn't see scars or tracks – a vein-line from needles. But the polygraph was on the blink, so I can't report on his truthfulness." I couldn't explain my impression because I hadn't reached a conclusion. "Let's say I didn't get enough for a lengthy obituary on the guy."

Looking down at my watch, I uttered, "I'd better get going. Charlene will be home in an hour and I need to stop by Arlen's and pick up a couple things."

As I rushed, I heard her say not to forget to pick up the loaf of home-baked bread and the sack of vegetables she'd packed for me.

Also, I was to make certain Lea wasn't burning down the kitchen. Or flaming up over a guitar player.

Momma required a lot of attention come to think about it. I sighed. How many clicks is infinity? Is the omnipresence of middle sisters ordained by a creator? Will Charlene be in the mood tonight?

I knew that finding a parking place in front of Arlen's Pump 'n Pop was nearly impossible some early evenings. Luckily, I parked near enough that I could have reached out and grabbed a pack of gum off the counter.

Arlen Denton was in his early sixties and had owned and operated the Pump 'n Pop since I was young enough to remember. At sixty, he'd seen the convenience store meet and beat all the calamities. A few robberies, thefts, fights, and complete breakdowns of electricity, leaky freezers, and tumbling shelves had all been dealt with by Arlen. Nothing daunted the easy-going, nice-looking guy behind the counter. Tall and large, with a huge paunchy stomach, the black man always seemed jovial.

From a child's perspective, going to Arlen's was a terrific experience. Some of the shop owners didn't want to be pestered. Arlen never complained or got grouchy. Smart aleck teens and young adults would attempt to give him fits. But he grinned and kept the peace as best he could.

Momma said that he told her, in confidence, that he didn't care how stupid, stinking, or how much of an asshole a customer might be. The money wasn't stupid, didn't stink – and could be an asshole if it wants.

Momma didn't criticize his language. Grandma chuckled each time she heard the story.

When I stacked my armload of goods to be purchased on the counter, he welcomed me. "Vicky, how are you this beautiful summer afternoon?"

"Great and you?" I slid my charge card to him.

"Me and the Mrs. are dandy." There was a pause where he usually had inserted several sentences about Mrs. Denton. "Well, we're a little concerned about Derwin lately. He was in way after dark last night. He had to get some soda bicarbonate for his Ma. I followed him out and some fellas a couple years older – well, I'd say maybe preteen – going into teen – were waiting for him."

"Rats! He's only nine," I divulged. "Dottie says that dark is his curfew. But she doesn't watch him."

"Well, those boys were lots bigger. I go out and watch. Keep a lookout. I warned the two of them to be walking the other way. And if they didn't, I would call in the law. They took off, and I watched Derwin until he got to the corner. Kids pick on him. And there are a lot of rank strangers hanging out."

"I know." The thought of the poor kid being bullied hurt like evil debris. And if a perv got him, that would be it. "Look, you've got all of our phone numbers. Just give any of us a call. Momma can be here in five minutes and I can be here in ten."

He nodded. "Damn kids call him sissy. It isn't right."

"No. Kids shouldn't need to endure that. In my day, I got teased for wearing clothes that weren't feminine enough for *their* tastes." The scent of loneliness suddenly surrounded me as I dug back into my memories. Expulsion from the popular kids was a given for kids like me. Expecting some of the hip kids to be friendly was like watching the carnival pack up and leave the county.

"I remember when you were small, just before your daddy took off. Simon and me were talking about how people had their prejudices and probably always would. I'll never forget how he said that he hoped his daughters didn't need to deal with hatred."

"Arlen, you knew my father. Did he ever tell you why he left?"

There was a long pause. Arlen packed my items into a plastic bag. "I think him and your mother had problems back then. Maybe he didn't think they could be solved. One day, he just loaded up his beat-up old car and left."

"He just loaded up and left us." I repeated.

"He stopped by to fill up his gas tank. Seven dollars. Thirty-plus years ago prices for half a tank. He didn't need gas – he stopped to say goodbye." Arlen's blinks rushed – drying the mounting tears. "Said he was filling 'er clear up because he had a long way to go. When I asked the whereabouts, he said he didn't know." Arlen glanced back from the cash register to my face.

"Your daddy always talked with complete clarity. But that day, he seemed all bewildered. He was a man who had always cared for his family. He paid his bills and I don't think he ever missed a day of work at the factory. And I took it that he loved you all."

"He left us. I'm not sure how that converts to love," I responded.

"Maybe he was planning a return trip, but it didn't happen." Arlen was thinking my thoughts.

Maybe he was dead. Sure, he could be tucked into the soil. Or maybe he was incarcerated or institutionalized. "It didn't happen. He never came back. And I don't think he ever will."

Wisdom is reaching inside for truth. But, I questioned, what if the truth is unresolved. Life closes off things, people, and even wisdom. We can never know about the future. If destiny holds an auction, we never know what to pay for any given thought.

"Thanks, Arlen. Have a good evening. And please give us a call if it appears that Derwin is endangered. Or if he needs a ride home."

"I will. Tell your Momma that those vegetables she brought us were appreciated. Me and the Mrs. fixed us up some delicious stew."

"I'll tell her." Grabbing the sack, I left the store. Once securely in my vehicle, I drove through scant traffic. Music had been turned down to a whisper. Then I remembered. "Aw, shit. I forgot the cayenne."

I hoped that my beguiling lover would provide even hotter spice.

As I was driving near a liquor store, I decided to pick up some wine. Charlene usually did the vintner visits because she knew wine. I only knew it was wet – and sometimes too sour.

The final leg of the drive home went smoothly. Most of the traffic had drained off Littleton Boulevard. Even Littleton, Colorado had traffic crunches at drive-times.

Before parking in the apartment lot, I looked up at our window. Charlene was watching for me and her wave told me that she was indeed in the mood. That has to be what *lucky* really means.

I loved her so much, and to my astonishment, she loved me. Charlene's love latched me to her. It didn't matter if we were in the same room or across the world. We knew we authenticated one another. She called me the butch princess, and I teased her that she was my ornamental bitch with cleavage.

She could certainly do better, but for whatever reason, she *thinks* I'm better. There's an ease with trust. Yes, there is that certain eloquence of trust.

Truly, with the exception of Char, I'm earth's stranger, I thought stoically. I glanced back up at the window. She was still waving.

My heart was still uplifted.

Chapter 10

My heart was racing. "Holy blazing entanglement! Sugar Lips, you rock the pelvis of love," I murmured.

"Remarkable," she lulled. Her word was as soft as newly mowed Kentucky Blue Grass.

"Our bed must assume we're a couple of flesh curlicues." Our love sessions of orgasmic pleasure were never a quick frolic. I glanced up at the window. Beyond was a thinly sliced sliver of moon. "I'm glad the moon can't give reports of our activities."

Charlene began to giggle. "Your post-coital words of passion make me laugh. You are indeed a mattress dandy."

I held her smoldering body as we bundled together. "That's it?" I kissed her temple.

"I fell in love with your words. How you see the world – you interpret it differently. Well, actually off-kilter. I first noticed that about you. Remember when I told you not to take any liberties with your first assignment – it was a speech for some dignitary?"

"I remember. I didn't take it personally, but I did wonder why you admonished me to make it boring."

She smirked. "I so loved your words, no matter if they rained their way down to me, or needed to be extracted one-by-one. I enjoyed them. Your verbal imagination makes me think."

Our embrace intensified as she kissed my clavicle. It was obvious I was smitten each moment I was in her company. "You are the most incredible woman I've ever known. I need to be reminded what you could ever have seen in me." I kissed the tip of her nose. "I don't deserve you. You're alluring, and I don't think I could make it without you. But loving you so much – sometimes scares me. Char, I love you with everything, and I'm never sure that's enough."

"Our evening pleasure is plenty." She began caressing my back. I felt the tender drag of her nails climbing across my skin. "Your words tickle my soul."

"Ah, you love me for my titillating literary skills. I'm certain I would be kicked out of most writing courses. No wonder I'm insecure about this phase of my life. I'm only a product of genetic programming."

She leaned up on her elbow with her chin in the cup of her hand. "Vicky, your blogs are really getting lots of hits. With this possible windfall, I want you to really give some thought about working part-time and devoting yourself to a book."

"I like my work. There are a few twits. But yacking with a twit once in a while is actually great entertainment."

"You're meant to write a book," she was insistent.

Sighing, I turned my face to the wall. "I'm not sure I can sustain a story from blog to book. Not all runners are long-distance runners. Some are sprinters at heart."

"Maybe you need to go into seclusion. Your family uses you to intervene."

"Yep, I'm like this intervention ramrod."

"Like your mother sending you after Lea today. Your mother is not a bar-the-door transparent kind of woman. She's a little on the devious side."

My pause was a relief. Thoughts gathered. "Maybe Momma does send me off to spy and be the bad sister. She might not want to teach corruption by example when it comes to apportioning snoop assignments. She is the director – she points out the dilemma and figures we should deal with it." I hadn't thought that one through before. "But she loves us."

"She does. I evaluate each sibling's place in line differently. Isabel is the head-start child. She feels responsible for making certain you and Lea do what tasks she imposes. She's a dismal failure at that one. You are trying to solve the problem with two sides – a controlling older sister versus an unruly, ditzy kid sister."

"Yes, I agree."

"There's more to it than that, Sport."

I then added with a nearly muted concession, "I do feel as if I'm in the center of a game where I'm the one getting trampled." I wanted a different, more descriptive allegory. "Isabel is always at her own racing track meet. She sets the regulations, she runs the race, and she declares the winner. Lea is living a constant life of basketball rim shots. She never seems to come up with a score. She just keeps aiming for the backboard and missing."

"And you're in the middle of a pre-won race and constant losing?"

"Pretty much so." I took a deep breath. "Yep."

"I'm so glad I'm an only child. When I was small, I resented not having a brother or sister. Now, after seeing your family, it was worth the childhood loneliness not to deal with all the problems of adulthood."

I snuggled around her protectively. "I'm glad you're my sugar lips and sugar hips."

I loved the feeling of Charlene drifting off to sleep in my arms. Just as I adored waking up with her next to me. My head could be thick with sleep, but the mornings were still recognized as glorious because Char was there. Just touching her had always been a kiss of sunshine on my heart.

Reminiscences of first meeting her marched through my mind. When we first got together, I treated her as if she were a live electrical wire. She mesmerized me. One day, all my insecurities tumbled out. She laughed and said everyone has those feelings of the unknown.

Unknown. Talking about writing. Considering having more time – it was all unknown until a great fortune happened to my family. I wondered if the good-fortune fairies had suddenly made a clerical error.

Last weekend had brought a life-changing bonanza – and ramifications were like huge question marks hovering. My mind swirled as I considered all the changes that money makes in life. Future expectations were simply to provide for myself. A large chunk of money was never part of my dream's splashiest rendezvous.

Some people have their dreams listed indelibly on the wall of their mind. They know exactly what kind of goodies their best fantasies were made of. I was clueless when it came to material treasures.

The night skies outside our bedroom window spelled it all out. As mere human beings, we keep detecting new galaxies. We make them ours – we want to believe they are. They should belong to someone. We all should.

I noticed the sky's darkening pattern as the moon slimmed down to a sliver. When the night is darkest, it sometimes seems as if the atmosphere becomes inhaled away. Light was extinguished into near blackness.

Somehow, I felt it analogous to the moment. At least my pulse had quieted down, and I enjoyed the post-orgasmic feeling of being carted off by the Goddesses. Well, my Goddess in particular.

Making love with Char was like gathering orchids.

Chapter 11

Charlene had hurriedly rushed from the apartment to arrive on time at the weekly corporate breakfast. I'd renamed it the Eggs Benedict Arnold Special with a side of Executive Moaning and Rancor.

I was left behind hunched over a bowl of stale cereal and curdled milk. Neither of which appealed to me. Checking my messages, I found that Momma had left several. Thankfully, among them was an invitation. She said she was off to work, but if I hadn't already eaten – I should drop by and heat up some buckwheat pancakes she'd left in the refrigerator.

The other messages were asking if I had done a background check on Ari yet, would I please take a loaf of bread and a sack of veggies to Isabel, and please awaken my lazy sister, Lea. Lea should be in pursuit of a second job. Three afternoons a week did not a fortune make – especially if Lea was sneaking off to chase after a man. Momma's aphorisms were often greatly imperiled by her emotion.

Obediently, I showered and dressed – readying for my delivery service rounds. I'd arrive at work a little late, but I'd say I was doing work from home. Although I put in my hours, I did my share of hour swapping. The work was done. My employer was pleased. My family was taking advantage of me constantly – so they were pleased.

I would work at double-time speed – both on delivery and writing a bunch of propagandized crap for hire.

Momma's cooking was always worth the drive. She'd carefully stacked the pancakes and readied them for their microwave adventure. I ate with delight and with streams of butter and maple syrup. I'd also warmed the coffee – so I was on a happy camper high. Or maybe it was the syrup that was giving me a sugar high like a glucose jump-roping contest.

Then I braced for the tough part of my assignment. I went downstairs and across the hall to my sister's room. She'd been given her choice of staying in an upstairs bedroom or having the privacy of downstairs. She'd wisely opted for privacy. Well, Momma didn't *really* believe in privacy. We were all very aware of that fact. But the decision was based on the fact that Momma wouldn't be so quick to climb down the stairs.

"Rise and shine or Momma will get a bad report," I threatened – but with a deliberate joke skipping around in my raspy voice.

"Not so loud, Vicky." There was a shift of the bundle she was wrapped inside. "Damn, it's early yet." Her face was of an adorable child from one side, and on the scarred side, it was like ruffles and wrinkles from night's bloating. I rarely ever noticed how terrible the disfiguration was. We get used to things. We glance across the reality of them.

"Momma said you should be making phone calls and sending out resumes online. Come on, she has to work. I've got to work." Sitting on the bed beside her, I gave her shoulder a playful shove. "You'll show Momma how you can succeed."

"Are you the dyke cheerleader today?"

Glancing around the disheveled room, I commented, "I see your dust-ignoring maid hasn't been to work in a while."

"You and Momma are a matched set."

"Lea, she would say cleanliness is next to Godliness. I would just say this place is a pig sty," I pontificated. "Momma is tyrannical, and I'm merely suggesting you get your ass out of bed and hang up some of these clothes. It looks like fabric is flooding the room."

My sermon was a big dose of zero. She glared at me. Then with a thorny, morning voice, she snarled, "Screw you. I've got a cramp in my shoulder."

When all else fails, a grin and a pat on her head usually helped. "Working out cramps is easy, just move around. There are pancakes in the fridge, and I'll even fix a fresh pot of coffee. And have a cup with you. I just finished eating. I took the plate with the most pancakes because I'll need the stamina to deliver some things to Isabel."

"Isabel. Better you than me." She rolled over.

"I'll be waiting. I'll be expecting you in exactly five minutes." She mumbled something as I made my exit. I didn't ask her to repeat because I probably didn't want to hear her tell me where I could go or what I could do to pleasure myself.

Although I hadn't set a timer, she did make it to the breakfast table by the time I'd made a fresh pot of coffee. Breakfasts are most generally a gentle, almost timid time – like mornings.

Both tables – in kitchen and dining room, were round. Grandma believed in round tables. She said you could view everyone's eyes. Make certain they're on the up and up. And if you need to throw something at someone – you have a clear view when you take aim.

As Lea ate, I noticed her glaring at me. Finally, she said, "You know Isabel is going to talk you outta sticking up for me about the sundial."

"Admittedly, she'll give it her best try." I took an overloaded gulp of coffee. "For what it's worth, I'm not changing my statement. I'm sticking by it."

"Hummff. You'll buckle. You always do. But even if Momma resists and keeps saying the will stands – I think she'll still give us each a fourth share."

I took another gulp of coffee. "Maybe. I know Isabel is going to be at Momma for Tad's right to be the inheritor. She claims he has the legitimate lineage to the sundial."

"That bitch never once visited me in prison."

"Maybe it would have hurt her too much." I tried to see Isabel's side. It was a huge ripping of the heart when you see your baby sister behind bars. The rat-fuck clothes are more than enough to lend heartbreak where sisters are concerned.

"What a hell of a burden for her. I was in the correctional institution. She wasn't."

"She didn't embezzle."

"See, I knew you'd end up on her side."

"I'm not on her side," I protested. "But I know she cried a lot when we talked about you." It seemed everyone in the family became a little sadder when Lea was sentenced. Although not entirely devastated, our happiness meter certainly dropped in intensity.

Grandma felt she hadn't done her job in watching Lea. Momma thought she was a derelict parent because she had to work, and also feeling as if she'd delivered those criminal genes to Lea. Isabel, as the eldest, figured she should have beaten the crap out of Lea a few times and it might have trained the wild child. I knew it was *my* fault.

"You're all against me."

"Lea, Isabel balled her eyes out. We all did."

"She cried because of embarrassment. Not because I was dying in that goddamn place." Hostility was oozing. "At least a portion of me was dying."

Wanting to diffuse not only the hate, but also the hurt, I offered, "But she did send cookies. Treats."

"Sure, an oatmeal cookie will make up for not seeing me."

"I'd a traded places on that one. I'd gladly given up seeing Isabel for four and a half years. I wouldn't have even insisted on the flipping cookies."

She grinned. "You'd a baked the cookies and given them to her for her staying outta your hair for that amount of time."

"Yep. No doubt about it." With the mood slightly elevated, I questioned, "What's on your play-card for today?"

"I might pop over to see Gypsy. And Ari."

"Momma's concerned about things with Ari getting too serious too quickly. You are planning on going slowly?"

"No." She resumed her hostility. "I'm going over there and take the guitars off the counter and screw him right there." She seemed to be in an unusually volatile mood.

"Lock the door first."

An unexpected bursting laugh was issued. "You never change, Vicky."

"Nope."

"Look, I'm not going to make any mistakes. I know Momma wants to have him checked out. But he's a nice guy."

"Momma is used to looking out for your best interest. Time will tell about your best interest."

"Momma wasn't looking out for me when I got this." She pointed to her face.

"Lea, it was an accident. Momma wouldn't have allowed you to be hurt if she could have helped it. She and Grandma always protected us."

Tears formed in the corners of her eyes. "I know. Vicky, it's just that I'm feeling self-pity."

"You'll be fine," I lied.

"Ari is real sweet with Gershwin, the dog."

I wanted to reply that Hitler loved his German Shepherd. But I didn't. It might have been a spindly hope, but I wanted this Ari to be a good guy, too. And I didn't want Gershwin to take a bite out of me.

Loading up my delivery, I knew that my next leg of the journey would undoubtedly be even worse than the first. Before this potential 'treasure' was cast upon the family, my life had been relatively easy. If I was with Momma, I would simply nod, mumble agreement, then leave. Now there were plots, plans, instructions, and investigations.

Before the sundial crap, Lea's chatter would impede on my day, but I would let most of it go – to be disbursed into the clouds of conversation. Some of Lea's gibberish was about new shoe styles. Other prattle was placed in a huge 'talk tube' labeled the 'gossip and nonsense' channel. Ignoring most of what Isabel had to say, I only attempted to glean enough of her blathering complaints to use them as a comic source. Charlene was greatly entertained by Isabel's nasty drivel. One might even say she was amused by it.

Now, family words had become ugly accusations and mistrust. Words took aim at any and all. We were all one another's fair game. Firing on one another left a yelping soul after each encounter.

No rule book was being used in this game. Unless maybe one considers the actual legal document – Grandma's Last Will and Testament. And if that hadn't been botched with some legalese, the winner of the shooting match was Momma.

Another piercing of pain hit me when that thought occurred. What would Grandma think about this travesty?

She'd probably flush the flipping will right down the toilet. She'd be determined to live forever – because all those left behind would bungle it. She'd scold us all. She never played passive-aggressive like Momma did. Grandma would kick us to the curb and not look back. She often stated that we were all too big for our britches. She was probably sitting up in heaven cursing us for our muddied accusations against one another. I can hear her saying that we'd pay the piper.

I often ruminated about Grandma – and what she'd think. The current goings on would most probably throw Grandma into an all-time rotten mood.

Well, I had a lot of her genes – and that's what I would do. Maybe she would have turned out nicer than I projected her to be. She'd forgive us for being greedy little carnivores.

I braced for the toughest part of my assignment – that would be Isabel. Isabel would be fuming. She'd wail about my recollections of Grandma giving Lea the sundial. Her face would be coiled up with her vicious eyes zeroing in on me.

Charlene was right about Isabel. Sometimes she did wear a snaky, reptilian expression.

Grudgingly, I started my vehicle's engine. I glanced down at the sack of produce on the passenger's side seat. Tying the top of the plastic bag, I then put the vegetables down on the floor for safe keeping so nothing would fall out. I cautioned myself – I couldn't stand dealing with soggy tomatoes and Isabel's dour face all in the same day.

I gave way to the giggle of my daydream. I would roll down the window and pitch the damned vegetables out and hit Isabel's porch. Delivered with the acumen of a seasoned newspaper carrier – I'd hit the spot nearest the door.

Suddenly, there was the problem of being serious. I couldn't let Isabel see me yuk-yuking. She didn't respond well to giddy sisters.

I recalled when I was about thirteen and Isabel was fifteen, we were looking up at the cloud formation. We'd always had a game of finding things in the skies. Clouds. One formation was very interesting. Isabel said it looked exactly like some green beans. I said that it appeared to be a vagina. She stomped several times and told me that clouds are not vaginas. She also said, for the very first time, that I was a lesbian because I always saw breasts in the clouds. And then vaginas.

I accused her of being a gourmand for believing the cloud formation was green beans.

She responded by saying my allegation was very unbecoming. Only Isabel could believe *gourmand* was a dirty word.

Chapter 12

Isabel's hands flapped like she was swatting at a herd of bumblebees in hot pursuit. She even seemed in-flight as she filled each tiny candy bowl then moved rapidly across the kitchen to fill another. "Slow down," I suggested. "Remember how Grandma used to tell us we'd combust on fire if we didn't stop rushing?"

"Well, thanks for dropping Momma's bread and the veg. But I've got my canasta morning and I'm just not ready. I want you out of here before the group arrives."

A quick glance down at my cargo shorts and tee-shirt verified a reason for my dismissal. "I'll be leaving now," I muttered as I backed away a few steps.

If Isabel's feminine dress code was all it took to scram out, so be it. I could go way butch and get out even faster. However, I couldn't just skedaddle mid-sentence and her words began again quickly. Too quickly for a rapid-fire escape.

"Just tell me about this Ari guy. If he has a record, Lea is going to be in trouble hanging out with him. You were supposed to check." Her hands dug deeply into her apron's pockets.

"I'm checking today, at my very first chance."

Her sigh was one of utter distain for my procrastination.

However, while she had me there in front of her – the inquisition would continue. "Victoria, this family has trouble. And you know what I mean. Lea has always been boy-crazy and now she's man-crazy. If he gets her mixed up with anything shady, that would be the end of Momma. Seeing her youngest back in prison, well, that would do it."

"I agree," I spoke solemnly.

"He's not from around here. California." Her eyebrows bobbed and she blinked rapidly. "If you get my drift?"

Charlene would call Isabel a xenophobe. A reptilian xenophobe. "I get your drift," I answered.

"God knows what he got up to in California."

"We don't know that he's ever been in trouble," I argued. "His father, Eli Tanovich, was a well-respected merchant in Littleton. Ari was cooperative about giving me information. He even got out his driver's license." With a giggle, I added, "He knows he's under surveillance."

"That's not funny." She was stern. "Growing up, Momma always said you were a precocious little goober."

"She called me a precocious little whippersnapper," I corrected.

Isabel's glower was that of a flame-thrower. With a tip of her head, she asserted, "It's the same thing."

She was going to be smug and intolerant. She flourished in that role. "I need to get to work."

"Another thing," she bristled. Then words shot out like arrows. "You're flapping your mouth about hearing Lea say Grandma was giving her the sundial. For all I know, Lea offered you a share of the take if you back her. You're in cahoots."

"I'm not backing her, Isabel. Momma has the will. Anything could happen." I sidestepped, pulling back across the room so she'd have more room for her dramatic whirling dervish swirls as she dispensed candies into the candy bowls.

I remembered watching an old TV shows with Grandma called *The Loretta Young Show*. Loretta's wild entrance on her show was with swirls, twirls, and drama up the yim-yam. Isabel must have seen the show a time or two as well.

Plunking small cracker trays on the counter in haste, she missed a couple of the trays, and crackers hit the countertop. Angry with the miss, she pitched them back in the bowls with force. I thought she would chip at least one, but she didn't. "Vicky, you are a disappointment to me. I always thought I could count on you."

"You pretty much can." My mouth waggled. "Until we know more about what is happening, we just need to keep calm. You know – end hostilities."

"I should just open up and tell things I know – about how Lea's accident happened. Is that what you want? I can do my reminiscence." Her head ticked off the words as she mimicked me. "Grandma promised it to Lea. I remember the conversation." Her words were like a secret hiss coming to the foreground. The lash was meant to get my attention.

My mouth might as well have been super glued and clamped. Add to that, my brain was clogged completely. Rats, she could smell my fear. She knew how to leverage her power.

As if x-raying my shame, she'd cornered me. She asked, "Well, missy, what are you saying now?"

Suddenly, I remembered thinking about something. I would spring it on her. Change the topic of concern, as it were. "There might be a far greater problem."

She stopped, as if skidding. She turned. "What kind of problem?"

"Say Momma gets the money from the sale of the sundial. But what if our father is still alive and what if he returns to claim it?"

Her eyes nearly sprung out of their sockets. "Oh, my God. Dear Jesus!" Pale wouldn't have begun to describe her coloring. She grabbed a tea-towel and waved it in front of her face. Stiffly, as if she were being lowered from an imaginary harness on a pulley, she sat down onto the kitchen chair. "Do you think he could find out about it – if he were alive?"

"The program is going to air on national television. It is possible he could find out, certainly. Maybe he's in touch with someone back here. They would tell him. See, when someone vanishes, you don't know where they are or what they're doing. But they know where you are and maybe know what you're doing."

Her words became frail, "Yes. I hadn't thought about that." Her frown was so deeply dug in that I could have planted potatoes in the wrinkles on her forehead. "Legally, I don't think he could waltz in here and take Momma's money after thirty-five years." She sucked in air. "He ran out on us. Abandoned us. There must be a law about him being gone so long."

"In the news you hear about crap like that happening all the time. I mean, he's only two years older than Momma. Sixty or so.

He could be alive. He could get wind of Momma's fortune and hustle back here to sign off on it."

"Oh, my – blessed Jesus, Mary and Joseph!" she exclaimed. As if she were one of those caricatures – where the eyes pop out on stems, hers bulged further out.

I figured she'd be inconsolable for at least another few minutes. So I continued on. "In some of those cases, one person wins a lottery or whatever, and the other comes back to poach the winnings. Then they spend the whole shooting-match on attorney fees. They come out poorer than they began. So, what I'm trying to get at – is that maybe we should sort of stick together. In case that type of scenario was to happen, we'd have a rank and file going on."

"I see your point." Her lower lip trembled. Her hands were fidgety. "Momma would never take him back. They'd be like strangers. Remember that trip to Omaha Sully took a few years ago?"

"That company union meeting?"

"Yes. Well, when he got back here after just a couple days, it was like we had to get to know each other again," Isabel divulged. "With Daddy, well it's been decades."

"Do you remember much about our dad?"

"I was only five – or nearly five-years old. So I don't remember much." Thoughts transported her for several moments. "He wasn't mean. When it was time for him to get home from work, I'd wait for him at the gate. If you were up from your nap, you'd wait for him, too. He'd bring us little hats made out of paper folded from newspaper. Sometimes he'd have candy."

"I wish I could at least have had one thing to remember."

"You were a toddler then. But he picked you up sometimes. He'd swing you around and you'd laugh. Then he'd swing me." Suddenly, like a burst of memories, she said, "He was usually happy – but sometimes he would be sad – for no reason. I'd ask Momma why he'd go in the bedroom to be by himself. She'd say he was in one of his moods."

"Why do you think he left?"

"Maybe he stopped loving us." Her eyes flickered with pain. A pain I hadn't realized was there inside her. "Maybe it was all too much for him – supporting three kids with only a menial job."

"I wish I could remember getting candy and a paper hat from him."

"It was usually M&Ms." Isabel crossed her arms. "If he'd only been gone a week or a month, I'd be glad that he'd returned. Not now. He doesn't belong here now."

"And it could be an expensive return," I suggested.

"Well, let's just hope for the best. And pray. Let's go to church tomorrow and pray. Wednesday Mass – and that will be our holy intention."

I walked to the backdoor for my hasty retreat. "I'd like to, but I'll be working."

"Well," she dispensed her harshest frown, and continued, "Vicky, you can pray *anywhere*."

"Yes," I muttered. I wasn't certain how she would suggest that prayer go. 'God, please, if you haven't already, kill off Simon Brent.' Or maybe, it should say if he still is alive, that he be struck blind so he wouldn't see the program. Deafness so he wouldn't hear of Willa Brent's amazing blessing. The entire thing sounded like out-of-context sorcery.

I wondered if my father had been in a bad mood, so he picked up and hauled it on out of our lives. Or maybe he decided he was tired of dispensing candy and hats. Maybe it was simple. Maybe he was fed up with swinging a couple of brats and tired of baby poo.

I didn't know if I should feel noble for having shared my thoughts about the return of our long-lost father with Isabel or satisfied that I'd derailed her rant. Either way, it felt as if it belonged in my win column.

Chapter 13

"Who did you say you are?" the pleasant-sounding woman's voice asked.

"I'm doing a background check. According to my files," I tried to sound authentic, "you were married to Aristotle Nickolas Tanovich ten years ago. And I was just verifying."

Her chuckle was muffled. I must have caught her on a good day. I waited for a response. I was certain that she was suspicious. "Ari. Yes, we were married for four years. A long time ago." The blank spot in the conversation was probably her wondering what I was doing calling her – intruding into her day. "We weren't ready for marriage, really. Nothing to tell. We split with decorum and amiably – that's one of the modern ways of saying peacefully. We talk once or twice a year, and e-mail oftener. Just to check to see how we're doing. Why are you investigating him?"

"Not really investigating," I quickly reported. My search into his background had dug up a marriage and divorce. From there it was relatively easy to locate his ex-wife's phone number. I'd expected she might want to joust - with either him or me. Thankfully, that was not the case. "Just getting a background. You know – his finances, prior criminal record."

This time her laugh was booming. "Ari would make a piss-poor millionaire. If he ate money, he couldn't have shit a nickel's profit. Bucks never impressed him. He would have made a worse criminal. Yah, he'd be an ineffectual enemy of the people. Clueless."

"No drugs?"

"Minimal grass – for a time. We were kids and in a band. After the band broke up, and he was doing studio work, he became a suburb dork."

"Does he have a temper – fighting and all?"

Her laugh sashayed. "God, no. He was always sweet tempered. Quiet." There was a pause. "Where are you getting your information?"

"Just general questions," I answered. "Any other details you can offer?"

"Well, if you're looking for criminal behavior and lots of assaults and batteries – you really can't be serious. Ari and I are two terrific people who thought we might be in love – but weren't. We were in *like*."

"It sounds as if you still like him. Respect him."

"I do, and he's a heck of a guitar player." As if remembering, she said, "Last time I talked with him – that would be last winter – his father was ailing."

"Mr. Tanovich passed away recently."

"Oh, damn, I'm sorry. I didn't know. If you're in contact with Ari, please give him my condolences. I loved old Mr. Tanovich."

"We all did," I said without thinking. That oversight undoubtedly blew my cover.

"I heard Ari moved to Denver. Sold out here and went Colorado. He must have changed phone services – so if you talk with him, please tell him to give me a call."

Before disconnecting, I had thanked the prior Mrs. Ari Tanovich. Of course, she knew I wasn't from some agency. We both played along splendidly. Now I could report my findings to the family – and that should sooth everyone. I felt better.

The other search I'd embarked on was much more complicated. I'd typed in my father's name a dozen different ways. But searching the world was an expansive search. His family was originally from Florida. I did a quick check and found they must have all scattered to the wind. Like my father. Relatives had their own disappearing act that spiraled into the corridor of the unknown. They'd all vanished.

The remainder of my work day was putting in my employment time speed writing about the benefits of luxury vehicle tires. The suckers rolled like cheaper tires, were inspected like less-expensive brands – but their posh name advanced the safety and elegance-on-the-road satisfaction of driving. By the time my blurb was done, I wanted to go out and buy the miraculous, comfort-oozing things. Maybe even make love to them.

I'd mentioned to Momma that Charlene had a business dinner – public relations group – and usually attended the dinner every month. So I'd stop by to tell her my findings about Ari Tanovich. By the time I reached Momma's, it was late afternoon. She was in the garden chopping the crap out of runaway weeds. "I thought I'd find you back here."

Continuing the assault, she answered "For a fact, these weeds populate like there's no tomorrow. Now what did you find out about Ari Tanovich?"

"Good news, Momma. Ari doesn't have any kind of record. And I found that he'd been married."

Her cautious gaze lifted. "He's got a wife?"

"No – he had a wife. He'd been married from when he was twenty-two until he was twenty-six. She was still in the L.A. area. Momma, she likes him. That's positive when an ex-wife likes you."

Her mouth pursed. "He might 'a changed."

"She talks to him every so often she said. She seemed to paint him as being boring. And you know we're really jumping the guns on this one. We don't know if Lea and Ari have any intention of even dating."

"They're dating all right. She is with him now, and they're planning to go to a movie after they have a takeaway meal. Besides, Lea's face lights up. Well, the way your face gets all bubbly when you talk about Charlene. That's why I knew it wasn't doing me any good to resist giving you my blessing."

"I'm glad you did, Momma."

"I figured with other women it was only something you were going through. But mothers know. We do." She stopped smashing weeds. "We want what's best for our children."

I gave her a hug. Her shoulders always seemed to get smaller each time my arms wound around them. Maybe she'd forgotten that for so long she'd been mortified about my settling down with Char. "I'm thankful, Momma."

"I want Lea's happiness."

Stepping away, I noticed an expression of distance. I wondered if she might be thinking of my father. "I had a thought about this entire bonanza thing – the sundial. Momma, what would happen if our father returned? You always hear stories of a spouse coming back for a share of the treasure."

She chuckled. "Vicky, I may present myself as dumb as dirt. But I read stories. All the time I'm reading things. Once I read about such a case – the lottery winner's runaway wife comes back. Well, I called an attorney right away. I had my marriage dissolved. Dissolution because of abandonment was what it's called. After so many years, you can file for divorce. Done," she announced as she snapped her fingers, "marriage gone."

"You never mentioned it to us."

"I never even checked it with the priest. I just did it. Well, at that time there wasn't any treasure. But there was Grandma's house. I didn't want to be on the wrong side of Grandma if she wanted the house passed down to you girls, and I'd failed to protect it."

Nobody wanted to be on Grandma's wrong side for anything, I was fully in agreement and compliance. Grandma had come from a different era, and she knew her stuff when it came to reading people. She didn't like mistakes. Not when you should know better.

"That was really smart to do, Momma."

"I'm pretty bright about some things." Her eyes blinked to a close for several moments. "If your father is still alive, I'm married in the eyes of the Lord – but as far as the State's concerned – I'm an unattached woman. A crafty unattached woman."

"You're crafty about *most* things," I concurred. A serious frown suddenly congealed on my face. "Do you ever wonder where he went? Or," I asked with trepidation, "why he left?"

"Musta been his own reasons for leaving. There's no clue about where he might be now. Could be in the ground buried *tightly* – for all I know." She emphasized the word *tightly*.

"Does it ever make you sad – not knowing?"

"Of course, I think about it. But we aren't always the whipped frosting on our spouse's cupcake."

"Most people move out, separate, divorce – they leave a trail. They don't just run away."

"Your daddy had some good ways. But he also had some strange ways about him. He ran off for his very own reason."

Momma wasn't the type to emit wails of grief. I'd never once seen her sob for my father. Her unsettling gaze went back to her gardening.

Dead, destitute, or deranged – I liked my alliterative thought. Speculation was all up for the grabs of fate. I supposed that there was something more behind my father's gallivanting. But who is ever to know anything unless a mystery is solved. The shouts of time are a mystery.

Had he gone off to become a hidden famous hermit? Was he lost – and couldn't find his way home? Were his moods a private isolation he couldn't explain?

Trudging to my SUV, I considered that the family might have glossed over something in his past. If I were writing about his moment of going missing, I would make him a cavalier character that was in love with adventure. He side-stepped the mundane life and hit the action trail.

I'd recalled Grandma once mentioning my father read poetry. It was when I'd read some in high school and she noticed it. I asked her and she said she had no idea what kind of poetry he liked. Then she said she'd considered it might be the reason I had a way with words. I got that from him.

She believed that people have other good things in their hearts – not just poetry. But it mattered to me. There were no poetry books on Momma's bookshelves. Maybe she'd tossed them away – or sold them at a garage sale. Maybe that's why my father boogied on out of Littleton – she sold off his poetry.

Or perhaps he was weighted down by guilt. But I'm weighted down by guilt, and I'd never leave my lover and my family behind.

Perhaps writers are nature's stealthy visionaries.

Chapter 14

The furnace of summer's dry, high-altitude heat was upon us. My investigatory skills were certainly not red hot. I'd uncovered very little. That meant the really big news of the afternoon was a scant, but colorful culinary hint about what might have happened to my father.

My parents weren't the matching whipped frosting on one another's cupcakes.

Intrigue and mystery happen in most families, I presume. Perhaps my family wasn't destabilized beyond the chaotic norm. After all, we are each unitary souls. A family tosses units together under one time and area. From there, we navigate through the various mixes and complexities. While we do, regardless of the differences and multitude of problems – love occurs. It is undeniable. It could be an impediment at times and a blessing at others.

Maybe it comes down to our desire to belong.

I felt like a flipping carrier pigeon. Around my neck was this wire that transmitted messages to each of the other family member – from one another. I'd scurried to and from each, and they would tie different messages – like dangling post-it notes. Over the past days, I'd become the to-and-fro Brent family emissary.

When Charlene checked in with me, I moaned about my plight since the revelation about the worth of the damned sundial. She'd phoned just after Momma had called to ask me to keep an eye out for Derwin. Once again, he was MIA, and Dottie finally realized he was missing. The shrew was a menace – as mothers go.

I complained to Charlene. "Just guessing, but I'd say vodka sales are up at the neighborhood liquor store." Grandma used to say Dottie kept the cheap booze market afloat.

"Vicky," Charlene interrupted my thought with her alluring, lush voice, "why do you always get lumbered with everything?"

"Maybe it's because the wrong one in line gets slapped," I offered. "I'm usually the wrong one."

Her throaty laugh continued. It turned me on – even through the mayhem of this week, she had heart-centric appeal. I was throwing sparks when she laughed.

"Babe," she responded with her argument, "they've always done this to you. Your devotion astounds me. Just don't let it get you down. I don't want you in a depressed funk."

"I'm fine. It will settle down after things are figured out about this sundial. Until then, I'll pretend to give a crap."

"The problem is you do care."

To take up the phone's dead air, I questioned, "So what's on the menu tonight at your little banquet."

"Cardboard chicken and soggy, month-old vegetables. Naturally, that will be followed by some unimaginative dessert that should be tested by the Federal Food Administration. And I'll bet your mother will have a mouth-watering, lip-smacking cherry pie with a dollop of Ben and Jerry's topping it."

I couldn't deny her version might be correct. I didn't want her food-tortured – so I just shut up about cuisine reviews. "If I can't find Derwin, or if Momma calls to tells me he's home, I'll grab something on the way home."

"I've got to scat now, Vics. Wish I didn't have to go to that boring damned dinner. I'm in the group to advance my career. I think it's a waste of time. But it beats your volunteer career of family and neighbor butt-wiper."

She laughed, so I did, too. I wouldn't tell her that I'd just been thinking the exact thought before her call. She knew it was bothering me. She always was aware – and she would give me an emotional pat-down, if for no other reason than to let me know she commiserated with me.

When I drove past the bank, I considered the safety deposit box. It held so many dreams, and as Momma said – blessings.

I wondered why I felt the sharpness of some vast and deep inferno. All that the sundial represented seemed to be hurtful. I didn't want our family torn apart any more than it already was. It was leaving scuff marks on my heart.

Up the street, I saw the plod of Derwin. It was, as always, restless, and with a gait of perplexed wanderlust. Each step was as if he were expecting a trip-wire. Damn, the poor kid could so easily get snatched, beaten to death by bullies, or could die of his mother not even caring about him.

Well, we, the Brent family cared. We did. We'd all gone on one reconnaissance mission after another. Me, mainly. I do care about the kid. If some of us feel we might be EveryWomyn – yet not quite, I think we can spot EveryKid. Derwin was an EveryKid with a learning disability. There was a sweetness, a shyness – that made him a unique EveryKid. He didn't represent the 'typical' child. But something about him was softly, gently reinforced with innocence and trust. When he unfurled a smile, I noticed that it was so true that his meaning it could never be disputed.

Sometimes, I wanted to peer into his soul. How does someone feel when their own mother doesn't see them as anything but a burden? But Derwin wasn't into 'show and tell' with his truest feelings.

Wondering if part of what kept him silenced might be fear I swallowed hard. Yes, he might fear that he wouldn't get by without Dottie. He might not think he had anyone else. But maybe we Brents cared more for him than he knew – or we knew.

Maybe I could mention it during dinner. Of course, I'd take him with me to dinner.

I'd already talked myself into a juicy burger, a load of sweet potato fries, and a chocolate malt. Carb, sodium, and sugar-jammed – and not as good for me as Momma's meal might be, I opted for the ole coronary calamity meal. I usually allotted myself one wildly out-of-bounds meal per month. I was up to my eyeballs in sinister family finagling. Treating myself seemed appropriate – even mandatory.

Parking on Littleton Boulevard – Main Street, I honked my horn to get Derwin's attention. "Hey, partner, I'm on my own this evening. How about joining me for a burger and malt?"

His eyes brightened when he saw me. Climbing into the passenger's seat, he said, "Sure, Vicky." He gave me his lopsided grin that appeared to dangle off his face. "Wow, yah."

I called Disaster Dottie. I told her I'd found him and would be taking him to dinner. Then I'd bring him home. I instructed her to please call my Momma.

"You got your phone in your hand, why don't you call 'er?" was her grumbling, unappreciative response. When I didn't answered, she screeched, "Well, why can't you make the fuckin' call?"

"I just found your wandering child, the least you can do is call my mother. And yes, I'm asking you so that I don't have to. Not that you usually get the message right when you do remember to call."

Giving Dottie instructions was always very 'iffy.' What she usually relayed wasn't precise. At times, it wasn't even decipherable. But when she slurred, she always gave you a look that you could interpret. She questioned your hearing, intelligence, or both.

"All you bitches do is complain about every little thing." Dottie was clearly sloshed. "You and your old lady just keep up the insults. I can't help it if the little fucker runs off."

"You need to watch him closer." My voice held my emotions in check. Yet anger was escalating.

"He's with you, so he's okay."

"Why don't *you* take care of him?"

I could visualize her fleshy lips oscillating around to find the truth.

Her theatrics astounded me. Although she pushed all of Momma's buttons – Momma said we should be charitable. I disconnected quickly before I called her a roach.

When I hung up, I immediately called Momma to report that Derwin was safe. I didn't want her to worry. She read when she was worried and particularly, when awaiting word about the kid. She'd have been sitting by the telephone, agonizing until midnight if I left it to Dottie to call. I could hear the relief in her voice. Before hanging up, Momma said thanks twice.

When I pulled into the restaurant's lot, I gave Derwin's shoulder a pat. "What do you say? Should we go inside or go through the drive-up window?"

Without a miss to his beat, he replied, "Inside. Inside takes more time. We can talk more stuff when we have more time."

Holy, blazing crap! The kid might end up a cross-contaminated politician.

Chapter 15

Carefully and systematically, Derwin unstacked the tomatoes, lettuce, and onions that blanketed the huge burger. He squished pillow packets of ketchup, mustard, and mayo on the burger's top. Rebuilding, he placed the bun perfectly center, and then pressed it down as if his small hands were a Panini press.

The eating process was nearly a fulltime career for Derwin. There were times when he would be the last one sitting at Momma's dinner table – after we'd all excused ourselves. Momma said to pretend not to notice. He was being entertained.

Amused, I observed the way he laid out the French Fried potatoes. They were all stacked and going the same way. He'd built a log-like mound – tribute to his dinner, I supposed. With his lips placed delicately on the straw, he sipped. "This is so good," he commented.

"I like the malts they make here." I chomped into the juiciness of the burger. I'd ordered the one with guacamole sauce and bacon. I didn't mind the sauce dripping from the burger.

"This is delicious. Vicky, you know the best places in town," he complimented. "I'm glad you take me with you."

"I'm glad, too. Glad you hang out with me." I wiped my mouth as I cleared my throat. "How's your mom doing?"

"Mom gets wobbly sometimes. She loves to sleep. That's why I go outside. Well, in winter and bad weather, I just go to my room. But sometimes, I get bored in my room. That's when I think about going somewhere. I like going over to your mom's house best. But other times, well, I just want to see how things are going everywhere."

He'd called his mother wobbly. I considered that translated to drop-down drunk. Sometimes, she needed a floor chart to walk across the room. Sadly, she couldn't take care of herself, much less a nine-year old child.

"Does she ever help you with your lessons?" I inquired.

His eyelids pulsed. "No. She doesn't like it when I miss something – when I get something wrong. I try to study, but I'm not good in school. Sometimes, your momma helps."

"School gets harder and harder. More to learn. I actually liked learning most things, but there was so much – even back when I was in school. But let me know if I can help."

"I find stuff out when I visit with your momma. She's knows lots of garden things. Yard things. Your mom knows all about gardening and outside things."

"She taught us to plant gardens."

"Me, too. She let me plant lots of small boxes of herbs, too. She'd plant them before summer. She always said to tuck 'em in gentle like. We didn't want to crush the baby plants. So I know all about how to plant seeds and tiny plants."

"I remember when I was young – I'd always worry about breaking one of Momma's delicate seedlings. She'd say the roots are the feet and legs."

"And your grandma told me all kinds of neat things to learn."

Thinking back, I recalled it was my grandmother who instructed me in so much about life. A staggering hurt was a flashing current through my limbs. I missed her. She could certainly be prickly, and at times, had a surly disposition. After raising a daughter, she took charge of raising three more girls. Then, it seems, she continued by raising a young baby boy – Derwin.

"I know my grandmother thought a great deal of you, Derwin. She enjoyed you as if you were her own child. Or grandchild."

"I love your family more than mine. You're all good to me. I like spending time with you and your family. That's why I love your family better than I love my own mom. I probably wouldn't wander off if I was your boy."

"Hey, Der, we all love you, too. And I worry about you – we all worry about you – when you wander off. You shouldn't be out alone. It isn't safe. And we would be heartbroken if anything happened to you. You are our boy."

His head lowered. "You aren't mad at me, are you? I mean, my mom gets so mad at me."

"Naw, I'm not upset. Just concerned that no one hurts you. Like when kids give you a rough time. They shouldn't do that. It's wrong."

He wrestled his next words out. "Sometimes, they're just having fun. Joking with me. That's what they say. When Arlen chases them off, they say I gotta be a good sport. So I guess it might be all okay."

"It's not really okay, Pal. I'm telling you. If they rough you up – that's not okay. You should be respected for who you are."

Warily, he stared across the room. Even his voice seemed skittish. "I can't be a baby. My mom says not to be a baby. I should grow up. I think she wants me to leave home, really." His words withered away.

"And that's why you run off?"

"Sometimes. I used to go to visit your grandma. Then she died. Your momma works days. That's what I mean about your grandma teaching me stuff. I noticed your old sun clock is missing. Your grandma taught me about how it told time."

I sat up straight. He was so observant. Once he told me Grandma's Hummels were out of line and out of the placement she'd selected.

"It isn't missing. We still have it," I stated.

"Good. Cause if all of our watches break and the electricity turns off, you can still tell what time it is. By measuring the shade," he proudly offered. "The cast of sun – and the shade – shows time."

Grandma had often positioned the base of the sundial to show my sisters and me how the shadows were cast. The indentures on the dial kept our ancestors on time. How life's odometers have changed, I considered. My body's mileage ticked with time. *Time* needs to be encoded information – for historical reference, but also to keep us together. It is used in nearly every phase of our lives. What other measurement is so intrinsically important to us?

That gave me an idea for my next weekly blog – or the following week. I was always on the hunt for good topics. I'd pun that the sundial would always be *timely*. I'd put it onto my list called Blogs to be Blurted.

"I recall Grandma taught me that, too." I nodded, and then a laugh escaped. I quizzed, "Anything else we have out of place at Momma's?"

"The cats in the corner curio." Derwin explained, "I didn't want to touch them though. Not without super-super-vis-ed – vision."

"Next time you're at Momma's, just tell her. She'll help you." Grandma's collection of three and four inch high porcelain kittens were always a hit with kids. "My grandma loved cats."

"Her last cat, Diva, was my favorite. Diva loved your grandma, and me, too."

Diva, a stray, had been part of the household for years. She died only months after my Grandmother. "Diva was loved by everyone. I remember when I was a child we had one named Silver the Cat. We always had a cat around, and they were fun to watch. But after Diva died, Momma said no more cats for a while – until she retires."

"My mom won't have cats. She chases 'em off. Even throws stuff at 'em," he said disapprovingly. "You don't have cats either, do you?" There seemed to be a mild resentment, which was an emotion Derwin seldom showed.

"No. Charlene and I have talked about getting a dog or cat, but not yet. We both usually work all day and don't have regular hours to let a pet outside."

"Charlene is beautiful. Like Lea is beautiful."

"They are, yes." With a jocular, easy chuckle, I asked, "How about me?"

"Sort of," he answered with a frown.

The huge burst of laughter made me nearly spill my malt. "I'll settle for that." I admired his honesty.

"You're cute," he stated. "You got cute ways."

With a wink, I expressed gratitude. "That's one of the nicest things anyone has ever said to me." I meant it. Derwin's affection was never glossed. "I think you're mighty cute, too."

He joined in giggling, and together, we toasted with our malts held high. Nearly every dinner we'd shared together had at least one toast. Derwin loved that idea. He loved celebration – and he showed it. It was visible. What I worried about was the invisible. I was concerned that there were dark places in his dreams. And his heart wasn't designed to be a dark dream kind of place.

Glancing down at my wristwatch, I realized his dinner had taken two hours to complete. At least there had been joviality.

My decision was made though. Next time we'd grab our sacked burgers as we raced through the drive-up window. That way we could go back to Momma's house for a quickish meal. He'd only eaten about a third of his food. I suggested we get a container to take the rest home because Momma hadn't had a chance to chat with him.

Derwin's talk was really about his lack of family life. His treatment at his own home was demoralizing. A long and somehow painful dinner, I thought. Maybe he needed to chat more than I didn't need the painful reminder that there were little kids all around the world who were ignored by their families.

Another consideration was that maybe Derwin was destined to be a womanizer. He appreciated Lea and Charlene's beauty. Who can tell? But that being the case, I figured I ought to get out my softball mitts and give him some pointers. Sports might as well be called chick magnets.

The interest shown by women in sports was a huge reason I played ball when I was in high school and college. I wanted to impress the girls, I acknowledged. That, and I wanted an outlet away from home – the fuss of two sisters was going strong even then. Ours was a matriarchal home – with a feminine sibling rivalry. Well, I was on the lower rung of the feminine part.

Derwin and I jabbered the entire drive home. I promised we would try to get together more often for burgers. He seemed to like the idea of a little baseball. He usually wasn't interested in playing catch for any more than half an hour. Same thing when I'd taken him fishing. A little outdoor stuff went a long way with Derwin.

The evening really had been fun. It also pointed out something that should have been more conspicuous. Derwin really was part of our family.

Chapter 16

As we crawled into bed, I thought about the evening with Charlene after she returned from her business dinner. Laughs seemed to come in multiples. Explaining my family's behavior as exotic, well, that didn't do it justice.

Charlene tittered slightly, setting us off again. "Cupcake frosting!" Her explosive laughter chained with mine. Tears slid down her face as she caught her breath. "I nearly collapse when I think your mother actually said that. Spouses aren't always the whipped frosting on one another's cupcake." Our laughter seemed charged with visions of Momma actually saying those words.

"Bye-bye trouble – and by trouble, I mean the entire Brent family. And off my father went – taking his frosting with him."

She leaned toward my shoulder as we rested back on the pillows. "And Isabel is on a prayer mission so that your father never returns – that I really don't get. I mean, she's the only daughter who was old enough to remember him. I've never heard her talk negatively about him. It wasn't like she hated him."

"Half a million inheritance is at stake," I reminded her. "She'd take the polish off anyone for a share of that kind of money. I'll bet she can ramp her campaign up to some major indulgences, prayers, and yes – a bulky contribution to the Altar Society."

"But he's your father. I don't understand the lack of concern for him." Charlene snuggled nearer.

"I guess we couldn't care less. He left – we didn't. So since we had no control over being fatherless – why do we need to mourn a stranger? I'm well-aware that he may be skid-row destitute or even dead."

She sat up a moment. "What about good old forgiveness? Hell, Babe, it isn't as though he mistreated anyone."

I leaned near her and kissed her temple. "Forgiveness is another word for 'I'm coming back for another serving of your disrespect.' For instance, if I ran out on you, leaving you with three children to bring up, how happy would you be to see me come back?"

"We don't know why he left. He may be an innocent old codger." She hesitated. "As for you, of course, I'd kick your ass to the curb. Just remember, Sport, if you'd even think about it – you'd be so single."

"I never would leave you. Char, you make me feel as if were weaved together. I couldn't be without you."

She smiled a thin smile for just a flicker of a moment. "Not that I ever would, but what if I hurt you – would you write me off like you've written your father off?"

I considered the other side. "Seriously, it might depend on what he did. Maybe his life was somehow smudged. Or what if Momma was the transgressor? What if she did something unforgivable? He might have had a reason. But it's highly unlikely." I sighed mightily. "So I'm sticking with my original unforgiving thought."

"And with me?"

"I'm not certain. But I would know what happened if it was between us. In my parent's case – I don't know the facts. I just have to pick who stinks less."

Snickering, she asked, "And you're a churchy. Shouldn't you be offering unconditional forgiveness?"

"I'm a cafeteria Catholic, Charlene. Some things I believe in and some things not so much. I'm trying to make everyone happy." I felt the warmth of her body. "I hope you're happy."

"Yes, I am." Her smile issued approval. "I'm happier than I've ever been. From the moment we met, there was something about me that felt your happiness."

"And I felt your return happiness leaning up against me." I recalled, "But I worried about my family bugging us."

"In spite of your family constantly interfering in our lives – I'm happy."

"Me, too," I agreed.

"They have improved over the years. No more snarky *hell* comments. Maybe they've gotten to know me better."

"Yes, and I think they've decided I really am fortunate to have you. Now they're obsessed with Ari. All I know is that he's not on the ten most wanted list."

Charlene assessed, "It could be a marvelous event in your sister's life. I hope Lea is having a leg-kicking night of it. However, I'm with Isabel for once, so I hope she's not having a propagating night."

"Let's not even consider the consequences of a reckless action. She's savvy enough to use birth control. She sure as hell wasn't celibate before getting pitched in the penitentiary. "

"For being Catholic, I'm amazed Isabel didn't have a herd of kids."

"I'm guessing Sully only got a little once. Tad."

She sighed. "Unless he slipped her a little once and awhile when she was preoccupied. He probably hasn't had a very sensual time of it. Sully is a saint."

"You, too. I just hope Ari is prepared for the family. Lea is wobble-dobble enough. Add in her family – well, poor Ari."

"What's 'wobble-dobble' mean?" she questioned.

I shrugged. "It's just a made-up word."

"Vicky, I wouldn't use it in your blog this week."

Charlene was right. Some of my words couldn't fly if they were riding the back of a hungry hawk. My blogs were free-word zones. I would take the clothes off words and let them run naked. Teachers always commented on my assemblage of words – thoughts. I always vowed to one day allow free-rein to those notorious notions. I wouldn't expunge a single letter. Except when Charlene recommended it. "Okay. No wobble-dobble."

With a tender kiss on her neck, I heard her low, sexy moan of potential lust. "I've been horny all night, Vics."

My eyebrows playfully bobbed. I could read the fervor on her face of sublime desire. Could luscious carnality be far behind? Blessed endorphins, I thought. "Come here, lover."

There was no reason for her to love me – I'm not a centerfold. I'm not rich. And certainly not powerful. I wanted to ask her if she ever looked for an upgrade. But now was not the time or place. She was in my arms.

"My cupcake frothed over," I uttered. We both began choking laughter. Before I could take the words back, I'd broken the romantic mood. "Aw, hell. Yumberry the Muffin!" With trapped giggles that dissolved into a lengthy kiss, we knew there was an entire night for spreading the frosting.

"I am so in love with you," she whispered.

Showing her how much I loved her was on my midnight agenda.

Chapter 17

I always considered Wednesdays to be the weeks middle-ground. Last night with Charlene had put a day-long smile on my face. Assuming that Ari had also been in the land of Happy Bed last evening, I thought I'd pay him a morning visit.

This was after Momma had phoned to say Lea didn't get home until morning and was now resting. "That girl better get herself to confession," Momma admonished.

"Yes. Be a good Catholic and go to confession. But be a bad Catholic and be sure to use birth control," was my amatory word to the wise.

"That would throw a wrinkle in where it's not wanted," Momma declared. I envisioned Momma doing half a dozen signs of the cross. She'd probably end up bruising her shoulders someday.

"Lea and Ari like each other. That's not a bad thing," I tried to stick up for my baby sister. "He's been vetted, so I don't see it as a problem." Not that doing a cursory search that provided a clean record, and the unimpeachable witness ex-wife, made any difference to Momma. Her youngest child had already shown that there was a streak of corruption in her luxurious body. Momma searched out thorny contents of a story. Once, in my mind – I had called my mother a battle-worn woman.

Isabel was probably becoming battle-worn. Lea was – or had been – a sadly battle-worn woman.

Forever I would believe that Lea had been tricked by life. She was impulsive. The crime she committed hadn't been planned out. She always seemed set adrift – and she reached for the golden ring – and ended up regretting it. Lea always tended to look to the future with optimism. Even when the face of tomorrow looked mighty crabby, she believed things would be okay. I'd hoped she could recuperate from the jail deal. Incarceration has been known to sterilize ambition.

How did Ari figure in? Well, if Lea was already battle-worn, maybe Ari could renew her.

I wondered as I parked my vehicle in front of the music store, was I wishing for good things for Lea because of sisterly goodwill or because of my own guilt? Did she ever question if I were the guilty party – where her accident was concerned?

Crossing over into another person's thoughts may be a way of losing one's self. Reality is all swerving and speeding. Each act we commit puts wear and tear on our tread. Lea ended up with a scar. And I ended up with the interrupted silence of guilt that screamed my name each time I thought about it. Guilt is some self-avenging emotion.

"Did you telephone my ex-wife?" Ari blasted me with his question of the day.

"What?" I squirmed. The one-word question was to buy time. Ari knew I'd called his ex-wife on my prowl. He knew I was the only one who might have been skulking in his background. If he hadn't guessed – I would have considered it high-resolution stupidity. He wasn't dumb, by any means.

He leaned against the counter. It wasn't threatening. He wanted to make me aware he was on to me. "You heard me. Someone called my ex checking on me. She called a couple of my friends and finally got my new phone number. You were in here on a hunt. You wanted to know if I'm good enough for your sister. So, with that, I narrowed it down to your family wanting my history. I'm not sure playing a private investigator is your mother's style. And Isabel would crap her bloomers."

I chuckled. "Yep, she sure would. Look, I won't lie to you. I wanted to check you out. I love my kid sister. I'm not TMZ. I don't give a flip about your background. Other than, I want you to treat her right – and not be a bad influence on her. So if you hate me for protecting my sister, hate me."

"I don't even know you, much less hate you." As if he'd tackled me and was now reaching to help me up, his grimace converted into a smile. "Lea is the kind of woman people want to protect."

"Ari, you sound like a decent guy. Another point in your favor – you're tall."

His face creased. "Lea mentioned that. She's five-foot nine and said she likes six-footers."

"It's a family joke that Isabel is five-three, and I'm five-six, then came Lea. Momma said if she had any more kids – it would be like manufacturing a woman's basketball team."

"Lea is just right for me," he gushed like a foolish high school boy with a crush.

"She's the pencil thin one. As you can see, I'm husky – well, maybe a little over-husky. And Isabel is a tad plump. Momma must have liked variety." I wouldn't mention that Isabel questioned Lea's parentage. From descriptions, my father was not much taller than me. He didn't have light coloring like Lea, and his eyes were bronze – like the rest of the family. In Momma's defense – recessive jumps generations.

"Just guessing, sweetness worked its way through the lineage. Isabel is cranky, you're feisty, and Lea is pure sweetness." His grin was again flashing like a neon sign going on with its wild blink. I could almost hear the sizzling whistle of the neon light.

"Feisty about says it all. Ari, I know you think I'm terrible, but actually, I was coming in to apologize and tell you about the phone call." I stuck out my hand as an offering.

His large, thin hand warmly took mine. Mine nearly disappeared in the handshake. He shrugged. "Okay – we're okay now. Any more questions?"

Pausing, I frowned. "Yes, I do have a question. Why do you chase kids out of the store? Are you just mean-spirited or do you hate kids."

His laughter was musical. "You're a tough act, Vicky. I'll try to explain it. I'm a sensitive guy." He was serious a moment. "Look, my father recently died. I've been in pain about that. I should have come here to help him. Make things easier on him. I offered, but he insisted I stay in L.A. I was about to have a major sale of some of my songs."

"I know what guilt is all about." I hesitated and looked away toward a vacant corner. "But he was proud of you. And with his

112

heart problem – well, there probably wasn't anything you could do."

"I came back here. But there was no longer the joy here that there was when Dad was alive. This place seemed like a mausoleum when I arrived. It felt constricting – and it hurt. I knew I wanted to be here, but I also knew the sadness I was dragging around. Kids pick up on things. They know if you're sad. I didn't want my sadness to permeate their lives."

His dark eyes were dim for many moments.

"I'm sorry, Ari," I apologized. Truth was there – intricately appearing through his anguish. "I know you loved your father. And your father loved you."

"I talked with that old man every single day. He continued to encourage me." His head lowered. "Now, well, the kids can come in and mess around with the instruments. I've got happiness back."

"How so?" I hoped for the correct answer. I could vouch for the fact when sunshine comes into your life – living converts to happiness. A dozen years ago, it had happened to me. No matter what goes wrong with a day, I go home and happiness greets me.

His face beamed. "Lea." He gave his answer and it was correct. "Romantically, I've been happy before but never this happy."

I grinned. "It doesn't bother you that Lea has a record?"

"Naw. My father thought she was a great lady. He'd always tell me if she'd come in. He said she was beautiful and that she cheered him. When she was going through everything – well, he said she was innocent."

"She admitted to being guilty."

"She wasn't guilty. In her mind, she was fixing what had happened to her. She was desperate."

"Even so, she shouldn't have done it. She knows that now. Our family thinks she got too much time. But prison didn't change her to a bad person. I'd hoped it wouldn't."

"My dad said her letters indicated that she realized how wrong it was. She wasn't like some of the women who were mean and awful. Maybe as a person, it strengthened her resolve to never do anything like that again." Ari was convinced. "It was all about her scar."

I concurred, "I think it just got to be too much for her. She endured it for as long as she could."

"Do you know what happened to her when she was a kid – how she got the scar?"

"She probably told you. She was in a wagon, and Isabel and I were outside in the backyard with her. She fell out of the wagon." My words sounded rehearsed. "Her face took the brunt of the fall. Momma took her around to many surgeons. Fixing her face when she was small meant that she could have nerve damage that might end with paralysis. Years ago, Lea found out that they had new and improved methods – medical techniques and surgeries that could make a complete, safe recovery possible. She tried to save money – and I tried to help – but it never seemed to be enough. Flipping inflation."

"She took the money to make her life normal."

"She knew it would break my grandmother's heart. And Momma's." I took out my lip balm and spread a heavy glaze on my dry lips. When I was nervous, I fiddled. "Lea is a good person."

Nodding agreement, he said, "I know. I think I'm falling in love with her. I started writing a new song. I haven't written a song since before my dad died."

"I'm glad you're happy. But just a footnote – don't hurt Lea. If you encourage the wrath of the Brent women – it will be your sad day. Do we understand one another?" I threatened.

Amused, he answered, "Hell, I wouldn't want to tangle with any one of you – much less the four of you."

"Keep that good, healthy respect. Be glad my grandmother isn't also here. She was a hellion on steroids." With a wave goodbye, I added, "And the most *vicious* of us all is Isabel with full bloomers – she's to be reckoned with only if you're the devil."

Amused, he commented, "I figured the most worthy opponent would be your mother."

"Her, too. She's the commander of the cafeteria. After careful evaluation, she tells the kids in line what their having. She slaps more veggies on some plates and more protein on others. The kids know better than to argue with her. Or they'll get her 'you need more muscle mass' lecture."

We both laughed. The sound of our laughter hadn't been smothered by self-consciousness. It nearly ricocheted off the walls where a few of the guitars hung.

With a nod goodbye, I realized that it was a very good conversation. That was a relief. Climbing back in my SUV, I felt satisfaction. Although he'd nailed me immediately as being the private investigator, he had underestimated Isabel. But then, it's difficult to get a take on any one of us. When there is crazy going off all around, where do you point first?

Thrilled that it went well, I realized Ari had feelings for my sister. That was the important thing. Ari and Lea certainly eyed one another as if they were trying out for a TV Cialis ad. My sister was smitten. Lea tickled his sadness away. His songwriting days were being spurred.

Thinking of Charlene, I wished everyone could have such a wonderful romance as we have. Recalling last night's love-sharing, I thought of her warm, magnificent fit against my body. Her lips were sultry, joyful whispers that touched mine. Her eyes were filled with delight, praise, sensuality, and they were mine. When she uttered 'come here, dandy' – my poker face was demolished. I was all in.

Well, I had a million reasons for cherishing her – passion was only one of them.

How could I not want this kind of love for every single human being? It was belonging, sharing, and desiring.

Love – long may it flourish!

Chapter 18

Just after I'd arrived at my workplace, my cellphone rang. It was Tad. My nephew, the heir apparent, rarely called me, so I wondered what might be up. Yet somehow I feared that he'd been encouraged by Isabel to badger me.

"Aunt Vicky," he began with pumped-up salutations.

I immediately recognized the sound. It was the voice of Isabel telling him that his Aunt Lea was trying to steal his inheritance. A phone call to Aunt Vicky might turn the tide. I limbered myself up for a skirmish.

"Hi, Tad. How's the wilderness camping trip?" I kept my voice pleasantly conversational. Maybe he had merely wanted to chat with his aunt. Sure, and maybe nobody I know wants a well-aged sundial.

"Everything here is great. I'll be back tomorrow night. I guess the family is going to have a photo session on Friday."

He was getting right to it.

"Yes. Exciting news," I continued the hypersensitive conversation. There was still nothing controversial. Perhaps he *had* missed me. Or maybe he needed information on how to seduce a woman. Not that he'd take my advice of thinking like a woman.

"It's all I can do to keep it a secret from my buddies, but Mom said not to tell anyone." His voice was deep and sounded a great deal like Sully's. But his father didn't talk in a commanding voice. Tad's inflections were learned from his mother. Isabel was a graduate of the Drill Sergeant's Tech Academy a.k.a. Older Sister's Club.

"Do you have your camera ready?" I inquired.

"Sure. I always have it." Suddenly his vocal demeanor jumped track into a completely unrehearsed enthusiasm. "Aunt Vicky, you should see some of the great shots I got. Grandma Brent will love my wildflower photos. There are a lot of little critters. I spent two hours taking various studies of birds. I'm telling you, there are photo opportunities everywhere I look."

"You've always been great with the camera."

"The new camera I got with graduation money is amazing. It almost takes pictures by itself."

I laughed. "You have to provide the artistry. And you do." I complimented his photos because he did catch the nuances of shade and sunlight beautifully.

"Thanks, Aunt Vicky. I'd really love to become a professional photographer."

"Thoreau said," I quoted, "'In the long run, you only hit what you aim at; therefore aim high.'"

"Who's Thoreau?"

My throat choked up. "A poet." I once heard that a poem should both open the soul and body at the same time. I wasn't certain who might have said that. And if I had a name – I was plenty certain Tad wouldn't recognize it anyway. "Just a poet," I concluded with sarcasm at full blast.

"Oh, yeah," he muttered. As if shot from a cannon, he recalled what he'd called for. "Is it true Aunt Lea wants to take the sundial?"

He was sending out the message. The true reason for the call was now presented. "Tad, she believes she was given the sundial by Grandma Donnell."

"Mom said you're saying you heard the conversation."

"I did. But I think Momma legally owns it. So it's probably not important what Grandma said to Lea. I suspect Lea is just saying it so that she won't be excluded. I'm not sure. Time will play it out."

"It was passed down to Grandma Brent – and by rights, it really should belong to me."

"Tad, I can't say I haven't got knowledge of something I heard. I've got to honestly tell exactly what transpired." My heart froze up a minute. Where was the little kid who shared his toys with me when we would play? He'd even give me his best baseball glove when we'd play catch. "Tad, I know it would seem that it should be passed down – but Momma will decide."

"No one else has kids. The lineage should be continued, like my mom says."

"Lea is in her mid-thirties and still of childbearing age. And who can say – maybe Charlene and I will have a child one day."

"They don't let homosexuals have kids, do they?"

"In fact, they do." My jaw was suddenly clamped so tightly, I felt like a gangster spitting out a threat.

"I didn't know that." He was perplexed.

"I'm sure you didn't, Tad." Zap.

He was spewing the kind of rhetoric Isabel had been hand-feeding him. Lesbians are second-class citizens. We shouldn't marry. We shouldn't raise kids. We aren't worthy. Yes, that came directly from Isabel. I could almost hear her saying it. That would be followed by my sister saying '*if you get my drift.*'

With her superior airs, she would tell him sin by sin – what the Bible says. That was a backup to be interpreted to say whatever made Isabel superior.

He muttered, "Mom said it should be a family member to inherit."

"The lineage isn't set in concrete," I added. "I could be inseminated. My uterus isn't any different than any other woman's."

"Well, as of today, I'm it. I'm the forth-generation heir."

You sure are, Pal, I thought. "If there's a court battle, there probably won't be much left. And Momma will probably get that. If we piss her off by fighting – she isn't likely to give anything to anyone."

He became silent for many seconds. Thoughts were cascading through his brain – the treasure was passing through his fingers and onto a garbage heap of legal maneuvering. "I don't want fighting either," he finally spoke.

"Then there are at least two of us who want peace in the family."

The remainder of the brief conversation remained cordial. He'd wanted me to throw in with the Sullivans. I hadn't.

We'd both won the booby prize. Soul-speaking wasn't doing my vitality any good. Family dynamics astounded me. I'd always been the family flub-up. Push Vicky to the right; pull Vicky to the left; smack Vicky downward; shove Vicky upward.

Did Tad really think I was going to fold? Holy blazing horseshit!

Maybe tomorrow evening when I planned to write my blog – it would be about family. The true thoughts were undoubtedly grudge-driven. Sort of a zygotic mess – family. Towers of words stacked over the decades. I'd try for exhilarating paragraphs. But really, so much of it had been said before. Life is copycat theatre. Greed. Disappointment. Well, hell, it had all been written before. Stereotypical plots. Mundane egos induced age-old riddles. Dogmatic drama.

Maybe because this particular week was so f-ed up, I would take a week off from the blog. But for the past many years, I'd never missed releasing a Saturday morning blog.

Right now, times weren't fun – and they weren't even formula. After hanging up – thankfully, the call from Tad had been severed, I felt drained. One of my coworkers placed a cup of coffee on my desk. After thanking him, I took a huge gulp.

Anger roiled – I loved that word *roiled* – it was absolutely flushed from the tongue. Why was the family agitated when everyone should be joyful? Mind puzzles began. I was in hopes that Ari was as good as I thought he might be. Lea marries him and they have half a dozen little inheritors of the damned sundial.

The kids would all have Lea's niceness and Ari's sensitivity. They would become my favorite nieces and nephews.

Decades from now – they would stand around my gravesite and weep for me. Tad would be there with a nasty smirk. He'd pulled my life-support plug. He'd offed me so he could get the massive fortune I'd accrued from selling blog books. Those collections finally were worth something. Tad had finagled to steal it all from his cousins.

Lea and Ari's kids had the financial acumen of a toad. They were so honorable that they wouldn't have known how to thieve. Hell, their mother pulled time because she didn't have a clue. And their father was plunking his guitar for donut money. His first wife said he'd make a piss-poor crook. Tad could rule the roost and be off with the takings. He had Isabel's inclinations.

My next swallow of coffee nearly choked me. Vicious Isabel had made me vilify Tad. He really wasn't such a bad kid. Everyone says to listen to your mother. He did what he was told by society – by church. And then by Isabel.

Until further notice, I instructed myself, no more daydreams.

Chapter 19

A great dividing point of the day was lunch.

Charlene requested we meet at a cute little restaurant that specialized in salads. Momma always sent bread and pastry, and often times, entire meals. Char and I attempted to compensate for peach pies and caramel silk cake. I was always loaded up with arms filled with calories after visiting Momma.

Snagging a parking place on Littleton Boulevard, I quickly glanced down the street. Littleton, Colorado seemed like the sweetest small town in the world. There were shops on both sides of the street for several blocks. Anything from intimate bar and grills to exotically romantic restaurants – were lined up. There were specialty shops with scents of spices, teas, and coffees. Interspersed were boutiques, craft shops, and elaborately smart galleries.

Not that I'm a PR person for my town, but downtown Littleton was named one of the ten best places to live, shop, and work. Even Bloomberg Business Week proclaimed my sweet city one of the best places in Colorado to raise kids.

Not that Derwin was included – because he must not have been counted. His mother was a mean drunk, a total twat – and she had no interest in him. Kids picked on him and he was told to toughen up. Stand up, pull those balls out, and be a man. Nine-year old kids with learning disabilities aren't the ones responsible for holding their own when confronted by a herd of bullies.

I spotted Charlene. I tried to rescue a smile, but was too late. "Are you stepping on your own teat or just in a miserable mood?" she questioned.

She could entice a smile any time she wanted. "Naw, I'm in a miraculous mood now that I'm seated beside you."

On the restaurant patio, my lover and I gazed across at one another. Ours was far from a new relationship. However, we always tried to make it feel new by experiencing fresh, exciting times. We'd been to this cafe before, but today, we'd ordered something they'd advertised as a new menu item.

"I was just thinking about all the amazing recipes Momma has," I mentioned.

"Every time you return to the apartment, your mother sends a sugar rush." Char paused. "I wonder why she never stops by the apartment."

"Because she wants me at her house to do something, fix something, et cetera. For example, today after work, she wants me to fix a barrier around part of her garden. The rabbits are foraging her crops. So I said I'd fix up a little chicken-wire fencing. It might detour some of the wildlife."

"A rabbit fence."

"She'd also mentioned sawing some lower limbs of the apple tree, but she might have gone off the idea."

"Why?" Char asked with a frown. "She knows you can deal with the landscaping."

With a crisp laugh, I answered, "You're not going to believe this. She said she worried about the birds. They used the limbs to sit, stand, sing, and whatever. She was worried if I removed the limbs, it would be like stealing their furniture. So she probably decided against it for now."

Charlene's chuckle began like a chop, and then lifted. "Oh, my God. Furniture?"

"Yes. She worries about birds. No working on the trees until the baby birds are out of their nests. Now, she's worried about the bird's décor. You know Momma and her ideas."

"Wildlife was here before her family moved to Colorado."

"Precisely." I was always glad that Char pretended to understand.

"That doesn't really answer my question about why she rarely visits us. I mean when we were first together – she never came over. She didn't approve of me. But now, she knows me."

"And she likes you, Char." Frowning, I considered that Momma never even talked about visiting. Both Char and I had

122

invited her. "Maybe," I said timidly, leaning toward Char as I spoke in a half whisper, "maybe she's afraid she might sit on an errant vibrator."

Char's giggle sounded explosive. With her napkin up to her mouth, she shook her head. "Don't do that to me when I'm about to have a drink of water. I'd have sprayed you good if I had a mouthful of water when you said that."

The sound of her laughter was always worth the scolding.

I answered her question again, "Just so you know, she rarely visits Isabel's either."

"And she knows damned good and well she won't sit on anything errant at Isabel's. And Tad's phone call..." her concentration was interrupted.

Delivery of the salads was testing the server's skill. Whoever built the architectural delight, was a construction champ. Mounds of salad were covered with grilled salmon, snow peas, and dripping avocado sauce.

"Tasty," I commented in between bites.

"I recall having something similar when I was at that conference in Spokane." She chewed delicately. "Well, this is delicious. If your mother insists on loading your arms with calories, at least this helps."

"I should exercise tonight. Maybe we can when it cools down this evening. After I've built the bunny fence."

Laughing, she said, "You should run every night."

Grinning, I shook my head. "Interested?"

"Sure. Or we could play a game of tennis."

Debating, I finally agreed. "Okay, tennis it is. It's just that you whip my arse nearly every set."

"Hon, you're better at things like softball."

I poked the salad, and then stated, "Look, they've put down celery ribs crisscrossing on the bottom. Looks like pallets holding the salad up."

"Probably the chef's signature."

As we ate, I enjoyed the time with her. She leaned back in her chair, looking relaxed and lovely. Wearing an amazing summer dress with splashes of coral and soft turquoise colors, she was elegant. Yet her wardrobe always reflected a playfulness. Her hair was pushed back and her slender neck enticed a kiss.

"Holy blazing flips," I exclaimed. "You are so danged beautiful."

"I got all foo-fooed up for you, Babe," she flirted. "That's one thing I love about you, you always notice anything different – and let me know you like it." She also had the expression of wanting to delve. I recognized the glimmer in her eyes when she picked up where she'd left off.

"Of course, I notice you. I've notice you every moment we're together."

Sitting straight up and with a serious intonation, she asked, "Now, let's talk about your conversation with Tad."

"I told you exactly what he said. The entire dialogue was obviously regurgitated from Isabel."

"Vics, Isabel is such a manipulator. She wants you on her side. Everyone is lining up now. Your mother, Isabel, Tad, and they want you against Lea, too."

"I'm not changing my story. Isabel knows that. Tad isn't going to sway me."

I never thought there would be this problem. I assumed that Momma wouldn't fall off her perch anytime soon. And I figured when she died, she'd have everything precisely divvied up – with instructions for the house sale, etc. Or else, maybe all her funds would be spent keeping her in an assisted home residence.

"I'm surprised Tad would be so transparent."

"I was on to him when the call came in. He knows I've always doted on him, so I'm sure he was amazed that I didn't join the Sullivan side."

"I'm not sure your mother has a side. Although, I recall that one time she told me that as far as moral pillars go – you're pretty much it. At that time, Lea was just going into the slammer and Isabel had disowned her sister. Your mother didn't like Isabel's attitude toward Lea any more than she liked Lea's misappropriating thirty grand."

"To be honest, I think I had more respect for Lea."

"If I've said it once, I've said it a hundred times – Isabel is very, very reptilian. I know she's your sister, but she is so sanctimonious."

"I agree. We sisters shouldn't be fighting about this. If Momma gives me ten bucks – it's ten bucks I didn't have before."

"Hey, let's pretend you got a whopping tenner. Look at this." She pointed to the menu. "There's another new item on the menu. Chocolate soufflé cake with raspberry and rum sauce. Orgasmic."

"Caloric. We just ate salad. Now you want to blow our well-intentioned lunch order on dessert?"

"I'll make sure you run your ass off playing tennis."

"One dessert – two spoons?" I inquired. "I'm not above bargaining for pounds. Two spoons."

"It's a deal, Sweetheart."

I was besotted by this remarkable woman. "I love you so very much," I said with a soft, nearly silent voice. Then I looked around to see if anyone heard me.

She was enjoying my being uptight. She ran her hand along the length of my upper leg. Medium loudly, she replied, "I love you, too, Babe."

Trying to hide the case of jittery eyelids, I glanced in the opposite direction.

She wasn't done with me. "Darling, did you hear what I said?"

I whispered, "Yes, I did." I was attempting to rein my primal coping skills. "I heard you."

She upped her volume, "Good. Now which one of us will pick up our wedding invitations?"

Chapter 20

Isabel and Sully's lawn had been neatly mowed and trimmed. Presumably, it met with Isabel's inspection. My guess was Sully had done the honors since Tad wasn't there to do his chore.

Momma's car wasn't there, so either she'd dropped off what she had in the way of bake goods and scrammed or she hadn't arrived yet. Although I'd parked my car in front for a fast getaway, I didn't turn and run. I should have.

I'd never been any good at showdowns. Especially not with Isabel. However, I did plan to inquire why Tad was calling me about the Lea deal. Although I realize he would be told about the sundial because he had been asked to take photographs, I didn't think it was necessary to tell him about Lea's laying claim to it. Of course, Isabel was using Tad to work on me. They'd figured I wouldn't refuse my nephew. I would recant my testimony about hearing Grandma give Lea the sundial.

"Have a seat," Isabel pointed to the kitchen table. "Sully decided to have a beer with the fellas after work, so here I am alone. It is so quiet without Tad in the house. Vicky, I just want to cry when I think he might be going off to college in a couple months. Tad's talking about going off somewhere. He wants to spread his wings. We have a perfectly good college a few blocks away." She carefully poured two glasses of iced tea. Placing one in front of me, she whined, "Well, if there's money enough for him to go."

"Isabel, I'm really pissed off." I noticed her eyes clamping for a moment after I'd used the word *pissed*. "Tad called today. I don't know why he has to be privy to what's going on with Lea."

"He's my son. *Family*. Of course, I told him." She looked away. I caught that little moment of her face flushing. She was flustered at the thought of my being unhappy about her big mouth. "I have every right to tell him. As the legitimate heir…"

"No, you don't have a right to tell him my business. You told him that I corroborated her story." I took a sip of the tea. "That put me in the middle of it."

"You are in the middle of it. If Tad loses his claim to the family treasure – his rightful inheritance – he'll know who to blame. It isn't *just* Leandra."

I gave a huge sigh. "You're making trouble about something that needn't be addressed until we see what's happening. Momma would be furious if she knew you were trying to influence Tad against me." I stepped up the game. "She might even be mortified."

"Momma doesn't know what she's going to do. She's confused. If you get my drift."

"Confused! I sure as hell don't get your drift," I repeated with an objection in my voice. "You, good daughter Isabel – Daughters of the Altar, or whatever the hell you call it. The two of you churching and lapping up Commandments like they're good candy. You would never hear a bad word about Momma. You used to say *Momma means well.* That was your stock comment. Momma means well. Morning, noon, and night – Momma means well. So now, when she isn't bending to your command, it's poor, confused Momma. She isn't meaning well now?"

"Since when do you talk to me like that?"

My eyes narrow into a sharp line. "That would be since your persnickety airs began pissing me off. Since you decided to stir up problems between Tad and me. I resent that!"

"Don't you call me a stirrer. Victoria Lee, you're the one causing trouble. You're going along with Lea's lie. Well, you're going to be sorry! You'll lose me and you'll lose Lea when the truth of the accident comes out."

"I'm not sure I have any allies. Not really. I'm too different to ever be close to you." I realized my hands were squeezed into fists. My grip was strangling the air within those fists.

"I've told you that I accept you." Her act went haughty again. "I was one of the first to say I love you in spite of your abomination."

"Damn it to hell," I shouted. I began to swallow back the words I wanted to say to her. Finally, the words won and they came tumbling out. "I don't want to be *accepted!* I want to just *be*. I don't have to accept you for being straight."

"Because straight is normal."

I stood, nearly spilling the tea. "You are normal, and that means you are acceptable, and you are better than I am. That's what it comes down to. You're training Tad to be another undercover bigot. In your image."

Slamming the door on the way out was an afterthought. It fit right in with the drama. Why, I pondered, did she always have such a terrible impact upon my tranquility? She was acting as if it was heroic to have started a problem between my nephew and me. I was substantiating the conversation between Lea and Grandma, because it was exactly what I'd heard.

I felt as though my sorrow was being spent faster than I was even earning it.

I aimed my vehicle toward Momma's house. Looking at my watch, I realized it was later than I'd thought. Building the rabbit barrier would take some time. I strode into the backyard. Momma was smacking the crap out of the bindweeds.

Derwin was sitting cross-legged with two softball mitts and a ball in his lap. His smile bloomed when he saw me.

"I been waiting for you," Derwin announced. He tossed me a glove. "Your Momma found these gloves in your old room."

Momma greeted me, "Vicky, he said you promised to play catch with him." She started toward the shed. "I'll dig out the fencing material, so you can play a few minutes with Derwin."

Fitting my fingers into the glove, I motioned to him. "Come on, Der. Let's burn 'em in."

After pitching a few very weak balls at me, Derwin shrugged. His thin, weedy arms had very little muscle. His legs were scrawny, and yet I knew he got plenty of meals from Momma. Food was always available for him here.

While Derwin and I tossed the baseball, I saw Momma coming from the shed. She had retrieved the chicken-wire, posts, and a sledge hammer. "This oughta do it," she said as she dropped everything near the sidewalk.

I turned back to Momma. "I came to tell you that Isabel is creating a big mess."

"I just had a word with her," Momma acknowledged. "So don't feel you need to load me up with your side. I'm not a stupid old woman. I know your side. I do know what side you're on and I know what side Isabel is on. You're both pathetic brawlers."

"I'm pathetic. I'm *pathetic!*" I stormed away.

After pitching all kinds of wild balls toward Derwin, I realized it might be giving him practice, but being angry when I played ball wasn't helping me. I slowed down. The poor kid had no coordination. He was way too timid with the ball to ever think of making it on a ball team.

"Okay, Champ," I said, holding up the ball. "Enough for now. Practice tossing it up in the air and catching it."

"I will, Vicky. I guess I better go see how my mom is doing."

I nodded. Taking the hammer from Momma, I asked, "Do we have some of those little U nails?"

"I'll get 'em and you have your pleasant face on when I return. You never used to be so moody. Reminds me of your father."

I stopped in my tracks. I watched as she went to the shed. My entire body felt ice cold. That was the only time I could recall her saying anything like that to me. When she returned, she saw the tears building in my eyes.

My shoulders slumped as I asked, "Why did you say that?"

She turned away from me. "I don't know. I'm sorry." As she walked away, she said, "I'm just upset about this whole thing. Maybe I'm taking it out on you and I shouldn't. Take no notice, Victoria. A mother doesn't like seeing her children turn on each other and on her."

For the next half hour, I pounded stakes into the ground. With all my strength, I hit them with the full force of the sledgehammer. Then I attached the wire around the vegetables. Tapping the U-nails in was tedious.

It did give me time to reconsider. Momma didn't want us going after one another.

After I'd finished, I put the tools back in the shed. When I entered the backdoor, I saw Momma with her head down on the kitchen table. She was crying silent sobs that were shaking her body.

"I put the fence up, Momma. Charlene is waiting for me." I started to leave then moved back to Momma's side. I leaned to kiss her forehead. "I'm sorry. I shouldn't get in such a bad mood."

When her head lifted, her eyes were still rimmed with tears. Seeing them was too powerfully sad. I walked away – my damned puerile behavior had hurt my mother. I didn't want that.

My nerves were bundled tightly as I half ran to my vehicle. I wanted to smash something. Anger was building. One thing was certain, the tennis game would do me more good than just taking off a pound or two. My wild velocity-jammed serves would definitely be on tap. Char liked it when I gave her a little competition. She hated my 'I don't give a damn' volleys.

As I drove through traffic, I wanted to pound the steering wheel. Maybe kick out the windshield. My family didn't really accept me. Not completely. My soul felt impoverished. Of course, I wore a scowl. My mood had never been put to this kind of test. Maybe I was inflicted with my father's bad genes.

Tired of my coded life, I realized even if I were completely out as a Sapphic – something inside me was still, and maybe always would be, hidden from view.

My family could never understand why I felt miserable – they sometimes created the misery.

How could I possibly be miserable? When I had the love of an amazing woman? Each night, with a flood of moonlight, I would hear the melody of her laughter. Love radiated from her eyes. Char called herself my lust goddess. My romance Muse. Well, hell, she was everything to me.

She loved me forever and was willing to make a permanent commitment. She told me we should get married. It wouldn't change things – really. It would however be a dream she had shepherded since we met. I was constantly considering it as well as constantly resisting it.

I didn't see marriage happening until my mindset was ready. Why wasn't I ready for that? Was it another way to appease my family? Turn down Char's bid for permanency – it made no sense.

Even when relationships of our friends were cracking and crumbling – we were strong. Char said there are animals that mate for life. After all, her parents had a solid marriage. She would always joke that it was because no one else wanted either of them. She used that addendum as an example of what a good relationship was all about. Humor. We had that by bushels.

Certainly, there was no one else I wanted to be with. I thought of the trail of her hair against my nakedness in the night. There were her warm, slow caresses I so loved. The tenderness of my woman was a seamless beauty in itself. Char's love was the only love I felt was valid. I questioned why I couldn't simply trust and agree to marriage with the woman I adore?

So why not?

Was it because my own guilt was so heavy? Was it because my father had skedaddled and left me? Left the family? Now I wondered if it was because I was in his image. Maybe my own tumultuous spirit was kin to his agony.

I felt the sudden relief of the truth I wanted. My smile began skinny – then spread across my face like a huge bloom. Hell no, I was never like my father. If I were good at running away, I wouldn't be in all these messes. I wouldn't care.

The reason I rejected the marriage deal? Okay, maybe it was as simple as I didn't want to get all gussied up for a wedding. While I shared most of my inner thoughts with Char, I thought I'd keep this one to myself.

She had never before called me a *jockstrap* and I hoped she never would. Why chance it with a wayward thought?

Chapter 21

The morning was brightly splashed with fresh, clean sunshine. I'd showered and dressed quickly. There was always so much on my Daily Agenda List. Even my list had grown appendage lists. I'd dressed in my usual garb of golf shirt and cargo shorts. Since it was early, I felt a little chilly. Crisp Colorado mornings – I loved them.

Charlene was in the kitchen. She'd put on the coffee, and she was seated at the breakfast nook. She carefully aimed the coffee mug for her lips while reading the newspaper.

Upon opening the refrigerator for the cream, I exclaimed, "Holy blazing crap! What happened to our fridge?"

"Yesterday afternoon while I was waiting for you, I called two of our neighbors and asked if they needed fresh produce. I took every damned bit of the garden you've been dragging home and gave it to them. I told them to pass it around."

Giggling, I pulled out the box of cereal. "It looks great. There's room to put the cream back without spilling it. Momma will have another bundle for me to bring home today."

"Yes," Charlene agreed. "And she goes very heavy on Thursdays and Fridays. She must want us fully prepared for entertaining dozens of vegetarians over the weekend."

"Thanks for reminding me it's Thursday. Blog night – first draft. This week has seemed like months. All because that flipping sundial became valuable." I wondered if Char could tell how much I resented the sudden family wealth. She knew me too completely, I thought as I caught her stare. She was looking over the rims of her reading glasses. "I'm not certain what I'll blog about."

"You always come up with something. How about familial greed? That seems to be a topic of the day." She refolded the newspaper that was beginning to send out tentacle pages. "Greed is always a good story. However, before your mind whirls into a place where you'd rather it not be – just wait for your Muse to shower her voluptuous ideas. Write something very, very provocative. Pure raw sex."

Chuckling, I spewed. "I thought of that. But Sully reads my blogs religiously. He would tell Isabel. She's already instructed me to keep her name out of my blogs. She doesn't want to be associated with me on any level." My comment was half said and half spit out. "X-rated is something she'd never get over."

Charlene suggested, "Maybe you should wait to write the premise tomorrow night. After the Friday fights have been completed." Again, she gazed over the rim of her glasses. "I wouldn't expect a love-fest – that's for certain."

Thinking about how there would be Momma, Lea, Isabel, Tad, and me there at the photo session, I wondered how riled up everyone would be. Five venomous agendas. It could get hellfire hot. Everyone tugging away at their agenda could easily provide a blog. The spasms of selfish energy would be going to town.

It was never a given that we would all get along when we congregated in the best of times. But with everyone claiming the sundial, it could get contentious. Fangs were already showing and jaws were snapping.

"Aw, I think they'll be okay," I replied with optimism.

"It will be delightful, I'm sure." She gave a sardonic sounding twist to the end of her sentence.

"It could become intense," I muttered.

"Intense! Everyone will be near enough for physical violence. Chaotic."

"Chaos on stilts and steroids – I agree, it could be."

"Maybe you'll need a police escort," she teased.

"At least a wrestling referee would be nice. I'm hoping my entire quirky, excitable family will be on good behavior. Momma doesn't like ruckuses. Grandma used to say we shouldn't get in a dither over things. So maybe we'll handle it like gentry and aristocracy."

We both laughed simultaneously. "Vicky, there will be hysterics, ambushes, and maybe even the pandemonium of a brawl."

I stood, took my dishes to the sink, and then whirled around. "Well, I better get going. Get my work done so I can come home early tonight. I need to work on the first draft of my blog. That blog isn't going to pitch itself upon the pages."

"No topic at all?"

I leaned down to her and kissed a circle around her neck. "I could write about the strike of lightning I had in bed last night. That bolt made me proud to be a Sapphic. Whew, darlin', you are incredible. Your kisses encouraged my every nerve to tingle. You are lava hot!" I caressed her shoulder tenderly.

"You, too, Babe. You are my sensuality savior."

Her smile of satisfaction, along with a lifted, arched eyebrow, made me long for a morning seduction. I loved mornings where we swam through the balled up sheets toward one another – and her eyes were always polished jewels inviting. Love sharing was whatever mischief we exacted.

I teased, "Our morning delight would make a great blog. I could call it, AM Affection."

Charlene's frown lifted. She quizzed, "You aren't really planning on divulging our bedroom romps in your blog? At least, not before my demise?"

My head shook negatively. "I won't hit the 'publish' button until the first shovel load of dirt hits your stylish coffin, Sweetheart. Then it's tell-all time."

She snickered. Then she threatened, "If you go first – I'm going to be deleting every f-ing, incriminating word you ever wrote."

My arms surrounded her shoulders. "I love you so much. I don't mind that you're an oversexed, erotically-charged woman."

"Let's keep that a secret," she joked.

"Your lips are the most expressive form of love I've ever seen. Your eyes are gentle with a sweetness known to every romance. And that body of yours can wind me up and send me spinning."

Her raspy morning voice whispered, "Vicky, go to work or stay here where you'll risk getting a pre-eight o'clock ravishing."

"Save up for tonight, lover. We'll place electrified gleams on one another. We'll have a nocturnal romp like no other."

"Well, I'm hoping you aren't creating those words for a new 'tell-all' blog." Her chuckle seemed to topple over when I didn't join in her amusement. "Babe?"

"There will not be a word on my blog about wanting to nuzzle your thighs." I gave her a salute, and then left for work. Charlene never failed to have confidence in me. That made me stronger. It impacted my words. Writing a blog about how she ignited my desire would be exciting.

Seated in my SUV, I wondered if my blog readers would enjoy a sexcapade blog. I turned the key of the ignition as I was thinking about what a swell blog it would make. Amazingly, I drove at a nice steady pace.

I was convinced that my mother had me on radar. I'd just pulled into the parking lot of the office building where I was employed when she phoned.

"Listen, Vicky, what I said yesterday – take no mind. We're all wadded up so tightly. We can hardly breathe over this sundial business. I shouldn't have said what I said."

"That's okay, Momma. I shouldn't have spoken either. You're right, we're all tense."

"Wound up tight as ticks, for a fact."

Her pensive words sounded as if they were fighting their way through her lips. I figured she would be residing all day Saturday in the confessional.

"It's all forgot, Momma. Like Grandma used to say – fresh start."

"Vicky, can you pick Lea up at the house? I'm at work, and she has some early appointments at Angelo's. She said Ari's already got the music store open, so he can't come get her. She's in a terrible hurry."

"Sure. Okay." As I started the car back up, I asked, "You think things will be amiable tomorrow? I mean, we could meet at the bank where everyone would behave. Surely, no one will trade punches in that small vault room."

"We've just got a little family spat going on. We need to be kind. We surely don't want anyone knowing that the sundial is valuable."

"The bank employees must know. We had to rent a large lock box to fit the damned thing in. Our faces were colored purple. Plus we all stuttered nervously."

"Well, let's just stick to my plans. The old sundial would be more comfortable in my house while being photographed. Also, it's more like we're including Grandma."

"Sure, Momma." *Including Grandma!* If that was the premise, I considered maybe we should go to the graveyard for the photo shoot. Stick the damned sundial on top of Grandma's marble memorial – then do the photo shoot. Tad could snap photos and we could tell what time it was – it would be like two benefits at once. Grandma would say that we'd taken care of the whole *shebang*.

Momma continued with her instructions. "Oh, and I got you a sack of veggies to take along with you. It's in the fridge."

"Thanks, Momma." My eyes automatically rolled. I wanted to say my neighbors would love it, but I refrained.

When I parked in front of Momma's house, I knew without being told that Lea wouldn't be on the steps waiting for me. Lea – who was in a flipping hurry – was probably still fiddle-farting around with her hair curler. I wasn't going to hurriedly rush in and wait for her. I saw Derwin on his front porch.

I sauntered over. "Hey, Pal," I greeted him. "How you doing?"

"My mom is feelin' poorly."

I sat beside him. "Sorry to hear that." Shit, she was *poorly* every other day. Vodka flu can make anyone poorly. Dottie poured drinks like a faucet with no stopper. "But don't run away, Derwin. We worry about you when you run off."

He was silent, which meant he wasn't giving me any guarantee that he wouldn't be hightailing it.

Finally, I commiserated, "I used to run off once and awhile. Usually, when Isabel or Lea was blabbing to Momma about something I did. Tattling. I tried to get out of trouble by hiding out."

"Where'd you go?"

"Sometimes, I'd wander down to the Littleton Depot Art Center. You know, where they have the antique caboose car as a memorial. It's on a short section of tracks. I'd just hide on the steps of the old caboose. Sometimes I'd hide under it."

"That sounds like a fun hiding place."

"I also remember one time I went clear over to the gulch. That was when I realized it's too dangerous to run away."

"What happened to you?" His eyes were popping with curiosity.

"It was stupid of me to run away. There's too much danger. Everyone said to never go there alone. And it's really dangerous around the creek. Snakes, wild animals – and Momma said vagrants hung out there. Anyway, I was terrified. There's a little brick building off to the side."

Later in life, I learned that it was a hook up place for making out with a date. But back then, when I was small, it was a mysterious place. During the day, it wasn't so bad, but even as night approached – it was scary. And I never went alone again.

"Did you stay in the building?" he asked.

"No. It was locked up. After a couple hours in the dark, I was terrified. Well, that was the last time I ran away."

"What did your Momma say?"

I laughed. "She saw me all trembling and terrified, and she said, I should come in and not play outside in the dark. I told her I'd been clear back by the gulch. She said I was making it up. Well, her exact words were – *a likely story.*"

Derwin laughed heartily. He then requested, "Can you tell me that story again?"

Laughing, I ruffled Derwin's short hair. The top was growing. I suddenly had an idea. "Have you got any hair-gel?"

"Mom does."

"Your hair has grown out a little…"

"Mom says she's taking me to the barber this weekend, but she sometimes forgets."

"Bring me the gel!"

He rushed inside. It only took him seconds to find it and return. "Here. You need some gel on your hair?" he inquired.

"Nope." I opened the container and inhaled the fruity scent. "Let's make you cool."

I put some of the gel on his hair, and then forced the curls upward into a faux-hawk. The spikelet stood to attention in the front. I slicked back the sides. He looked cute, and I told him so. "Now you're one of the cool kids, Derwin. You got a spiky, trendy hairdo."

"Can we still be friends?" he asked as he looked into the windowpane glass reflection. "I remember you said you weren't the cool kid in school. And they didn't like you either."

"Well, when I got a little older, I played softball. The team liked me. Sometimes you just have to find the place where you best fit. You'll find yours, too."

"But you'll still be my friend?"

"Always."

"Good, cause you're one of my very best friends."

I looked up to see Lea leaping through the door and dashing toward my vehicle. "I have to take Miss Priss to work." I put the twist cap back on the gel and handed it back to Mr. Cool. I gave him a thumb's up signal. "Very cool, Der."

Lea was in her hurried mode. At the vehicle, she jiggled the door. "Gypsy will be upset if I'm late."

"I'm upset that you didn't get up sooner so you'd be able to walk a couple blocks. Instead, I'm spending my time waiting on you."

"Vicky, I got back home late. I was with Ari." She fluffed her multi-colored skirt. She called it her square-dance skirt. I called it a garish foo-foo miniskirt. "Ari is so wonderful."

"Things are going okay for the two of you?"

"I think he's the one. I mean, I know I've had poor judgment in the past where men were involved. But Ari's like his dad. Kind and considerate."

"Life is better when you find someone who really cares."

"Yeah." She was silent a moment then asked, "What is it you lesbians want your ideal woman to be?"

"Germ free."

"Vicky, can't you be serious just once?"

"We want them to be nice. To love us. And to be red hot sex maniacs."

She failed to appreciate my humor. She moaned a moment. "Sex maniacs are too much like most men."

"I was joking. Sorry, I didn't think you'd object to a little early morning banter." There was silence. "Love is what we're mostly all looking for."

"There were some women in prison and they chased after me. It was terrible." Her eyes glazed with hurt, and then her eyelids lowered. "I hated the tough dykes," she disclosed. "They didn't care about love – just sex. Getting satisfaction."

"I'm sorry you had to go through that." I'd heard stories about lesbianism in prison. Some of it was harsh – and violent. How do you tell your baby sister that what she saw while incarcerated wasn't the real world? "Lea, most lesbians are exactly like straight women when it comes to loving one another. We aren't brutal, uncaring people."

Her nod was nonchalant. "Well, Charlene is very nice."

She pulled down the mirror to preen as I was parking. Then she twisted her neck. "Oh, hell. My nine-o'clock is already here."

When I'd parked directly in front of Angelo's, I said, "I'll go in with you and tell Gypsy it was my fault."

"Thanks. Just make it believable. Don't be funny. Be serious for a change," she implored.

Nodding agreement, I muttered, "I'll give my best Streep performance."

"See, you're already acting silly."

Doubting that Gypsy was even the slightest fooled, I spit out my story as if it were day-old, unrefrigerated slop. Gypsy was an amazingly good audience for my serious excuse.

"I'd promised Momma I'd bring Lea to work. Time slipped away, and I was driving against the traffic. Then I had to stop and talk with a friend for a moment. A neighbor and I couldn't get away. Well, it was my fault."

Gypsy's loud chortling continued for a couple minutes. "Vicky, that was the best *late excuse* I ever heard." She turned to the half dozen people either getting their hair fluffed or fluffing hair. "Did you all hear that? Hell of an excuse. If I need an excuse, I'll give Vicky a call."

The eyes of both patrons and two hairdressers were glued to me. All I saw was a smattering of curlers and hair sticking out in various directions. One hairstyle was cascading. It made the woman look like she was a whoopee girl with the world's largest mop of hair. Another had a plethora of pleating locks dripping from the top of her head.

"Oh," I gulped. "Well, I tried."

Gypsy slapped my back. "Girl, I would drop that excuse like a stinky turd."

Nodding, I grinned. "Have a nice day, Gypsy."

Chapter 22

"Is Isabel really such a scaled-up bitch as Lea makes her out to be?" Ari asked.

"Lea probably didn't exaggerate. Isabel isn't an easy person." I'd decided since I was within walking distance of Tanovich Music Shop, I'd drop in on Ari.

The shop was homey and he seemed relaxed. The background song was B.B. King singing 'I'll String Along With You.' B.B. King puts a song down with its magic growing.

Complimenting, I said, "Love your music selection."

"It's a beautiful day. B for beautiful. So it was either B.B. King, Bob Dylan or Beethoven." Ari was in denims with a midnight blue cotton tee-shirt. On the front of his chest was the message: Cole Porter Wrote Night and Day.

All types of information can be gleaned from a drop-in. I remembered his first comment. "Exactly what did Lea have to say about Isabel?" I interrogated.

"She said that Isabel is very, very religious, and vicious." His face beamed as he leaned into a secret. "Don't tell Isabel that Lea said that. Leave it at very, very religious."

"Isabel is in the pews of hell," I commented. I leaned against the counter. "And what did my baby sister have to say about me?"

"She told me you're okay. Even after I disclosed how you did an investigation of me by contacting my ex-wife. I thought that was a little extreme."

I liked the timbre of his laugh. Well, I liked him. "Ari, I probably shouldn't have, but Momma tends to prod me into these things. She doesn't want Lea mixing with the wrong crowd. Mother's never get over watching out for her children."

His face became serious. "I know. Dad may have died, but I feel him with me. Watching after me. In fact, I'll tell you something I haven't even told Lea yet. Over the years, each time I talked to Dad, he mentioned Lea. Maybe I fell for her through his eyes first. I liked her from what he said about her. So I know that I have his approval of her. Things seem to be going quickly, but it isn't at all like we just met. It's like I knew all about her from Dad. It's like I *know* her."

"And does she know you from what your father said to her about you?"

He went around the counter. Pouring coffee in a paper cup, he asked, "Cream and sugar?"

"Cream, please."

When he handed me the coffee, he explained, "Thought you might need a cup of coffee before I begin. Yes, Dad talked about me to her. Funny, it's like Lea has had prior knowledge of my life. From my family pets to when my mother died. All about me. I'll say my favorite food is Mexican and she says cheese burritos. I start to mention my favorite song and she says the title. I know those things about her, too. Because my father always told me what she was doing."

Although I considered my sister a flake at times, I also knew she didn't just hop into bed with men. Not that she was any good at selecting before now, but at least she'd vetted them for several weeks.

"And what is your favorite song?" I questioned.

"Elvis Costello's 'She' has been my favorite since I first heard it. What is your favorite song?"

"Gershwin. 'Our Love Is Here to Stay.' It's Charlene and my song." Before I could turn around, I heard the paws of the dog, Gershwin, headed my way. I bent down to pet him as he stepped into my arms. "Must be his favorite song, too."

"I wouldn't be surprised," Ari agreed. "So what's Isabel's favorite song?"

Chuckling, I answered, "I'm not sure she knows what a song is. But I'm sure she's got a few favorite hymns. That would be h-y-m-n-s," I spelled.

"Isabel is so different from Lea. Lea is so warm, and you're friendly – now. Now that you know I'm not going to implicate Lea in any crime. It's hard to believe Isabel is such a witch."

"Isabel has some oldest sister complex. I used to call her the dragon lady. She wants to be in control. She gets nasty when she doesn't get her way. Lea is a gentler spirit."

"I know. Lea didn't commit a crime because she was bad. She never would have hurt anyone. It's just that she wants her face fixed. Well, I think it's silly to go through all the pain of surgery."

"She's a beautiful woman," I commented.

"Yes, absolutely. But she sees the scar as a detriment to that beauty. My take on it is that it doesn't matter. I mean," he said as he lifted his hand to demonstrate his words, "with men, a scar on our face is a badge of honor. A battle scar is because of something brave. It becomes admired and revered."

"Her scar doesn't bother you?"

"Not at all. Other than the pain it caused her, but she doesn't remember the pain. She told me since she was only two-years old she has no recollection of it. She suffers vanity now. That's why she wants her face fixed up. I don't really want her to have to go through surgical pain – but that's up to her. Whatever makes her happy." His frown deepened. "Maybe I'm being selfish."

"Selfish?"

"Yeah, the thought occurred that if her face was repaired, some flash, shallow guy might sweep her away from me. Maybe it would be for the wrong reasons. She deserves a devoted love. I can give her that."

"I think she's pretty sold on you, Ari."

"I hope so – because I think she's planning to get the operation when the money comes in."

My heartbeat pounded. I couldn't move. I felt as though I had been stapled to the floor – paralyzed. When I finally did move, it was with a stagger.

Damn, Lea told him about the sundial. She broke the family bond of secrecy. I shrugged as I repeated, "When the money comes in?"

"Yeah. You did me a favor when you called my ex. While we were shooting the breeze, my ex asked if I'd sold all the songs I'd written back years ago. I told her no – that there were a few left. She said she knew a producer and asked if I minded if she showed him my work. Naturally, I'm not opposed to selling my songs, so I emailed her a list of the ones that were available. I attached the actual songs. Well, anyway, she called last night to say they wanted them. Half a dozen – and I got the overnight contract early this morning. There was even an advance included. The songs were for one of the top country stars in the nation. I'm getting a record deal and the money should cover the operation."

"*You're* going to pay for her operation?"

"Sure. Between what the songs are selling for and what I can borrow from the bank – it ought to be enough. Once the songs are released, I'll get a cut on that money, too. It will pay back the loan."

"Wow. That's generous of you."

"I think my dad would have liked to know Lea is being taken care of. You know, she'd come in here and make him happy. There's no price on that. Maybe this is my way of paying her back for all the joy she spread in his life."

I was beginning to tear up. Humor saved me from sentimentality. I asked, "Do I get a finder's fee for getting the ball rolling?"

He responded with a laugh, "No, I think I'll just give you dispensation for being a prying snoop bitch."

When I got to the door, I turned back. "Thanks. You know, my sister could do a hell of a lot worse than you. On the other side, I don't think there's any way she could do any better."

The walk back to my vehicle was with a much lighter step. I gave a tremendously pronounced sigh of relief. There was always a part of me that pitied Lea. The looks people gave her were both sympathetic and repulsed. I have always known that she feels as though she's different. I've always been plain – so although no one ever made over me about being cute – they did pay attention when I said something unique – or I made them laugh. So I honed in on humor as an entrée into being accepted. Without that skill set, I was hopeless.

Lea's beauty set her up for the role of perfection destroyed. And she bought into that role. She allowed pity to become her cross to haul and her chain to drag with her. There wasn't any compensation for beauty pitied. She shrunk into her own world.

She knew that withdrawing was her best bet. In grade school, each time she got up to speak, it ended in her crying. She got the brunt of people feeling uncomfortable. She knew that. Her tears would pour. A couple times, I'd been called into her classroom to take my pitiful younger sister home.

I resented being dragged into the situation. I blamed her for wanting attention. She only wanted sympathy, I thought. I wasn't certain why all these years past and it just started coming into view. As a kid, I couldn't *get* the pain she was experiencing. Because I wouldn't have felt that same pain – I wouldn't have appreciated its depth.

I thought because I was so unremarkable, so plain, that no one looked at me – so I had something about me that was substandard. Why feel sorry for a sister who was a true beauty – with a defect on her cheek? She was tall, willowy, and movie-star lovely. Even with a slash on her cheek, she was still better than someone that no one paid any attention to.

Now I was aware of how I'd miscalculated. Maybe my blog would be called 'Which is the Right Lane for Us to Walk?' I could veil it with generalities of sibling rivalry. That idea lodged in my brain as a possible blog topic.

But there was another thought that was stirring my soul. It continued jabbing its way into my heart. Lea had found a man who loved her regardless. She had a man whose love was purely *as is*. And his favorite song is 'She.'

Now that is riding the carousel of precision romance.

Chapter 23

Even if the day had been blistering hot with a huge searing sun, evenings in the Denver area and most of Western Colorado were cool – comfortable. Charlene and I were outside on the long terrace that is off both our kitchen area and our bedroom.

We snuggled as near as we could on the patio swing. My legs were extended, and ankles crossed in relaxation. My lady's head rested on my shoulder and my chin rested against the top of her head. Her hair felt silky as my hand brushed strands back away from her face. Kissing her temple made me want our embrace to go on forever.

"This feels so good," I whispered. I slipped a mini cheesecake square into Char's mouth. "Good wine, good tidbits. And delicious after-dinner kisses, Sweetheart."

"All that, and it's been a wonderful day. Now – end of the day, and we finally have a terrific family story. A love story actually, Babe."

"I can't get over how happy I feel."

"I'm glad for you and for Lea and Ari."

There was a moment of silence. We were both thinking of Lea's romance. I hadn't pictured the kindly, old Mr. Tanovich having a sensitive, engaging, and charming son. I finally spoke. "Amazing things are going Lea's way. Regardless of the sundial, she's got what looks to be a very good man."

The musical track playing in the background was now filling the moment with our song. "Our love is here to stay," Char sung the lyrics. "Our song. We haven't heard that in a while."

"I put it on. Ari and I were talking about favorite songs, and I told him that was our song. He said the song he likes best is 'She' – which is very romantic."

"It's also one of our favorites."

I gave a nod. "I'm lucky you're my *she*."

"I'm lucky, too. Ari sounds very nice. I hope he can withstand the Brent onslaught. Momma and Isabel will give him a run for his money."

I traced Char's lips with my index finger. Then I ran my fingertips over her face. Her eyes closed. I always tried to touch her in a relaxing way so that the stress of her day would abate. Even when I'd rub her back, it was to decrease my lady's tension. Without a doubt, she has a very demanding job. Pressure was built into her profession. So touching her did us both good. It relaxed her – and it made me feel good by witnessing her becoming soothed.

"Maybe I can blog about love being interfered with – by well-meaning relatives."

"I could even write a blog about that," she said with a chuckled. "Your family really put me through my paces. I was convinced they hated me. For a decade, I was terrified of them. I thought they might influence you."

"They could never have influenced me to drop you."

"Well, at the time, I didn't know that. I only knew you loved them very much, and they didn't approve of us. So there was concern on my part."

"I was frightened that they'd chase you away. Funny to think about it now. Neither of us were going anywhere from the beginning. And now."

"But they did attempt to pull you back to the fold."

I confessed, "Yes. They used faith. Maybe that was more to dissuade me from being Sapphic than to break off with you."

"I got the idea that they blamed me for you becoming lesbian."

"I told you they knew I was seeing women in college – and even when I was playing softball – precollege." I rubbed her forehead softly. "Maybe they thought it wasn't consummated before. But I can't imagine them not knowing."

"Oh, I think they knew you were sleeping with women – having sex. But I'm not sure it really registered with them. Some parents believe their children will grow out of it."

"A lesbian malcontent," I chided. "Yeah, maybe they thought I'd become infatuated with men as soon as I came to my senses.

Or maybe the religious hierarchy would drag me back to them and the church."

"It seemed like for years they were trying to tug you away from me."

"Then two years ago, when we had our ten-year anniversary, they stopped trying to influence me. I remember we took them out to celebrate with us. I love that charming little fondue restaurant. They all warmed up to you, I recall. And later, we joked that the fondue pots must have warmed them."

"Well, I've enjoyed the last two years of peace. Now, if I'd join your church, drop by to visit your mother oftener, and grow an appendage between my legs – complete acceptance would be mine."

I covered my eyes in mock shock. "Babe, you grow a wanger and I'm outta here."

She tickled me. Giggling, she said, "I can promise you, I won't."

"You are always invited to attend church with me," I offered.

"Church is probably out of my range, but I could visit your mother oftener. Kiss up to her more."

"Hey, that would make a terrific blog. I could talk about kissing up to the relations." I paused a moment. "Being accepted by the in-laws. You're an authority on that one."

"My parents loved you immediately. I could tell they did. And in fact, I knew they would love you before they even met you."

"I was terrified. But I figured I'd give them a good glimpse at me. If they didn't like it, I wouldn't have to waste my energy converting them."

"If I subscribed to that theory – I'd call the first ten years a waste of energy. But I hung in there. And I'm happy they seem to be accepting me."

"You'd know if they didn't."

"Okay, I'm heading to bed. You hit the office and write your blog." Pausing, Char leaned down and kissed my forehead. "Your blog will come to you. It will be there. Rest your mind and give it time to surface. You can do this."

"Thanks, Beautiful."

After she left, I sat alone – swinging, thinking, and wondering why this seemed such an uncomfortable blog zone. Hoping maybe my computer's face would prompt me I adjourned into the office.

Being a creature of repetition, every week I wrote the bones, blood, and flesh of the blog's first draft on Thursday evenings. Friday nights were for editing, rewriting, and finding any mistakes. Saturday morning, after a final read through – I would post. For years, I hadn't varied my schedule. Nor had I changed the basic script. Only the content of subject was changed. It was always light-hearted with a comedic view of life. I issued hundreds of words of encouragement in what was probably best described as light entertainment.

My demeanor was different tonight. I couldn't explain the emotion my mind was dancing through. Perhaps it was *sambaing* to a rhythm of music that wasn't slowing down enough for me to write. My brain felt imperiled. If I wrote what my heart was saying – what truth was chanting through my head – it certainly wouldn't be in keeping with my traditional blogging style.

Thoughts were coagulating – yet they were all naked. The term 'running on empty' came to mind. My language of observation and of participation was being ground away – demolished.

It was a soulful essence I couldn't describe. Nor could I unlock my literary voice. I wanted to glue back my previous ease of selecting a blog topic, and then roaring through to completion.

Seated at the desk with my computer, I was only capable of indigestible thought. My eyes blinked their nervous tick. That happened when I was overwhelmed. Bad vibes began piling up. Even time was heavier.

What if the way the sundial changed my family – it had also changed me? What if all the quibbling had silenced me? Nothing felt funny, humorous, or joyous. At this moment – to be happy was to be sacrilegious. What if I could no longer write copy for work? What if I couldn't make Charlene laugh – or satiate her libido with the charm of words perfect enough for her?

A summer's evening rain began to fall. Softly, but I could hear it striking the window pane. The weather had been clear out – but then clouds smeared the sky. I was under a rain cloud and there was definitely a spillage of water. How flipping appropriate. I was feeling exactly like thunderstorms were attacking me – and wham-bam – there it was. Overhead, it was exactly overhead. The rhythm of rain was converting me to morose.

I got up and went to the wine cabinet. Charlene had corked the bottle we'd had for dinner and after dinner. I uncorked it and poured a heaping dose. I rarely ever had more than a half glass of anything when I would write my blog. Did I think I might be lubricating my brain? Or maybe booze would kick-start a pattern of thought?

When I was seated at my work desk, the computer's blank face was just as empty and emotionless as when I walked away. Maybe I could do a list. When my grandmother died, I hadn't wanted to show my sadness. I made a list of some of the funny things she said and did. A list was better than a fraudulent blog.

Writing the first numeral, I congratulated myself on a start. Harnessing a topic line was an exercise in rudderless brainwork. Opening my dictionary, I saw the word 'lair' – it popped out at me.

Okay, 'life is a flipping lair' could be my line. For I now felt I was either hiding out from myself – or captured and placed in a cavern. I was cut off from the world with no more satire, parody, or mockery coming out of me. The world was safe from my ridicule, burlesque, and witticism. I'd once had the ability to say things that people read and laughed about. They never felt they might be the target. That was what I wanted. I didn't want any of us to recognize our foibles as belonging to us. I wanted to kindly point out the gamboling buffoons we all are.

My readers and I could ridicule and banter as a team. We'd laugh at faceless fools and nameless jesters. We were incognito – all belonging to the magical, mythical human species. I wanted us never to feel as though humor was heavy-handed and mean.

Certainly, I am amazed and entranced with the magnificence of humanity. I wanted to make them happy.

I was skirmishing to believe in kind humor. Believing in my ability to create jocularity was hanging wearily in my mind. My shoulders slumped as I lifted the glass to my lips. Sipping, I continued writing my list:

1. Surrender to seriousness.
2. Laughter melts away.
3. Dreams are broken.
4. Pain is an amazing event.
5. Jokes are bruised…

My eyes were twitching to the beat of the raindrops. I was so tired. Why did an event that should have been good fortune become a battle? I rubbed my eyes, and then examined what I'd written. In a low voice I said, "I'm renaming this blog – Ornament of Doom."

I suddenly heard myself laugh. It was the laugh of a quick slap at the sky. But it was indeed a laugh. I took two large gulps of wine, finishing the glass. Then I shut off the computer without having saved it. I would begin again in the morning. Or if I didn't improve words by the fraction, I would write an excuse for missing my blog day. Since beginning my blog many years ago, it would be the first and only missed blog. That stung for I loved the thought of continuance.

Pellets of rain were flicking against the window. I was sleepy. I was smoothly and satisfyingly inebriated. Goldilocks high – not too much and not too little of fine wine.

If I couldn't write my blog, I wanted to feel warmth from the woman I love. There might be a disconnect from my Muse. However, my Goddess was awaiting my heat.

Chapter 24

Sleep had provided a new day. Thankfully, night had filled the area of my brain where the blogs hung out. It had been an empty cavern – but words were jingling around in that space as I woke. Immediately, I rushed to my computer with a bushel full of words. *Fantastic!* I'd named my blog Fantastic! It was done in only half an hour. The premise was that we marginalize life. We don't appreciate its fantastic gift. In one of my conversations with Derwin, I'd mentioned that in each life we must go through things. Innocently, he asked why we *go through things.* Shouldn't we just *live?* Well, the blog was written without my usual flair, but there were a couple of laugh lines.

Amazing what cuddling with my sweetheart can do to pry open the spirit.

Wisdom is often well-hidden and simpler than could be imagined. Derwin got that. Thankfully, he was tutoring the rest of us.

I would need a huge dose of *fantastic* to get through the day. Friday was a day I'd looked forward to with pure dread. Since the plans were devised, I'd detested the thought of it. I called out sick from my work, which wasn't really a sick day, but 'free' day because I had so many sick days left.

However, one does not call out sick or free from Momma's precious photo-shoot of her treasure. She'd a been on a dead run to my apartment. She wouldn't have slowed down. She'd be jamming a thermometer up my butt as if it were a battering ram. Then she'd pour some salts and warm herbal therapy down my throat. For the sake of both ends. Ends, okay let's say it – orifices. That was her mission – keep both ends in proper working condition. It was a full-force serious prospect. For Momma, healing wasn't a delicate undertaking. Nor need it be.

I was nervous from the moment I pulled up to the house. Momma, Isabel, Lea, and Tad had gone to the bank to pick up the treasure earlier. Apparently, they hadn't considered I might ride shotgun. I was the only one who ever excelled in a P.E. course. Glad that I'd taken the extra time to finish my blog draft, I'd also missed sitting between Isabel and Lea on the armored car run. Some things are simply destined to work out in my favor.

"Just put it on the dining room table," Momma instructed. "And let's put down the embroidered tablecloth." Tad carried the old sundial with the reverence he carried the Holy Sacrament when he was an altar boy. Funny, before this, everyone sort of pitched the sundial off to the side. And dusting it was a task no one wanted. Now it had become this freakin' Holy Grail.

"Here, Grandma?" Tad asked if his location was okay. He was being Mr. Photo Savvy. He'd been able to assume the air of anyone since he was a kid. When he was a two-year old, I'd take him to my softball games. He would begin marching around with the little teeter of a toddler and end up stomping like a regular bull dyke.

Momma turned to her grandson. "That looks great. Tad, is there enough light?"

"Certainly, Grandma Brent. There's plenty of light. This camera can light up a pitch dark room." Theodore 'Tad' Sullivan squinted. With drama, he made a frame of his fingers and examined the table holding the half million dollar sundial. Then he reached down for the camera that was strapped around his neck. Carefully he focused, and then began shooting. He checked each photo. "I got several from this side. I'll get some from the other side."

"And Tad, get close-ups. I want every little scratch documented." Momma went into her administrative mode. After all, she was presiding over this ordeal. She ordered, "Tad, take some of only the scratches, too. You know, close ups that show every little dent."

While they blah, blah, blahed over the angles and positions, I thought about the dents and scratches. All those centuries ago, that sundial had been brand new. With pride, the owner must have polished it and bragged about it. The gleams would sparkle. Then the first scratch. What other stories were there concerning the scratches and dents? The pillages of war, catastrophic burials, and it had been relocated dozens of times. Carried across Europe. Then across the ocean, and finally, this relic of the ages was relocated to Littleton, Colorado.

Landing in sweet Littleton, it was now the subject of pissing and moaning like no other the Brent family object had ever been. The sundial probably hadn't been through anything in its past like the Battle of the Brents.

Momma tried to check over his shoulder. "That is perfect placement, Tad. Your digital camera is a honey."

"I got it with the money from my last birthday and graduation, Grandma." He glanced over at his mother in the kitchen making coffee. "I want to be a photographer," his announcement was issued with the silence of a whisper. He was well aware that his mother wanted him to become a CEO or politician.

"He's going to make something of himself," Isabel insisted.

He wasn't that corrupt, nor was he that superficial. He'd wash out of CEO school in a heartbeat. And he'd never even make it into Politicians 101. As Grandma would always say, perish the thought. I would hate to think he excelled in politics.

Secretively, he leaned and whispered. "Photographers don't need to go to college."

Like an alarm going off, Isabel yelled out, "*You are going to attend college.* Then, decide what you want to be." Isabel heard Tad's whisper as clear and loud as if it might be telepathy. She could hear a sparrow fart clear across town.

His mouth grimaced to the left side. "Mom, I just said what I want to be. College will just be a waste of time."

As she walked by him, she reached up and gave her son a swat on his head. His short buzz-cut hair was a so near his scalp that the rusty red had become diluted by light. Giving off the slight sound of a thump, his head jerked.

She ranted, "You're going to college, and that's final." With the resolve of a martyred saint, she whined, "That is if we can afford higher education."

Tad groaned. His moans were epic. They spoke volumes without his having to say a word.

I watched on as they all continued the drama. Lea rolled her eyes at me a couple times, and my grin wrestled back to the seriousness of this event. Momma wanted everyone at attention. This was a milestone moment. It was her spotlight – well, this and the TV production filming her trying to take deep breaths.

Once when she had to stand up before the Church parish – her contribution was being recognized – she nearly hyperventilated. So naturally, she was nervous when trying to spew a history of an item she considered worn, tattered, and ready for the trash heap. A camera was rolling. A microphone was recording. And Momma was terrified. That was her day in the spotlight. This day was more an after-event where she took over.

"Try to get a shot of it from the top downward," Momma instructed. She was working it for all she was worth. Isabel was showing motherly pride in the technical perfection of her son's camera work.

Glad that Charlene was safe and sound at work, I experienced relief. At least I wouldn't need to hear her bellyaching about my goofy family. She told me if she had my family, she would consider life a matter of one breakdown after another. She didn't know how I managed to hang on. I answered that I strongly suspected only comedy kept me kicking. Once I even heard myself telling her what might have been the reason my father did his runner. He'd either flipped out or feared he might.

A mediocre pounding of the backdoor disrupted my thought. I went through the kitchen and mudroom. "Hi, Derwin," I greeted.

"I come over here to see what you're all doing." He'd greased his hair into a point on top and in the front. It was just exactly the hairdo I'd designed for him.

Momma herded the young boy away from the dining room area. "Not now. We're busy with a project. Why don't you go on home, and we'll call you when we're done."

"My mom left for a while. But she didn't leave the house key." He sat at the kitchen table as if he'd been invited. But he needed no invitation. He also knew he must be on good behavior. Momma's demeanor shouted tension.

"Okay, just sit there. When we get done, I'll give you some ice cream," Momma said in a bargaining way. "I got both chocolate chip and peach swirl." She was certainly and visibly preoccupied.

"Your sun clock makes a pretty decoration," he said as he twisted around in the chair to see the sundial. "Not shiny, but nice. It looks nicer out of the curio cabinet. Grandma Brent said it come from England."

"Grandma also said it belonged to me," Lea stated with a precision clip to her words. "Said it and *promised* it." Her eyes blinked closed a couple times. "Promised it," she stressed.

Isabel jumped right in with both wedged-shoes she was wearing. "Grandma never said such a thing in her life, Lea."

"She did so say it," Lea said, then cast a blazing glance in my direction.

I coughed out. "I heard it, too." I felt as if my limbs were being pulled by a twelfth century wheel of torture. I was confessing in a very low volume.

Isabel's glare was equipped with the paparazzi's full interrogation. Tartly, she said, "Vicky, I have always backed you. Always. You know that. I could get my memory going and I'll bet you wouldn't be any too pleased."

She knew exactly how to get me settled down. Her look was with authority. I stammered, "I am just saying what I remember hearing."

Snapping, her statement sounded like a sledgehammer. "Your memory isn't always perfect."

"That would be because I'm not a perfect person," I retaliated. Why was life always concerned with dings versus perfection? Some dings might actually *be* perfect dings and scratches. Then what?

Momma was covering her eyes. "You girls stop that!"

"We aren't girls," I objected. "We're women."

"You're my girls, and I'll call you three anything I want," Momma's said with steely conviction. "I want you all to stop the nonsense. Or I won't give anyone anything."

"Momma," Lea said as she reached over and ran her hand along the highest point of the sundial. "Grandma wanted me to have it. By rights, it belongs to me."

"By law, it is mine," Willa Brent said firmly. "Your grandmother's will verified that exact thing. I'm to have the house and every blessed thing in it." For some unknown reason, Momma threw in a sign of the cross for good measure.

"Momma's right," Isabel reinforced. "That's the law."

"So what are *you* planning to do with *my* sundial, Momma?" Lea asked.

As rapidly as inserting a blink onto a face, Isabel answered, "It's an heirloom, and it should be passed down to the oldest grandson. Theodore." She gave Tad a sugary side-glance – then an immediate proud mother look that is the badge of all proud mothers. Tad's uncomfortable frame swayed from foot to foot. He was clearly embarrassed by most of what his mother did.

In my very early years, each time Isabel fussed over me, I wanted to run. When I did, she would snag me by the shirtsleeve and begin lint-picking and brushing. My collar was never properly formed. She would jerk it upright, and then fold it down – mashing it against my neck. It nearly pressed me to my knees. That was a place she thought I might be redeemed. On my knees with a starchy looking collar.

From the minute her child was born, I feared she would pester him to death. But at least it kept her too busy to bother me.

"That's not fair," Lea argued. "It's meant to be mine."

Quashing the conversation, Momma said with a gesture pointing out her heart and with a sweep of her lungs, "It is meant to be mine. And it *is*."

For several moments, there was a hush. Tad delicately moved the sundial to the opposite side of the table. Angling it, he then moved it slowly back to where it had originally been. It was as if the sundial might be migrating across the table. Tad was my sister's son.

"My throat hurts," Derwin said with a prickly accompaniment to his voice.

Momma's arms went up. "Would ice cream help?"

"Sure. I'd feel better with a bowl of peach swirl ice cream," the boy answered.

Who wouldn't? I considered. "I'll get him some," I offered. I needed to get back into some good graces. I would save Momma the trip to dispense ice cream. I was grabbing at straws – no doubt about that. After all, I'd become Lea's accomplice with my smattering of remembrances.

Derwin grinned at me as I scooped ice cream into his bowl. Giving him a wink, I added another scoop. While he slurped at the spoon, I had an interval of silence. It was pleasant not to be involved in everyone's sinister malevolence.

Not being able to avoid the din of everyone's sarcasms, I rested my cheeks in my hands. My elbows were carefully poking against the table top. Quizzically, Derwin said, "Do you know why everyone's fighting?"

"Greed. Everyone wants that sundial." I huddled nearer, confiding to him, "Everyone thinks it belongs to them. You know, like when kids on the playground try to take the ball you just caught. And they want to fight you for it."

"They mostly don't let me play." His eyes lost their glimmer a moment. "But I don't even want to be near the other kids. They shove me around a lot."

"Don't pay any attention. My sisters elevate my blood pressure without even having to shove me around," I admitted.

As if I'd activated a sore spot, his shoulders lowered. "I try not to pay attention. Except when they're shoving me. The mean kids push me around and call me *Tard.*"

"Turd?" I guessed.

He explained, "Like retard."

That's what I got for questioning his elocution. When talking with Derwin, things like that broke my heart. "If you're at school, tell one of the teachers. Do they call you anything else?"

"Faggot boy." His head lowered. "They say if I snitch, the kids'll kill me."

"They say things like that because they want to frighten you, Der. Tell a grown up if you can. If not, try to ignore them. I'm sorry you have to deal with bullies. It isn't fair."

"I know. Your grandma said it isn't fair. Then she said Jesus would look after me."

"Well, if I'm around, I'll try to look after you." I'd already decided Jesus might not be on bully call.

Winching, I felt exhaustion. Any comments I wanted to make would not be able to struggle through my mouth. He hadn't told me that before.

How could anyone harbor the entire world from being picked on? Mean people seemed far too devious. Bullies are far too good at what they do.

A sudden skirmish erupted, or perhaps detonated. I went to the doorway. Lea was in Isabel's face. "Don't you come at me like that. You used to be able to scare me, but that was before I met up with some really strong women," Lea flared.

We all knew who she meant by really strong women. They'd been convicted of some really strong shit. Beating, slicing, pistol-whipping, and murdering, were extremely strong events.

A flicker of terror from Isabel brought Momma into the skirmish. Momma could imitate a cloudburst. "You two settle back." Her arm protruded in Lea's space. "Now!" In Momma's vocabulary *Now!* could be translated to - don't mess with me. It was one of those words that exuded power.

Both women stepped back. Then faster than an electromagnet's pull, Lea made a leap toward Isabel. "It's my sundial. You take those Hummels and shove 'em. That's what the two of you wanted."

"Stop it, *now!*" Momma barked. "Nobody is getting a thing if this is how you're behaving. I'll give the takings to the Church," Momma threatened.

I issued an exhalation of pure misery. As if Rome didn't have enough treasures. Although Pope Francis would probably end up dispensing some of those treasures to buy food for the starving. He was my kinda Pope, I thought.

Tad coughed. "I think we've got enough photos." He clearly wanted the disenchantment to go away. And he wanted to get out of the fracas.

Momma pulled the sundial to her chest. She picked up the small canvas bag that she'd stored it inside. She'd began wrapping and twisting it protectively in a towel. When it was fully covered, she pushed it carefully into the bag. She uttered, "I'm going to hide my treasure away in the cabinet until we're ready to take it back to the bank."

She crossed past me, nearly knocking me down. Sliding the precious package into the kitchen cabinet, she scrutinized the corner of the shelf. She then fit the sundial behind a mixing bowl. Momma stormed back into the dining room. "If this is what having money is about," Momma pontificated, "it has reduced us to being a bunch of insects. Bugs."

Under my breath, and with full agreement, I added, "A bacterial colonization."

Chapter 25

Too much tension has always yanked me by the collar. It's as if I become suffocated by the strain. Maybe that was my reason for loving tranquility. Very possibly, it was my reason for appreciating humor. Humor could often shift those angry gears down. But not always, I thought as I stepped outside for air and quiet.

An inebriated Dottie Wake was fumbling with the keys to her front door. She would soon be over screaming the house down about finding her son. I went for a preemptive strike.

"Have you been out celebrating all night?" I questioned with my very best snarky accusation. She easily read my smirk.

"Yeah." She squinted, gawked, to make sure who she was going to cuss out in her tirade. She was unkempt – that was an understatement. Her coal black-dyed hair was like the top of a thick jungle. Her eyes were cautious, and the surrounding sockets were nearly charcoal-colored. Her ruddy complexion was redder than mashed raspberries. She'd obviously had little sleep wherever she'd last fallen. Her disheveled garment was mucky with a slept-in scent. Her body was tented with a loudly printed, satiny housedress. Color varieties were a mix of bold primary hues.

"Derwin is at Momma's," I divulged.

She gave a swat in the air. She was slowly taking charge of her stupor. "My kid should be home."

"I couldn't agree more, Dottie. He should be home being supervised."

Having caught my inference, she snarled, "I gotta life too, you know."

She was pathetic, yet in a very obscene way. "Your son should be your first concern. Children are priories."

Her voice rose to a semi-shriek. "He's fine. I'm a human being. I deserve some fun outta life. Men still wanna screw the daylights outta me."

"You're certainly welcome to my share of the men."

She gave a press upward to her sagging breasts. Her eyes honed in on me. "Stop looking at me like I'm a fuckin' slam hog."

I fired back, "Stop looking at me like I'm trying to sell you a twenty-year old yellow mongrel. You need to stop drinking so you can take your medication. Derwin deserves some normalcy in life."

"Normalcy! You Brents sure as hell ain't normal. You got an ex-con and a queer. And tight-ass Isabel. What the hell is she worth?"

I shrugged my agreement of her assessment of Isabel, anyway. "I have no idea what she might be worth. But I can tell you, your son has a heart of gold. He's a great kid. He deserves a parent who loves him."

"I love him. That's better love than the oddball Brents."

"It isn't even close. My mother and grandmother raised him more than you did," I reminded her.

She wasn't going to argue that point. She wanted to return to her offensive stance. "And your grandmother was every bit as much an old hatchet as your mother is."

Taking a deep breath, I then released a strong puff of air that could have knocked over a brick wall. "Dottie, you are drunk. You're pulling yourself in here at noon." All my words – the ones I wanted, they were lost between my brain and my throat. "Derwin is going to get lost, get kidnapped, get hurt, or even killed if some perv snatches him. He needs to be cared for."

"Tell him to get his ass home. And when he gets here, I'm tellin' him if he ever goes next door – I'm gonna whip him until he can't sit down."

"You touch him, and I'll have Child Services in here within the hour. So don't." I turned. I was angry and needed to calm myself. Although I'd had no intention of harming her, in the back of my mind, I was not treating her to a gloved boxing match. Those gloves came off when she called my grandmother an old hatchet.

Emblematic of the Brent women – we protected the name of my dead grandmother. Grandma was no saint, but we treated her like one when she was alive. And more so, we treated her soul like one when she died. Deceased Catholics tended to get better as time went on. Real scallywags obviously knew they'd eventually become an okay person. It's just that it took dying to get there.

Well, we all loved my grandmother – even though she was crotchety at times. The minute she died, she became a sweet old soul. She never warmed totally to Lea. I suspected she didn't like the name Leandra from the start. She'd grumbled over it being too different.

When Lea was in middle grades, Grandma had just begun walking with a metal arm-cane. We usually all played games with Grandma when we got home from school. Well, mostly we allowed Grandma to cheat at Chinese checkers. But Lea never turned a blind eye. She'd say, "You can't move that marble over there, Grandma." Grandma would become livid and smack the tabletop with her cane. The marbles would go flying, and Grandma would be yelling at Lea.

We loved Grandma in spite of her little foibles. But Lea did actually like her *less* than Isabel and I liked her.

So I was perturbed as I walked quickly back to Momma's. I gave a muffled chuckle.

Dottie wanted to press my anger button. Hell no, I wouldn't throw the first slap at Miss-able-to-get-the-daylights-bonked-outta-her, crazy, drunken – Dottie. I'd tell Momma that Dottie called her and Grandma old hatchets. Ret-ri-bution!

As I opened the door, I realized pandemonium had also made its home at the Brent address. The only one not saying a word was Derwin. It was just another day amongst *crazy* for him.

I dropped the conversation into Momma's lap. She balled her fists and her eyes formed some dangerous artillery. She began stomping next door. Both Isabel and Lea followed after her. They didn't want to miss anything. I motioned for Derwin to come sit out on the back porch with me. I figured I'd be able to hear any good parts from next door. Truth be told, I didn't want Dottie to take a swing at me. One swat from her could break my nose or loosen my teeth.

"Come on, Pal," I said. We sat.

Derwin's slow, pensive speech asked, "My mom is gonna be sick, isn't she?"

"Yep. Probably."

"What's the real reason your family is all fighting over the old sundial?"

"Derwin. It's valuable and so they want it."

He nodded. "I don't know what they want with it. It doesn't work." He was clearly perplexed. "When something doesn't work, we throw it in the trash."

"What do you mean, it doesn't work?" I questioned.

He shrugged as his head tipped. "Your Grandma said it only works in the sun. It doesn't work without sunshine. That's what she told me. When it goes dark, it doesn't work. It's like a night without time."

I'd never thought about that, but it was correct. "They like it because it's worth a lot of money. Not because they can use it."

"Why does somebody give them a lot of money if they can't use it to tell the time?"

"Because it is what they call an antique. People want to look at it. To see how people used to tell time." I watched his face begin to comprehend.

Suddenly, our heads lifted in unison. Derwin said, "Mom's getting loud."

A ruckus was boiling over. I stood. "Stick around. I don't want you going home until it gets quiet." I dashed over to Dottie's front landing.

"And you're a battle-ax," Momma screamed. My sisters had her by the arms, restraining her. "You can't talk about my mother like that!"

"Both of youse are the same," Dottie yelled back. She then advanced on Momma. "A couple of fuckin' old hags. And you think you can get up in my grill and yell at me. Shit no."

They were all acting like harridans-gone-wild.

Then Dottie widened her net. She was now dissing another generation. Isabel didn't like being called a holy roller and Lea objected to Dottie's calling her a counterfeiter. Dottie didn't know the technical terms. Embezzler and counterfeiter *are* different.

Both are crimes, but different violation. Dottie wasn't any kind of authority. The drunk-tank was as far up the ladder as she got, criminal-wise.

I figured I was next. She'd probably come out with some beauties to pitch in my direction. *Dyke* would have been too mild. I'd only have laughed at that.

Suddenly, it hit me. I needed to warn Lea. While I wouldn't throw a punch at Dottie, Lea might. I pulled Lea's arm. Those rough-tough *strong women* might have taught Lea how to defend herself. Or when to aim a sucker punch.

"Lea, you go back and make sure Derwin's okay." I then whispered, "If somebody calls the cops – you could get run in."
Her eyes went double-size as she made a beeline toward Momma's backyard. For wearing sky-high pumps, she was moving on out.

During the next several minutes, I pulled Momma back a couple times. However, Dottie would get in her face again. Isabel acted as though she might be part of some stage production. Her son had left when the combat started. Wise – maybe he wasn't as dumb as I thought he was.

Isabel was the next to surrender, which technically makes her brighter than me. I continued to try leading Momma away from the neighborhood disharmony. Finally, she whirled around and followed after me. Over her shoulder, she called out, "You are a soaker, and a wanton chippy, Dottie Wake. That's what you are." To me she blurted, "Did you hear her call my mother a hag?"

"She called you a hag, too," I unwisely reminded Momma.

Momma had replayed the entire event by the time we got to the empty kitchen. As if I hadn't heard a word of the exchange, she wanted to make sure I got the blow by blow account. Twice if necessary.

Derwin had gone home, I hoped. Tad had grabbed his camera and scooted. Lea had obviously poured herself a glass of milk, because she left the milk container on the counter – as she most always did. Then she'd retreated to the basement. Isabel had taken her sack of garden variety vegetables and egressed from the property as fast as her little legs could travel.

I was stuck. Momma guided me to a kitchen chair. As she pushed me into a seated position, I felt as if I were a hostage. If she had a roll of duct tape on her person, I would have feared for my life. She began, "I've never heard such trash. Talking like that about me and my mother. Why, your Grandma would have slapped her mouth."

Grandma could get plenty mortified herself. Come to think of it – it might be a gene thing – and Momma inherited. I could actually envision Grandma socking Dottie a good one. When that flash of hostility beamed from Grandma's eyes, it was like lightning smashing the ground. Hell, I thought – Grandma would have knocked Dottie's head clean off her shoulders. Holy blazing crap. Grandma's glare alone could scald.

One good thing – the bickering did transfer the ire of my sisters and Momma to the wild-mouthed Dottie. Temporary, sure, but at least it cooled the temperatures. The typical rocky times were simply little snipes at one another. Now, with the sundial on the line, it was as if the war that had always been undercover was now exploding. The world's most courteous arbitrators and diplomats wouldn't have a chance at settling this deal.

When Momma took a long breath, I stood like a jack-in-the-box. Amazed I didn't catapult to the door. I side-stepped quickly. "Momma, I need to run back to the apartment so I can add a couple things to my blog. If you need me to come back later to help you get the sundial to the bank, just call. However, Lea is right here, and Isabel is only a couple blocks away. But call if you need me."

"I surely will. If you see that bitch from next door outside don't you talk one single word to her."

My eyebrows shot upward. Momma had called her a *bitch*. And sure enough, she wouldn't want me to talk to the bitch next door.

I was feeling a little guilty as I scrammed out of there. Once in my vehicle, I peeled away from the curb – all the way to the corner. Maybe I shouldn't have told Momma what Dottie had said. But at least it got the Brents all on one side for a while.

I couldn't wait to relay the news to Charlene. I'd bet she wouldn't be so quick to turn down a chance to witness all the excitement. But then again, she got most of her laughing out when I replayed it for her.

Hoping that Momma wouldn't call me to help them get the damned sundial back in its safety deposit box, I even did a quick Hail Mary. I thought about how savage the neighborhood had become. Well, Momma's house, too.

Charlene was certainly going to get a kick out of this latest Brent episode. She would be a little disappointed to find out that Dottie hadn't gotten the chance to throw her fists. And she hadn't gotten around to lambasting me. Although Dottie probably would have loved to unleash all the synonyms she had for lesbians, but there just wasn't time.

Chapter 26

As she gulped for air, Charlene's snicker continued. She had arrived back at our apartment a few minutes after I had. I was glad that she'd decided to come home early because I had comedic events brimming from the photo shoot. As well as the knock-down between Momma and Dottie. Drama flourished, you might say.

Mid-afternoon on a Friday was a good time for Char to leave her office. She'd brought work home, so felt justified in taking off early.

Earlier on the phone, I'd started to tell Char about the skirmish. When I described the fight of the decade on Berry Avenue as being indescribable, Char said hold it until she got there. She would coax every little detail out of me. She would give me the sign to slow down or her hands would roll gently hurrying my story on – she directed the tempo of this episodic chronicle of the Brent family event.

When she'd entered, she held up her hand to halt me from starting before she was ready. By ready, I mean comfortable. She opened and poured wine while I tossed a few chips in a bowl. Then as we sat to toast, she gave the nod. "So, Snark Butt, let's hear how you converted from a sweetheart to a snark butt in one afternoon!"

Tittering a moment, I then began telling her about the day. I could still see Momma standing there with her hands on her hips, barking down to me – seated at the table – about how she told Dottie off – good and proper.

"And then Momma said, 'That oughta fry Dottie's fritters!' Well, I had to leave. I remembered one time Momma gave me a smack for laughing at her. She told me not to talk back. I said I wasn't talking back, I was laughing back. She whacked me again."

"I'm amazed that she'd stand up to Dottie. The woman is two-stories high and looks as if she could easily be a sumo wrestler. And your mother is a little stick of a thing."

"Hell, I'm larger, and stronger than Momma, and I stood back out of range from Dottie's fist. Momma got right up in the vicinity of a punch."

"Isn't it going to make it difficult when you see Dottie again?"

"She was staggering drunk, so I don't think she'll remember. She never does."

"Can she get help again?"

"Yes, I'm sure she can. It's just that she wants to drink. She even stops taking meds so she can drink. We've often offered to help her. Grandma used to say she's not long for the world if she doesn't pay attention to her health. She'd tell Dottie to her face that if she didn't lay off the sauce, her demise was near."

"I'm surprised your grandmother didn't get smacked."

"Dottie needs some detox again. I just hope she gets help soon enough to save her. Once when we were trying to talk with her, she said she couldn't help drinking. Having a kid who was slow was too much for her. Momma and Grandma tried to convince her that Derwin is a magical little guy. Dottie wasn't listening."

"She wasn't listening because that was her excuse to drink. She's sick. Anyone would be lucky to have a son like Derwin. But she needs some reason to drink. He's her reason. Heartbreaking," Char said as her eyes filled. "For everyone."

"Momma prays for Dottie – that she'll get help."

"Maybe one day she'll need to get help," Charlene said. "It's also sad for Derwin. He's a good kid. He has enough going against him. What do you think would become of him if something happened to her?"

I took a sip, and then another. "I don't know. Momma isn't ready to retire. At her age, Social Services probably wouldn't agree to give custody to her if she works. There's Isabel. She moans about Tad going off to school and her being alone. But Derwin has problems. He's slow. The jury is out as to whether he's homosexual. Isabel is not patient. Plus, she would be a fright about the gay thing – if that were his inclination."

"As a lesbian, she would be my last choice for a substitute mother," Charlene lamented.

"She insinuated that I could change if I would only give myself a chance to be straight. Derwin is going through a hooch-filled mother. Why give the poor kid another cross to carry. Besides, Isabel wouldn't be interested in being tied down with Derwin."

"No. Lea has a kind heart, but she works. And we both work. Is there any family beyond Dottie?"

"Dottie's family is certainly not interested. And his father – well, whoever Derwin's sperm donor might have been – finding him would take dozens of DNA tests. The kid would probably be collecting Social Security before he found his biological father."

"I presume that search would be much more difficult than finding your father. Locating your father seems to be impossible."

"So it seems."

"And your mother isn't the type to chase with men."

"I'm pretty sure Momma didn't do any carousing. Even if Isabel and I joke about Lea not sharing our father, or there had been a stork mix-up, I can't see Momma cheating on my father." I shook my head. "Nope, I just don't see it. After my father left, Momma sort of put the kibosh on romance. It was as if she abdicated her libido. It all shut down."

"Maybe she still loves him." Char poured another half glass of wine.

"I'm guessing, when it was over, it was over. I know she told me once that she'd checked with his relatives when he left, and none of them knew where he was." My jaws tensed. "I did try to find my father. I did. But where do I start? I can't search under every viaduct in the world."

"No." She reached toward me, taking my hand in hers. We both knew I was reticent about finding him. "If it is important to you though, we could hire a detective – you know someone who searches cold cases?"

"Naw. I did put him on a couple missing person's locator lists, but I doubt I'll hear anything back. He vanished." I sucked in a breath. "My guess is he lived a hard life and died."

"Let's talk about something happier." She lifted my chin so that our lips could meet. Her kiss was the warmest warm I'd ever known.

"Rats!" I said as my phone rang. The ringtone was a song I liked, but I did not like it when mid-kissing. "Slow down, Isabel."

"Come here right away. It's an emergency." Isabel hung up before I could answer.

"Isabel says there's an emergency. I better go. Wanna come along? An emergency could provide you with some big-time hilarity."

"Knock yourself out. But don't forget the details. I'll work on my Monday presentation. That will give us the entire weekend together."

Driving to Isabel and Sully's at a fairly rapid clip was unusual. An emergency called for expediency. Normally, on my way to see Isabel – my pace was slow, purposely taking my time. Preventing the onslaught of Isabel was a major decision.

But Isabel sounded panicked, so I was in rush mode. While I drove, I thought of the entire weekend with Charlene. I wouldn't even go to Mass. Momma wouldn't like it, but I would be loving it. And loving Char.

Parking quickly, I half ran to the door. I knocked and got no response, so I went around to the back. Sully greeted me. "What you doing here, Vicky?"

"Isabel said there was an emergency. I assumed I was to come here." I was confused.

"She's at your Momma's house. She probably called from there."

"So what's the flipping emergency?" I resented that Isabel was so rattled that she didn't say she was at Momma's house.

"I don't know. She got a call from Willa and off she went. She told me about the brawl this afternoon."

"It was quite a tiff. It reminds me that there's nothing quite as smooth as silence. Dottie can reach any high note you might request."

"She scares me," Sully admitted.

"Dottie is a danger to herself and others. I'm glad Lea went inside in case someone called the police."

"Isabel claimed she, *Isabel*, remained calm and attempted to settle things down," Sully said dubiously.

If ever there was an eye-rolling moment, I thought. "She said that?"

He chuckled. "Maybe the dispute is continuing. Wanna stay here. I've got an iced six-pack in the fridge."

"I'd like that, Sully, but I'd better head over to Momma's. In case Dottie might have gone off on Momma."

"Try to stay out of the wrangle and duck a lot." His husky voice warned with a laugh.

Back in the SUV, I felt a low-grade anger. Then the rush began because I figured Isabel was in a dither, or she would have mentioned she was at Momma's. It cost me an extra ten minutes, and I'd be blamed for not making it to Momma's at lightning speed. Momma's favorite saying when I'd dawdled along was 'If I told you I'd made a coconut cake, you'da been here twenty minutes ago.'

I said *fuck* several times under my breath. My language was not always pure. I usually blamed being on the softball team for that. My profanity had bloomed within the clutches of the team. Blasphemies, expletives – and any form of swearing – I learned every one, two, three, and four syllable cuss words from the locker room, field, and after-game parties.

I overdosed on saying *fuck*. When I was in college, I became so intimate with the word that I could nearly taste it as it slid through my lips. During that era of my life, the softball days took my mind off life's quandary.

Would I make it in life? I wondered. What was 'making it' all about? Now, for me, I could answer that I had made it. Charlene was all the hues, and tones, and textures that constructed the 'remarkable' making it.

Naturally, I considered myself blessed – fortunate beyond all my dreams. A minor part of my dream was that I would be employed by a national publication. I would have my own column, and it would be recognized. Or write a book that mattered.

Instead, I work at jamming words onto a page meant to encourage the purchase of tires and fresh orchard jelly and women's trendy handbags.

But I also write a blog. It was sort of a work-release program that allowed my spirit to yack about heart messages. I could jot down how the fragrance of scented geraniums impacted my world. I was able to explain what I gleaned from people's idiosyncratic motion. I once read that artists are nature's intermediaries.

One of my blogs was about listening to the bird's conversation, my early morning walks when I visited with sunshine, and the days that provided bird chatter. I was locked to the landscape for time so special that it made me grin.

So I assembled words. My blogs totally excluded the softball anthem of *fuck 'em all*.

Chapter 27

Momma was in hysterics! Lea and Isabel's glares were carving large chunks out of one another. I'd never heard Momma so utterly deafening. She kept pacing. Even her hands were ranting – well, whirling. It was like she was trying to throw her hands away and they wouldn't detach from her wrists.

"It's gone," she wailed. She did a rapid-fire sign of the cross. Then her hands resumed their flapping – undulating.

"What? What's going on?" I inquired. I was clearly out of the loop because I was the only one still breathing properly.

"The sundial!" Momma shouted. "Someone stole the sundial. The treasure is gone. Someone stole my sundial."

"My sundial!" Lea exclaimed dramatically. Her fake eyelashes blinked wildly. They were extenuating lashes – with the right side having a tenuous overhang problem. She pointed to Isabel. "She and her son conspired. They think they deserve it. And it's mine!"

"Yours!" Isabel was facing off with Lea. "Don't you accuse my Tad and me. You're the thief in this family!"

Quickly, I pointed at the table. "Everyone sit down and let's figure this out." Amazingly, they listened to me and the three of them sat. I went to the cabinet where the bounty had been stored for safe keeping. As it happens now, it hadn't been well-enough hidden. Where it had been definitely wasn't keeping it safely.

I didn't give a rat's ass about leaving fingerprints or smudging fingerprints. Anyone who had been in the house had left fingerprints everywhere. So it wasn't really relevant.

Peering inside, I saw that the sundial was definitely gone from where Momma had placed it. I looked on the other shelves – no dice, no sundial. I stood as I thought about Momma's old saying about things don't scamper off by themselves. That sundial hadn't walked away on its own. The cabinet was empty of a sundial. So much for following the blood trail. Like Grandma used to say, it was spick-and-span clean.

"They took it," Lea accused. "Greedy gut and her son took it."

"You," Isabel stammered at Lea, "you are the felon. You stole Momma's sundial that rightfully should go to my Tad."

"Stop," I commanded as I sat. "Okay. Who had the opportunity to take it?" I was sounding like Columbo. Grandma never missed a Columbo mystery. "Momma was with me, and she already laid claim to it. I was in her view all the time. She saw me leave empty-handed. "

Momma interrupted me, "I saw her leave. And like she said, she had nothing. She'd even forgotten to take her sack of vegetables."

I *hadn't* forgotten.

Momma continued, "I certainly would not have taken the sundial. I already owned it because the will said it was mine."

"Well, that excludes Momma. And I was with Momma, battling the drunk-hunk from next door." I paused. "Tad had been alone in the kitchen before he left."

"My Tad has never been in trouble and has never taken anything that didn't belong to him. He's been raised properly by Sully and me."

Momma began to rage. "Don't you be saying I didn't raise the three of you properly. You were all taught right from wrong, my girl – so don't start comparing us. You had a husband taking care of your needs."

"I'm not saying that, Momma," she quickly refuted. "Tad did not take it. And Vicky better keep her mouth shut about my son."

"Isabel, I'm only excluding the ones who couldn't have taken it. Relax a minute. Now where was I?" Continuing rapidly, so no one else would interrupt me, I said, "And afterward, Lea was here alone. For that matter, so were you, Isabel." Rather a bit too haughtily, I added. "I was in Momma's sight every moment. So I'm excluded."

"Derwin was here," Isabel indicted. "He could have stolen it."

Disclaiming her charge, I said, "He had the opportunity to nab it. But he didn't realize it was valuable. He kept saying it couldn't be worth anything because it didn't work. He asked me why anyone would want an old clock that didn't work most of the time."

"But he had the opportunity. He could have," Momma said. "He has to go down on the suspect list."

"He's almost grown up here. He's never once taken anything," I defended.

"Well, he had the opportunity," Lea parroted Momma.

"Okay. Here's the plan. Everyone take a room and begin searching. It might be in the house," I instructed.

"I want to search Lea's room," Isabel seethed.

"Go ahead and search my bedroom," Lea said. Her head lifted. "I haven't got it. It's probably in your son's room. Can I go over to your house and tear Tad's room up?"

Both women sprung to their feet in unison as if they were Radio City Rockettes. I almost expect a couple kicks. Lea was so much taller than Isabel that she could have kicked Isabel's teeth out. At this time, she probably would have liked to do just that.

"Start in this house and work our way outward," Momma commanded. "We can search the garage and garden next. I've read in detective books that they begin at the center of the crime scene." She elevated her head. She must have thought she was Queen of the Cold Cases.

"Great idea, Momma," I encouraged. "I'll run over to see if Derwin knows anything about it. Or saw anything to do with its disappearance."

"You think the bitch will let you in?" Lea questioned.

"She will. If not, I can get Derwin to talk with me outside."

As I trudged across the grass, I wondered if my health insurance was current. Dottie Wake was probably some kind of exemption. I also hoped my own 'one-page will' was up to date. And properly signed. Charlene didn't want my meager possessions and small insurance policy. She recommended I give any bucks I had to the gay and lesbian community center. I had done just that, and I was happy for my decision.

I was particularly gratified after now knowing the true nature of my family. Momma, Isabel, and Lea were all avaricious, selfish, money-grubbers. I was thrilled they weren't getting a nickel from my small pile of coins.

There were lots of terrific and needy gay and lesbian funds. There were educational funds to help kids who'd been kicked out of their homes. There was also a public relations group that promoted anti-bigotry ads and programs. And of course, there were the legal assistance funds.

All good causes, I considered as I thought about how badly the family was acting regarding the sundial. Muttering to myself as I walked onto the landing, I had no qualms about leaving my family out of my will. I wouldn't want to think they scratched one another's eyes out because I left an extra few bucks to any one of them.

I also wanted Derwin to have my softball/baseball equipment. I had few hopes that he'd ever use any of it, but maybe he'd find a home for it. My family clearly showed their colors. They'd rip the stitching out and sell the leather from the gloves and balls to some junk yard. Goodness knows what they'd do with the bats.

I wished I had one in my hands at this time for protection. Taking life and limb in my hands, I marched to the door and knocked. Before the door opened, I took a leaf from Momma's book and made the sign of the cross.

Chapter 28

As she leaned halfway out the door, Dottie swung a mug of liquid. It didn't spill, so when she made a crude gesture that would have upset Momma – I hoped she was just settling the mug business and her middle finger flew up on its own.

Momma would have interpreted it in the worst way. But not me. I must have awakened her from a sleep she dearly needed. With running mascara surrounding her rheumy red, bulbous eyes, she squinted at me. Smeared makeup caking her face – she looked a fright.

"I know we bickered, Dottie, but I really need to talk with you – and Derwin."

"Your old lady better stay clear of me. That fuckin' old weasel can kiss my sweet ass."

I had serious doubts that her ass had ever been sweet, but I wasn't going to mention it now. I was on a fact-finding mission and being conciliatory was part of my greater plan. "Momma's a little contentious, I agree. But we have a problem over at Momma's house. Derwin might be able to help us. He was over there when all the fighting between my sisters was going on."

"You Brents come over here like you own the neighborhood."

"Well, it wasn't really about that fight." As they say on the newscasts – and war was breaking out all over the freakin' place. "But let's skip to the other fight. Isabel and Lea were upset with each other. And," I paused to see if she was following. I was up to my eyeballs in fights. "And, well. That old sundial of Grandmas went missing. Since Derwin was over there – he might have seen something suspicious."

"Derwin," she hollered downstairs. "Derwin, you get up here."

I could hear the clatter of his shoes on the stairs leading from the basement. "What, Mom?" he asked. Frowning at me, he greeted, "Hi, Vicky."

"Hey, Derwin. I was wondering when you were over at Momma's, did you see anything to do with Grandma's old sundial?"

"I didn't take it!" he resolved firmly. His eyes did shift. But they often do.

"I didn't say you did," I corrected. "I thought you might have seen one of the others take it?"

"My kid didn't steal nothin' from over there!" Dottie began blustering. "My kid ain't a thief. You got the felon over there. And Isabel has always been a sneaky, highfalutin turkey-leg bitch. So don't bother tellin' me that your Momma is hard done by luck. She hasn't had any harder time than I have. Other than her odd assortment of daughters."

Her babbling would have continued, but I interrupted, "Dottie, I didn't say Derwin took it."

"Who wants any of your fuckin' trash?" She was getting belligerent. I could feel it.

"Let's ease off a minute. I'm not here to fight."

"Too bad, 'cuz I'm looking for a fight."

Solitude is sometimes my best emblem. But I felt mired in the dispute. Before Dottie began pitching fists, I would go for a resolution. I wasn't optimistic, however, that I could solve the poop-throwing contest.

"Dottie, nobody is accusing Derwin. I just needed to know. Better I come over than Momma comes over. She's in a terrible mood."

"Fuck her," Dottie shouted. "My kid ain't a kleptomaniac."

With a clandestine lift of my arm, I pointed toward the back, hoping Derwin would get my drift and meet me in the backyard.

"Well, let's just empty our chambers so we can be friends again, Dottie," I suggested. To Derwin I asked, "Want to play a little catch?"

He began to shrug. Dottie put a cork in that bottle. "He goes nowhere near you crazy broads. Tell all the Brents to stay the hell outta my life."

"You'll feel better after you're rested, Dottie," I said with a forced smile that was so bogus and crooked – I felt ashamed of myself. Being disingenuous doesn't come easy for me. It never had, and probably never would. "It will all work out. Let's not allow a few hasty words to ruin our neighborhood friendship."

The lie bell was going off in my head. Momma used to say if we told a lie, it showed up on our forehead. Poor Lea would lie her socks off, and then turn to ask Momma if her forehead said 'lie' on it. I almost hoped that the women behind bars had taught her a little street savvy.

Dottie gave a guttural sound that I translated to mean she didn't really give a damn. She was hoarse from drinking all night and shouting all morning. She didn't have time for the likes of me. I wished I had some throat lozenges to offer her. A peace offering that might soften her hostility up a bit.

I said, "Okay, I'll just be running along." I turned to leave. I should have backed away. A huge bourbon-scented mug came whirling past my head. If it had slammed me, it would not only have taken my ear, but the entire right edge of my head. It would also have certainly intoxicated me.

I broke into a hard run. I never knew Dottie had that kind of an arm. Geez, I was trying to teach *her* son to pitch? When I got to Momma's front door, I heard the Brent battle continuing. I wouldn't tell anyone about the mug nearly beheading me. It would only start another explosive rumble.

Things were way too high-strung in the neighborhood. I would try to get my pugilistic butt back to my sweet woman as quickly as possible. My mind was dancing with the thought of taking my honey-blond beauty, with her sparkling green eyes, in my arms and making love.

Love making. Or love sharing. Yes. I suddenly thought of the term *sexual intercourse*. What a miserable sound those words had to them. Intercourse – is not the most jubilant word in the dictionary. There's nothing at all romantic about it.

I longed to hear my lovely lady call me her sweet snark butt. I yearned to hold her near. Funny, but living with Charlene made me wake with a smile in the morning – just like she did.

Looking directly upward to the sky, I stopped walking. As if a moment of familial atonement struck, I thought about how I hated the recent scrapes I was constantly enduring. I wished I could decode my concerns. I never wanted to abandon my family. Yet, I was forever dancing to their weird musical drama.

This drama not only was tough on me, but also on my golden goddess. Thankfully, Char was forgiving. One time, after a mess, she said that we had taken one another lock, stock, and barrel. Families were a package deal that went with us. Well, her family is extraordinary. When they come into town, I rejoice because it is all so easy. My family is a different barrel all together. Everything needs to be conspiratorial and difficult.

Char definitely didn't get the best end of the deal.

Doubling around, I went toward the backyard. My pace was slow, thinking that maybe Derwin would join me. Thankfully, my saunter was worth it, because he ran across his backyard to meet me at our gate.

"My mom is already passed out on the sofa," he reported.

"I don't want you getting in any trouble with her."

His words were dragging, "Naw. She's out for the count. That's what your grandma used to say when my mom went to sleep. Well, she's really out for the count."

"Grandma always had sayings like that. Out for the count," I repeated. "Hey, how come you stopped wearing your neat hairdo?"

"Mom said I needed a haircut if it stuck up like that. I told her you helped me. She said that figures. I wish you sisters weren't all fighting." His trod was heavy with the weight of the neighborhood.

"Grown-ups should be better," I acknowledged. "I know Momma is inflexible at times."

"I love your momma. And all of you," Derwin said softly. "That's why I don't want fighting. I'd do anything to keep everyone from fighting."

Smiling down at him, I agreed, "Me, too."

"Too bad everyone doesn't make up." His face was swiped with concern.

"Derwin, my family needs to find that sundial. Are you sure you didn't see anyone take it?"

"Naw," he said shaking his head. "I never saw nothing and my mom said she saw me. I had nothing in my hands when I came home."

"I wasn't accusing you. I don't think you did it."

"Who you think did it?"

"Could have been Isabel, Lea, or maybe Tad. They all think it's rightfully theirs." I swung open the gate. We went to the swinging bench. As we sat, I admitted, "I don't have any idea who took it. But it's missing."

"They're all still fighting. You can hear 'em from here. I don't know why they're still fighting. The clock isn't really useful. And now that it's gone, they should stop fighting."

"You'd think. Well, they're looking for it now. Everyone is blaming everyone. Whoever took it is stealing from his or her own family." I stood. "I guess I better go in and help them. Or they'll be screaming at me."

His head went down. "I don't like it when everyone's fighting."

"Me neither, Pal. Mind you, it wasn't too terrific when they weren't battling. But now it seems out of control."

Derwin stood, dusted off his denim backside from where the swing was slightly dirty, and began walking slowly away. His head was still lowered. I wished he wouldn't always take things so hard.

Kids should be frolicking and having fun. When we were together and he laughed, it was as though the laugh escaped. It had been locked away, and suddenly fought its way out. It sounded nearly rusted shut – then there was a joyous getaway to safety. I loved when he'd release a chain of giggles. I always thought of it as soap bubbles being unbridled.

Derwin went to the gate and carefully opened it. He looked both ways and then scooted across to his house. It couldn't be easy being Derwin Wake.

The ruckus coming from the kitchen was getting even louder as I approached. It was like going from inaudible to a microphone on full blast.

Inside the place called 'us' – heart, soul, brain – was some kind of an inferno. I think everyone has one. Derwin's inferno would have to have been very large and uncontrollable.

My inferno is guilt for causing my sister's accident. It's all that's happened since the accident. Maybe I caused my father to skip out on us. Each thought that sends me back to the penalty box is like touching the radiantly hot inferno. I feel the burn throughout my body. I couldn't filter my memory forever – thoughts continued to seep in.

I wished it had been my face that got smashed. My mediocre face's destruction would be less of a loss of artistry. The tragedy of a great beauty like my sister was perilous.

How did that cryptically painful emotion figure into my feelings for Derwin? Well, sadness permeated my childhood. Now sadness is hurting a kid I care about.

Life's nectar pods aren't passed out like good candy to everyone. My childhood wasn't pitiably ruined. But the undercurrent of sadness never left.

For whatever reason, I couldn't really see anyone in the family stealing the sundial. Even if they felt justified in owning the relic, I just didn't feel as though they would take it.

I questioned if there was some stranger that might have snuck inside and carted it away. But there wasn't time. Not really, because a thief would have had to climb the back fence, and then figure out how to get in with all the people coming and going. Also, a thief would have had to know it was valuable.

It wasn't realistic to think of it being an outside job. But I wanted that. If it turned out to be any one of us – the dynamics of the family would be forever changed. I couldn't imagine any of our hearts that wouldn't be broken.

Now, if the treasure would be lost for good, everyone would suspect one another. None of their negotiations would work. Blame, I admitted, would tear my family apart. Dreams would be forever lost. I felt the exhaustion of stress. There was the pain of life that leaves us feeling empty.

I wanted to dash home to Charlene. I would ask her to remind me again why she gives me the love I don't deserve. I suddenly wanted to yell *fuck* a thousand times. I resisted the urge as I walked toward the backdoor.

In a few hours, it would be dark. I remembered what Derwin said about Grandma saying the sundial makes nights without time. Grandma was always on the money. She never allowed us to forget it either. Something inside me felt exhilaration when thinking of her. She'd know how to handle this mess. One of her favorite sayings was for us to keep in mind the importance of our family dynamic. The world isn't easy. But we're together.

Grandma said that there was Momma and her three brats. Every room had four corners. One for Momma and one for each of us. And, Grandma would sit herself down in the center of the room until we sorted things out. She would insist that we all face the music.

But how could we sort out a missing dream when the music was botched?

Chapter 29

My eyes clamped shut as I reached for the screen door. The blood-curdling shrieks coming from inside were from human beings with polyurethane hearts. Accusations were being hurled. I could almost smell the hatred – it was so thick. Beneath the accusations and name-calling, there must be a family.

Entering, I saw the anger – as if it were bright, blood red. It was all over. Mortified anger. Livid anger – all there. My words were nervously, but softly spoken. "Derwin says he didn't take anything. His mother saw him come in their house. He wasn't carrying anything. He also didn't see anyone taking it."

"We can't find it here," Isabel said with a disappointment in her voice. She had wanted to find it securely tucked in Lea's closet. She probably also wouldn't have minded finding a dozen vibrators so she could call Lea a pervert. Or maybe a set of lock-picks might be found when Isabel turned over her sister's room. Anything that might be in the least incriminating, Isabel would enjoy.

"We checked every cabinet and closet in the house, and nothing," Momma reported. "Also, I checked the shed. No sign of the sundial can be found." She issued a Columbo grunt. She was clearly enjoying the investigatory portion of this search. On her behalf, I wished she would be the one to find it. That would give her crowing rights in the neighborhood's largest crime.

Lea stated, "I even got up on a ladder to try to get up into the attic. But the paint was stuck. So it couldn't be there."

Attempting a miniscule touch of levity, I asked, "You didn't wear your platform shoes when you went up on that ladder, did you?"

Lea and Momma tittered a moment.

Isabel went on with business at hand. "Sully painted that hallway three years ago. Someone should check it now again and make sure you haven't got critters up there." Isabel gave a snort. "There could be a raccoon colony up there."

"Yeah," Lea said. "Once there were squirrels," she confirmed. "Remember that time? It was fun setting the traps. Then the fix-it guy came and spent two whole days repairing the gap under the roof's eaves. I think he was sweet on Momma."

"There will be no more of that talk," Momma insisted. Her tone was scolding, yet with just the slightest hint of pride in her enticing womanhood.

"Maybe we should call the police," I suggested as I sat at the table. It was like a war room.

Lea frowned. "Call the police about the squirrels?"

Now that, I agreed, was funnier than Lea's shoes climbing a ladder. "No," I said with a chuckle. "Not for the squirrels – for the lost or stolen sundial."

"We're not calling the police," Momma crossed her arms. "And it isn't lost at all. I don't know who took it, but we just have to find it."

Isabel asked, "So now we just have to find whoever took it?" She pontificated, "What a vile heart to steal from family! Maybe it was Derwin."

Momma deliberated. "Maybe Derwin wasn't aware of what he was doing," Momma said with compassion in her voice. "I don't want to believe it was taken by family."

I broke in, "Derwin *is* family. I mean, he's always been like family to us. Grandma looked after him for years. He's always over here. And his heart is the least vile of anyone I know."

"Then who *are* you accusing?" Lea demanded.

"No one. I don't know," I wisely answered. "But the damn thing is gone, so someone lifted it. And it sure wasn't me. I was in plain sight at all times."

The others looked around at one another. Isabel finally said, "Well, when we find the culprit, I'm going to expect some apologies for suspecting Tad and me."

"Me, too," Lea said with a machine-gun voice. "I've been called a felon thief all day. For nothing." Lea's shoulders twisted into a shrug. "Why would I steal it? I was planning on taking it to court and *winning* it. It belongs to me! Vicky, here, can testify that it was given to me by Grandma."

Isabel lifted her body upward. "Vicky is going to shut her mouth. She heard nothing like that." Her eyes narrowed, threatened, as they zeroed in on me.

Lea's piercing stare came from the opposite direction. "Are you going to stick behind me or are you gonna dump the truth and me? You know good and well that Grandma said it was mine."

Clearing my throat didn't take long enough. "I heard Grandma say you could have it. That's what I heard. I'm not going to lie about anything Grandma said."

Isabel wiggled around in her chair. Then she insisted, "You didn't hear Grandma say that. You never mentioned it until Lea brought it up." She had the 'command mode' in her voice. It was down to a precise art. "Right, Vicky?"

I responded, "Isabel, we've never even discussed the sundial before it became worth half a million dollars. But we never talked about Grandma's porcelain cat collection. All you ever talked about was the Hummel collection." Standing my ground was making me sweat.

"The sundial belongs to the legitimate next of kin," Isabel said. She was 'professional-grade' when it came to changing the subject. "That would be Tad. He's the heir."

Lea jumped right in, "Grandma made me the heiress."

Momma's fist hit the table with an alarming thud. "That would be me! I'm the only *heiress* that counts around here." We all looked at her. "You little snots took *my* sundial."

Throwing my hands out – palms up, I disputed, "I wasn't in on the sundial filching. I was in no way implicated."

"Sure you were," Isabel concocted the story as she was sitting there. "You and Lea probably have a deal to share the money if you testify in a court case on her behalf. You've been mighty chummy. If you get my *drift*."

Defending, I grumbled, "I wouldn't lie for either of you. I wouldn't lie for myself."

"You'd lie for Lea. You always favored her. Now you see a chance to get in her good graces and become wealthy."

Her allegation was infuriating me. Between my teeth, words were pouring angrily out. "Not that we even have the sundial to fight over. But I'm risking *your* tattling on me – even as we speak."

"Victoria Lee, whatever are you talking about?" Momma's question was insistent.

With a quick side-glance, I saw Lea's perplexed expression. Isabel was turning a dismal white-gray color. Her pursed up lips were so tightly drawn they looked like a butt-hole. She began to stammer, and it trailed off to a guttural sound.

As far as looks go, my face was probably the color of a Colfax Avenue whore's lipstick. "I'm sorry, Lea." My eyes began to brim with tears – tears that had waited for years to spill. "Momma, since I was small, for years Isabel has been holding it over my head. She saw me do it. I'm the one who turned over the wagon and spilled Lea out. I'm responsible for the accident. If it hadn't have been for me, when I was four-years old, it wouldn't have happened. Lea wouldn't have been scarred, and she wouldn't have stolen money and gone to prison. I'm responsible. I did that."

Momma's leap upward was like a runner going off her block. She stretched her body across the table toward *Isabel*. Her eyes were on fire. I'd never seen her so furious. "You told your little sister she'd done that?"

Words stumbled as Isabel answered, "Momma, there were only the three of us there. I didn't do it. So Vicky must have done it."

Momma's voice was an octave higher. "You told Vicky you'd seen her push the wagon over? Remember, lying is a sin. Thou shalt not lie."

"I didn't actually see it happen." Isabel paused collecting her excuse.

"You allowed Vicky to think she was to blame?"

Isabel's words rushed. "Maybe I did use it to make sure Vicky listened to me. I was the oldest, and she was such a wild girl. I guess I did use it to control her."

Momma pounded the table repeatedly. "Vicky did not overturn that wagon."

"How do you know?" Isabel questioned.

Momma answered, "Your grandmother saw the whole thing from inside. She was standing at the window – gawking out. Leandra was in the wagon. She'd been warned many times to sit still in the wagon and not crawl around or stand up. The handle was on the side, so the wheels were twisted. When Lea stood up, she leaned in that directions and the wagon tipped over. The scar was caused by the wagon's metal handle. She'd dumped herself over and landed hard."

"If Grandma saw it all, why didn't she say?" Isabel asked.

Momma answered, "Lea had been told repeatedly not to stand. She never listened. Grandma didn't want her to think it was her fault. She said Lea had been hurt enough, and punishing her for standing up would be an additional hurt for her. And at that point, we never thought it would go beyond." Looking at Isabel, Momma blasted, "And we sure as God is great never thought we had a little blackmailer in the family."

"Momma, I'm sorry. I guessed that it had to have been Vicky."

"You're apologizing to the wrong one, Isabel." Momma said, pointing to me. "And for the record – what Lea did – well, it was no crime at all compared to what pure crap you did to your sister. Shame on you, Isabel."

Isabel looked at me with both shock and some minimal shame. "I'm sorry, Vicky. I didn't mean to hurt you. When you were small, you were so difficult to control."

"Small," I shouted. My jaws were nearly locked in anger. "Goddamn you to hell. All these years I've lived with the guilt. Every time I looked at my baby sister – I felt self-vilification. I've been contrite my entire life. Now I find out I didn't do it. It's your fault for making me think I was responsible. You bitch."

Momma was silent. She wasn't going to reprimand my language at a time like this.

"Vicky, you thought you'd hurt me?" Lea asked, trying to comprehend it all.

"I've always felt I was to blame," I confessed. "I thought if you knew, you would hate me."

Lea's hand reached over and took mine. "Vicky, I wouldn't hate you. Even if you had hurt me, I would never hold it against you. You were a kid. I could never hate you. You always made me laugh."

Momma uttered, "Of all the things in the world, I want peace in my family. I don't think I could stand it if one of my daughters *hated* her sister."

"Well, that is exactly what you have now, Momma." I stood and walked to the door. "I hate Isabel. I'm not sure I've ever hated anyone before this. For over three decades, she's used emotional blackmail on me. She's continued to intimidate me. I've suffered more than any of you can imagine." I looked into Isabel's frightened, reddened eyes.

"Vicky," Isabel stuttered, "I didn't do it to hurt you. I only wanted to make you mind me."

"Mind you? You wanted to control me." I wanted to shout, but I couldn't gather the force from my lungs. I seethed my words out, "I hate you, Isabel. You put me through hell. And I *despise* you for it." I would never grace her hearthside again – ever.

"Vicky," she began. "I'm sorry."

Momma interceded, "Vicky, forgive your sister and don't stop loving her." Although she glowered, it was with a way of entreating my cooperation.

"Momma," I answered. "I've always tried to do what you said. But I don't forgive her and I flipping hate her."

"Please don't hate me," Isabel begged. Her eyes were filling with tears.

I wasn't sure she was feeling atonement or some inside anger at me for telling Momma. I didn't really care.

As I opened the door, I turned back. "Good luck in finding your damned treasure. If and when you do – go ahead and tear yourselves apart fighting over it. I sure as hell don't want it."

By the time I got to my car, tears were running down my cheeks. One part of my life was repaired. But another part of my life felt to be destroyed. I was no longer trapped in deep crevasse. Now I was snared in a different gorge. I understood this trap less than the one I'd been in for all those years.

I would never have to pretend to like Isabel. I would never again be subjected to her power. That alone gave me a satisfying exhilaration. There was also some weird gnawing at me – why had

I not stood up to her before? Fear? Of course, I feared her. I feared being hated by Momma and Lea for causing the damage to my sister.

On the other side of the coin – if I were a kind person – why would I not forgive Isabel? Using a word of Grandma's – I wouldn't forgive because Isabel was a *jackanapes*. Since I had no idea what a jackanapes was, and I didn't want to pull over to a side-street to look it up, I would call her another name. Char's favorite put-down name was jockstrap, and I would use it. Isabel was a jackanapes jockstrap and why should I forgive that?

I'd never told anyone in my family that I'd hated them. I'd never hated anyone in my family. Or anyone at all, I considered. I felt a surly mood coming on. I didn't want to ruin Charlene's day, so I figured I'd drive around awhile. Maybe go to the park so I could jog my trouble away.

Twice in my life, I'd left sunshine behind me. Once was when I was four-years old. And the second – it was today. Both could probably be attributed to hatred. Certainly hatred closes off the sunshine in lives.

Chapter 30

It was not one bit surprising to me that I had two calls from Momma on my iPhone. I didn't bother listening to the messages. Even Momma's dictates were of no concern to me now. She would begin by telling me to get right back there. She objected to her daughters walking out on her. It was a capital crime. I ignored the calls.

I pretended my wanderlust was born of freedom. Driving up the streets of my amazingly sweet little town, I thought of the childhood trips I'd take wandering through the streets. In and out of the small shops, I'd end up in a small candy store. I would purchase treats – buying each of my sisters and myself a freshly dipped and cooled piece of chocolate. They would be given to me in a small decorated box. When I would get them, I would examine them carefully. I always selected the one that was medium size for me. When I got home, I'd divvy them up, giving Lea the biggest and best. I'd take the middle size for myself. Then hand off Isabel's candy to her – the smallest portion.

Even back then, I knew I was being had by Isabel. She tried to make me believe she was hiding her information on my behalf. Deep inside, I must have known she was doing it to dominate me. She would exert her will – her commands. I hated it then, and I hated it now. But now, she had lost her power to keep me in line.

Foolishly, I thought my baby sister would hate me. Now I find that she wouldn't have. All the authority Isabel had once had now dissipated. The tyranny was turned off like a rushing faucet that ceases to spurt. No more gushing forth with the directives and ultimatums.

Momma now knew about what a deceiving, conniving plotter Isabel was. Lea knew her reason for disliking her eldest sister was well-founded. I found out the truth, and was vindicated of something I was accused of having done – but I hadn't done it. I'd always known Isabel was a schemer. And for Isabel – the f-ing chicken had come home to roost. All her goody-two-shoes laurels had been pitched away.

To boot, she'd always gotten the smallest piece of hand-dipped chocolate. If I'd liked her, she would have got the medium piece, and I would have taken the smallest candy. Lea still would have gotten the largest.

Glancing at my phone when it rang, I saw the phone call was from Charlene. "Hi," I answered.

"Hey, Babe, get over to your mothers STAT." Her words were rushed.

"I'm not going back there. My Momma has no right dragging you into this."

"It's Derwin. He's taken off."

"He's always taking off." I pulled my vehicle off to the curb and shut the engine so I could talk.

"Listen, he wrote a note to Dottie and left it in his room. He says he is leaving for good. Vics, he's got the damned sundial." She paused. "Did you hear that? He's running around with a goddamned sundial worth half a million dollars. He's run away from home for good. We've got to find him before he's hurt. His note said no one would ever see him again."

"Aw, shit." I covered my face. "Derwin has never left a note before. Or threatened not to return. Okay, I'm near Arlen's. I'll drop in and see if Derwin's been there. We've got to find him before it gets dark."

"That gives us three or four hours or so before twilight. The sky looks like we could get a late afternoon thunderstorm."

I gave a laugh of irony. "Just keep the good news coming." I looked at the skies. "Yep, storm-wise, it's going to be a bumpy afternoon and evening. Well, I'll check out the spots I know he likes to frequent."

"Do you want me to meet up with you? Honestly, I want to be with you."

"Yeah, why don't I drop by and pick you up. I can drive and you can search."

"Have you had anything to eat?"

"No. I haven't really been hungry."

"I'll throw together a sandwich for you. Also, I'll bring some bottled water."

I snickered. "How about an umbrella and a tent?"

"Smart ass." She allowed a few seconds to lapse. "Just drive carefully. I love you, Babe."

"I love you, too, Beautiful." As I drove, I pondered about Derwin's reason. He had taken the sundial. Obviously, for his own reason – but I'd bet it wouldn't have been for greed. Now he was out on his own. Knowing him, I figured he'd be terrified to come back home and face us. I doubted seriously if he'd ever stolen anything in his life. I had no idea where he would go. He was a rudderless kid who had let everyone down. This would be enough to keep him running for the rest of his life. He let down the people who loved him – the Brents. And his mother – she'd beat the shit out of him, and he knew it.

It hadn't taken long to reach the apartment. My 'boy-scout-prepared' lover was standing in front with a huge cooler. She placed it in the backseat. She smiled when she crawled in the passenger seat.

I greeted her as she kissed my cheek. "Did you think we're going on a flipping picnic?"

"Smart ass." She tickled my shoulder. "We might be searching all night."

"Yeah, my throat is parched. I could use a bottle of water."

She playfully shoved me as she reached back and dove into the cooler. "I should make you wait for the *picnic,* Sport."

"Okay. I'll cease with the snarky crap."

"You checked with Arlen?"

"He hasn't seen him. He'll call me immediately if he does."

"Your mother was in hysterics. What the hell happened?"

"Didn't she tell you?" I inquired.

"Just that you hate Isabel because she'd told you that you'd caused some accident."

"That's it in a nutshell." The car was quiet. Charlene didn't need to ask questions, only to allow silence to shrink me down to a babbling nonentity. "All these years I felt as though I was the one who tipped the wagon. I'd damaged my sister's face. I'd made her spend years of her life in prison for something I'd done."

"You'd done?" she questioned.

Explaining the entire story took several minutes. Conversations go so quickly when there isn't the comedic tales to spin in between the storyline. My eyes were filling with tears. I wiped them with my hand. I felt Char's fingers tenderly whisking them away, too.

Sucking air, I felt my tears and congestion in my throat. I admitted, "I even thought my father left because of me."

"Vicky, we will probably never know any more than we know now about your father. Some things just are unanswered. The mystery is unsolvable. We just have to accept. But trust me, no parent leaves because of a child. Accept that much."

"Sorry to burden you with this. And yes, that makes more sense. If one day I know why he left, fine. If not – I'll just have to let it go."

"You do realize the probability is that your family will never know?"

Deep down, I do know that. "Yes."

"What concerns me is that you've been on a guilt marathon all these years. Lea, your father – you've carried that. Why didn't you talk with me about it?"

"You?"

"Me. Remember me. I'm the one that shares a home, a life, and tons of orgasms with you. Wasn't I someone you could share that with?"

"Maybe I didn't want you to know how much I ruined the family."

"Hon, you were four-years old. That's barely out of diapers. Even if you had done it, it wouldn't have been your fault. I never have trusted Isabel. I think she's the saddest of all because she's such a showy emissary of good. Always has to have the reins. Now she's lost control, and she's lost the respect of her family."

"Momma is furious with her. Livid! That was Grandma's favorite word for *pissed off.*"

"So that's why your mother said she was disappointed in Isabel. Hell, your mother always treated her like she was the sweetheart of the Brents. Married, produced a son, not only goes to church, but is an unequaled do-gooder." Charlene, paused, considering.

"Momma is pissed off at me now because I said I hate Isabel."

"Do you hate her, really?"

"I've never hated anyone before. But I hate her."

"Yes," Charlene's words trailed slowly, "but in fairness, she was only six-years old."

I laughed. It was a dryly sardonic laugh – a jittery laugh. "All these years she's been holding it over my head. That carries it well into the age of consent."

"Agreed. But maybe she feels alone. You've always loved Lea. More than Isabel. And you were Lea's favorite."

"She was my favorite because I thought I'd harmed her. I gave her extra attention, and whatever I could. She was always starved for attention. So she loved that I did more for her."

I wouldn't mention the chocolate deal to Charlene. She was already immersed in an epochal, emotional skirmish of the Brent clan. There has to be a limit to what an in-law can take.

The waters of my family were muddied. Now the very skies of Littleton were beginning to pour. Those big Colorado gully-washers happened when the rains came up quickly and surely.

Predictable weather, I considered. For the next several hours, it would be raining until we'd want to put a stopper into the sky. Thunder began like kettledrums and lightening was slamming down to the ground. Waters were propelling earthward. The coolness in the air indicated hail could be expected.

I muttered, "Derwin is terrified."

Glancing over at Char, I could see her face transforming into concern. "I can't imagine what the hail will do to Derwin."

"It might knock down his little faux-hawk, but he'll survive. He's stronger than we think." Of course, I was attempting to comfort Char. Even with a little humor. We were both worried sick.

"Have you got hail insurance on the CR-V?" she asked, trying to get my mind off Derwin.

After taking a deep breath, I answered, "I do. But none of us have Derwin insurance. We've got to find that kid."

196

I felt Char's touch against my forearm – then a squeeze of encouragement. "We shall."

The screaming silence of pain merged with the shiny veil of rain that was falling. A shadowy blanket of clouds lowered into thick fog.

If there were to be a treaty with fate, I was praying that sanctions be lifted. I would do anything if we could find Derwin. I would even forgive Isabel if Derwin would be safe.

I issued a quick laugh. "Char, I remember talking with Derwin about you one time."

"About me?"

"He was saying how good looking you are."

"And?"

"I said if he was much older, and you were so inclined, you'd snap him up in a minute."

Amused, Charlene asked, "How did the little Romeo respond to that?"

"He said he was glad he was younger. That way you had to stay being my girlfriend. Because we belong together."

There was another silence. Char reached and wiped my tears away. "We do belong together," she affirmed.

Chapter 31

For over three hours, we'd been driving the streets, the allies, and the byways of downtown Littleton. We continued on through twilight and into the darkened summer night. We stopped to scarf down some sandwiches she'd lovingly made. I looked at the map app to find places I might not have considered.

When Momma called again, she sounded completely distraught, so I finally talked with her.

"Look, everybody here is sorry about today. Vicky," she coaxed, "you come home so we can talk. We need to be on the same page about Derwin. We're thinking of calling the police."

"Momma, if the police are called in, he'll certainly be taken to Social Services. Just give us another couple hours."

"Dottie opposes calling the police, too. She doesn't want them to interfere. He's money in her pocket." Momma's voice sounded as if she were completely disgusted. I could tell.

I shrugged my tired shoulders. "Momma, she makes money to watch him, and with his disability, and hers – she makes her living. Of course, she doesn't want him taken from her home."

Momma said, "It's getting late. Sully and Isabel are out looking. She said again how sorry she is about what happened."

"I'm surprised she's bothering to search. But they are looking for the damned sundial. Isabel probably doesn't give a damn about finding Derwin."

There was a pause. "I'm hoping she's searching for the right reasons," Momma answered. "She's really upset with herself for having behaved so badly with you."

"Momma, I don't believe that. Not really. She's sorry she was found out. Besides, after all the fighting and all the accusations, I'm not sure the family can ever be the same again."

"Both of your sisters apologized to each other for all the accusations." Momma was silent a moment. "Anyway, Lea said that Ari and she are going to be looking for Derwin after they close the shop. Maybe they already did, because they said they were going to close up early to go looking. I'm stationed here at home, sort of watching after Dottie. She isn't taking it good."

Charlene rolled her eyes and mouthed, *fuck her!* I held back a half chuckle.

"Momma," I argued, "Dottie is part of Derwin's problem. He should be able to take his troubles to her. He took the sundial. But if he had told her, she would have beaten him. She should have been there to comfort him." I felt like I was doing a closing argument. "If we find him, we've got to confront her about her taking care of him. Insist that she go through rehab."

"She's been through rehab twice," Momma stated. "She's always got an excuse."

"Yes. Always a peg to hang her shit on. But maybe if she thought she was going to lose a part of her income by losing Derwin, it might get her attention. Who knows, maybe she'll stop her sniveling and pick up her life. We'll see how this plays out. If she really understands that Derwin might be in major trouble out here alone – her motherly love might show. Even if it puts the idea in her head that her conniving games could cost her Derwin's love, she might change."

I wasn't adding my greatest fear. Someone might have beaten him up. Or taken off with him. Normally, he wouldn't have gone willingly with strangers. But the note he left behind indicated that he was in trouble. What, I wondered, would he be considering? Would he go with someone he didn't know or trust?

Momma interrupted my thoughts. "Maybe something inside her won't change."

"But it might. Sometimes it depends on the consequences. What it costs her."

"That child is out there alone. As a mother, she's got to see the dangers."

"Momma, I hope Derwin remembers everything we've told him. I hope he's safe. I just don't know where he'd consider as being a safe place for him. Certainly not his home. I want him to be safe."

"That would be one of my prayers answered," Momma said. "Are you and Charlene going to continue looking all night long?"

"I am," I glanced over at Charlene, and she nodded. "Yes, she is going to be with me. I was just looking at the map, trying to think of where he might be."

"Dottie and I told Isabel all his hiding places we know about. Then she and Sully looked at them all."

"I'm sure we all know the main places he goes. But this is different."

Charlene was motioning to me.

"Vicky, are you still there?" Momma asked.

"Yes. Char just said she has an idea. Don't go to the police before you talk with me again. I'll talk with you later."

"I love you, Vicky," Momma said softly.

Without responding, I hit disconnect.

Charlene's voice hurried, "You've talked with Derwin about hiding places. I remember you saying that you'd discussed it with him."

"What?"

"Okay, make a list of all the conversations you can remember having with Derwin recently," she suggested.

"I took him for a burger. We talked about his school." My memory unwound. "He talked about Grandma, her porcelain cat collection, and her cat, Diva. And he said you're beautiful. We didn't mention any place he might hide." I leaned back as I drove aimlessly through the streets in the downtown Littleton area. "Nothing is standing out."

"Okay, another conversation. Maybe when you were on the back porch? Or tossing the softball around?"

"No. I can't remember talking about it." I took a swig of water. Suddenly, I thought about him asking me to tell him again about the story of when I ran away. "I may know where he went," I said excitedly. "Yes, I told him I'd run away before. I had two runaway places."

"Okay, let's go. Where?"

"The Littleton Depot Art Center," I answered. I swerved at the next street to the right. "I'd hide behind the old building. There's that old caboose on tracks. I'd slip aboard and pretend to be going on a ride. It had just been placed beside the old depot. We've been there before." Someone bought the caboose as a display and it was placed on the old rails. It gave authenticity to the depot. It's even a historic landmark.

"Yes," she offered with a smile in her voice. "I love it. When we visit, I give my imagination free rein to think of the people who rode through Littleton on their way to the West Coast. All those stories."

"Well, I used to hide on the steps of the old caboose when I didn't want a scolding from Momma or Grandma. It made me feel as if I were going West during the gold rush. Walt Whitman even took the train through Littleton. He wrote a poem about it."

Charlene loved trivia. "You never told me Whitman as here in Littleton."

"It never came up."

Pulling into the parking lot, I watched for any shadows in the background. The depot had originally been built by the Santa Fe Railroad in 1888. I always loved its quaint building. It was converted to a lovely little art center.

Charlene grabbed the search flashlight. "Let's look around back," I suggested. "We need to search wherever a heartbroken, desperate little kid might run."

We ended approaching the caboose. I went to it and climbed to sit on the end landing. My eyes watered. Tears were mixing with the rains. My head went down into the V of my arm. Char hurried to my side.

"Vics, are you okay?" As she sat, I felt her arms slid around my neck. "It will be okay, Babe. We'll find Derwin."

"It isn't just Derwin. It's everything."

"Not everything. Your father abandoned you – he ran away. Even though you don't remember him now, you must have loved him because you're still hurting that he left. Now you love a little kid who runs away. And it hurts you. Don't you see the correlation?"

"You're saying I fear being left behind?" I hadn't considered that. Now, I thought, I would explore the idea. It sounded plausible. And perhaps it was right on the money. "You think that's part of my fear?"

"Exactly." She stood and stepped back down onto the ground. I followed. She took my hand as we walked. "It's romantic at night."

My head swung around, "Romantic? It's dark and we're here alone. It's a little too much detective story for me."

As we turned the corner, she issued a scream of fear. I jumped. She giggled, "You are the biggest scaredy-cat!"

"Yeah, and you just about became widowed." I took a deep breath. "Holy blazing crap."

"If we were married. An added inducement to matrimony is that it would completely piss off Isabel."

"Someday," I promised – however without commitment.

"Someday," she bantered. "Funny – that's a day that is not on my calendar. There is no date, no month, and no year."

"It's as near as I can get to calculating."

"Screw your calculations, Vicky. At least we can make it legal."

"Someday, we'll do just that. Right now, we're looking for Derwin."

"Babe, if we weren't looking for Derwin, I'd throw you on the ground and have my way with you. I'd be very, very brazen." Her flirty suggestion made me warm.

"Behave," I warned. "We need to find the fella. One more trip around the structure and the caboose." We continued wandering. With the light aimed at every area, we rounded the building again and the small train sections on the track. Dejected, I muttered, "Nothing, which means we go on to implement plan two. If I am shaking here, our next little adventure will have me in paralytic shock before we're done."

"Are you sure you told him about another place?"

"Yes. I remember because he wanted to hear the story again, and I didn't have time. Whoever thinks that kids don't listen is wrong."

"Derwin hangs on your every word. So where do we go next?"

"I told him I ran away and hid over by the creek – the gulch. I told him I hid out where there's a little brick building. It was for storage or something when they worked in the area."

"Let's go," she coaxed. "Is this gulch dangerous?"

"Of course, it's dangerous. At night, every wild area in Colorado is dangerous. There are wild animals around. You can see them in the daylight. Well, some of them mainly come out at night. Not only that – tonight there's rain. It'll be like a quagmire of quicksand. And who knows who is out there – maybe vagrants are hanging out."

"Well, hell, we might run into your old man and Derwin. Find both of them. Like a two-for-one special."

We both laughed. "You're serious, you want to go there? It's been decades since I roamed around there. I remember Grandma and Momma yelling at me when I'd wander off to play. You really want to go?" I asked again.

"If the kid is there, we've got to find him. He's in danger. We'll be okay."

I looked upward at a vicious shelf of clouds. The mood of the skies was terrifying. The serene storm was coming toward us and it was scowling. "We've got to find Derwin." I repeated.

Turning, I looked to see if there were any motions nearby the Depot. I'd wanted to see Derwin's thin frame. But he simply wasn't there.

Once back safely in my vehicle, I drummed my fingers on the steering wheel. All my life I wanted to pretend I hadn't been responsible for Lea's fall. Now that guilt was over, I was living my first guilt-free 24-hours in the gullet of certain danger.

"With daylight, the gulch isn't so bad. The dark and the storm make it a bad idea."

Charlene grinned. Her smile always knocked me sideways. She lifted her right eyebrow and blew a kiss to me. "Come on, lover. Be my hero."

The last time she'd said that – well, it was a star-studded night. I only hoped to survive this night.

It was then she delicately touched my chin. "Vics, I'll never leave you. I won't."

Chapter 32

The headlight's glow swam away into the distance along the gulch.

"Holy blazing fuck!" I exclaimed. That expletive was accompanied by pure trepidation.

Rain was beating down on us. I'd pulled into a parking area. The rain must have discouraged lover's lane folks from parking. Since I hadn't been there for a decades, I figured I might be out of touch. Rather than come here, chance getting stuck in the mud, or run off by the cops – kids are now cyber-banging.

Charlene grabbed the huge flashlight, an umbrella, and her rain jacket. I slipped my hoody on. It would be soaked in three minutes. "Let's roll," Charlene bravely ordered.

Our usual outing was a trip up into the mountains to climb or hike on a trail. That was fairly secure. We never hiked in the dark or in a rainstorm. Feeling the same fear as entering the alcove of hell, I mumbled, "You're sure about this?"

"Come on," she encouraged. "We've got to find him. Well?"

"I've always felt that I've been living a fixer-up life. Brave enough on the softball field, but this is a little terrifying."

"Vicky, you know what our favorite coffee barista always says — Go big; or go home!"

I thought about the young woman who fixed our cappuccinos. "Yes, but that was measuring the strength of coffee. We're talking fear." I pondered all the dangers. I heard the snap of thunder. "Aw, Geez," I whispered to the great dark night filled with unknowns. My shiver felt like dozens of squeezes per minute.

"We don't have an alternative. If we're terrified, and I'm not saying that I'm not terrified – think what a nine-year old kid is going through."

We exited my vehicle and began walking toward the creek. I could hear the usually timid waters of the creek slapping at the shoreline. When we'd sloshed our way to the dirt path that ran along the creek, we saw that water was pouring over the bank. "This is nuts," I commented.

Flashing the spotlight's cone of illuminations around as I led the way, I shined it over to the right. There was a rustle in a bush. I was happy my bladder wasn't filled. "I think it was just branches swaying in the breeze. Glad I took a leak when I was at Arlen's."

Char's chuckle sounded muffled by the rains. "Or as your mother says, 'use the facility.'"

"I'm pretty sure if Momma were here, she would instruct us not to 'piss our pants.'"

"Probably. But then she would make a sign of the cross." Charlene twisted around watching where the light was pointed. "I feel like making the sign of the cross here," she admitted.

"Momma would never be out here at this time. She never does anything dangerous without a confessional being available to her."

Charlene clamored, "I thought I saw something move over there."

I reeled the lantern back, swinging it in the direction she was pointing. "Mountain lion or bear probably." I teased. It very well could have been. Or a hundred pound possum. "I should have brought my Uzi."

She snickered. "Come on, Vics, think of the pioneer spirit."

I could hear the roaring splash of the water. "We're going to have to get off the trail and go through some of the bush area. The creek is filling quickly. This gulch is sometimes nearly empty."

"We'll just soldier through, lover." Her giggle was nervous.

I wondered if she thought we were on a park camping trip. The whoosh of wind was keeping tune to a Congo beat. She might be pretending she's in Africa.

I began silently praying. It wasn't a half-hearted prayer. I was all in. I asked the Creator to please allow us to find Derwin. I prayed for Derwin to be safe. If he wasn't here, I was out of places to look.

Moving nearer, I squinted, squeezing the rain from my eyes. The small structure was coming into view.

"I can see the little brick utility house from here." As we stepped down into the path, I grabbed her arm. Motioning, I said, "Stay over on this side. There's less chance of our butts getting swept away."

Hand in hand, we skirted the creek until we came to the small structure. Over the years, it had lost many of its top corner bricks. Other bricks sagged away, loosened by time. I saw the doorway padlocked. As we neared it, I recalled times when I was in my early teens. Afternoons, when school was out, I'd bring girlfriends here. I would sneak kisses from some of them. With the softball team, kisses needn't be sneaked. They were available.

Char evaluated the condition of the old building. "It is really a ramshackle old thing."

"If she knew you were coming, I'm sure Mother Nature would have tidied up."

"One would hope."

"Derwin," I called out. "Derwin."

I jumped when I heard noises coming from the other side of the building. My heart was battering my ribcage. I listened closely.

"I'm lost," his timid voice cried out.

Charlene and I hurried. He was curled up, leaning against the brick base of the old structure. When I leaned down on one knee, I felt his arms loop around my neck. "Okay, Pal. We've got you." I returned his hug.

"Vicky. You come to help me after I stole your old clock? I'm sorry."

Charlene comforted, "Everything's okay. Everyone forgives you. We're all worried about you."

I assisted him in steadying himself. Tears were rolling as quickly as the rains. "Why did you run away and take the sundial," I asked.

"'Cause I love you Brents. And your family is mostly peaceable. The sun clock made everyone mean to everyone else. I thought if I'd take it, everyone would go back to being nice again. Your Momma would bake cinnamon rolls and cake. Everyone would be happy again."

"Where's the sundial?" Charlene asked.

"I threw it in the creek," he answered. He formed those words proudly. Pitching that sundial was for the survival of the Brent family. In his mind.

I stood to look. Light from the lantern surfed the top of the rushing creek. As I walked carefully to the edge of the flushing gulch, I saw how quickly the waters were roiling. That word – yes, this was exactly what roiling *felt* like. The turbulence roiled. Now, I knew that word intimately.

Squinting, batting waters that were congesting my eyes, I surged. Suddenly, I could see the sundial. The top portion was sticking out of the canvas bag Momma had protectively wrapped it in. "It's out there."

Charlene was cuddling the crying boy to her. She said, "We can come back for the sundial in the morning. We'll bring rope, and try to lasso it in."

"No way. I'm going in for it now." I began my wade. My shoes sloshed as I entered the stream. "With this stream rush, it will be in Arizona by morning."

"No, Vicky!" she commanded. Standing, she came to my side. She was panicked. "Nothing is worth taking a chance. We know where it is. In the morning, we'll get it. Maybe Sully and Tad can help us."

I took another step into the cool, flooding waters. She grabbed my arm. "I'm getting that damned thing," I yelled. With a pull, I went to my knees, and Charlene slid on her butt on the muddy bank. I fought my way to my feet and began wading out toward the sundial. Carefully, I battled the waves. This was chancy and beyond stupidity. But Momma's dream was out there. I couldn't see it washed away.

Hysterically, Charlene was yelling something or other from the bank's edge. But I couldn't tell what she was saying, because the waters were now crashing. A roar blended with the fist of wind. Probably Char was calling me a blankety-blank goof. I didn't care. That stupid 'sun clock' that didn't even work meant so much to my family. I'd get it back for them – one way or the other.

Although I knew the dangers and that I could so easily be swept away, I continued. It became a compulsive act that I had no control over.

In pitch darkness, stars and moonlight were hidden by thick cottony cloud cover. I tried to see where I was stepping. Each step was with trepidation and care. Some of the rounder stones were difficult – and slippery with the goo attached.

Once every so often, a gush of water would hit me. My balance would waver and my feet fought. Then, when I was almost near enough to grab the sundial, I slid. My footing had hit the slippery rock bed beneath. I splashed as my frame did a body-slam into the creek. I fought the current to keep above the waters. Slowly, I was able to stand. There was a gash on my arm, but I barely felt it.

Charlene was screaming at me from the side. Although unintelligible – she sounded severely panicked.

"I'm fine." I yelled back at her. Then I reached out and pulled the bag toward me. Cautiously, I reeled it to me. When I lifted it from the waters, my sideline audience cheered. With my hands, I traced the feel of the sundial. Nothing felt broken or disturbed. The water must have buffeted its fall when Derwin threw it. Momma had also wrapped it in a towel. The canvas bag's handles looped around some branches that were in the stream – securing the sundial.

It had been a confluence of good fortune that saved it. Momma would say that it was a miracle. Now I had to save it by returning it to the bank of the creek.

Glancing inside, I saw it hadn't been injured. Pilfered, pitched in a raging drink with stones on the bottom, I was amazed that it wasn't busted to bits. Wrapping the handles of the canvas bag carefully around my shoulder, I began my sojourn back to shore.
It was a much longer return trip. I didn't want to fall on the damned thing and ruin it – after all that it had survived.

Besides, who wants to be impaled on a half a million buck treasure?

Grandma would have been proud of the sundial's endurance. I couldn't dare drop it or slip. She would want it safe. But then, everyone knew it had staying power. It lasted through centuries of pounding weather, and probably, the pillages that downed castles and occupants of those grandiose castles of olden days.

Both Charlene and Criminal Mastermind Derwin, were pulling me the last yard or two ashore. Charlene's tears flowed. She whispered in my ear, "I actually prayed," she divulged. "I actually said a prayer that you'd be spared."

Squeezing one another, I said, "Prayer may not make the difference, but at least it never hurts anything."

Nodding, she agreed. "Right now, I'm praying that you never scare me like that again."

"You saved it," Derwin exclaimed happily.

I looked at him and thought that maybe the sundial had saved us all. In a funny way, I thought about how I'd been freed from a terrible burden. My family loved one another. Lea would have forgiven me if I had pushed the wagon over, hurting her. I would need to forgive that horse's rear-end, Isabel. She probably doesn't wake up every morning saying, 'Please God, let me be a horse's ass today.' It just turns out that way for her.

"You saved it, and most importantly, *you*," Char said as she neared me. She took my face in her hands. With the coolness of this weather, I wasn't certain how her fingers could be so warm.

Derwin rejoiced, "Yeah, now that you got it back, maybe you can trade it on EBay for a new one that works."

"Maybe so," I acknowledged with a playful smirk. I reached to give his wet hair a swish.

I felt the warmth of Charlene as she hugged my body. This woman loved me enough to travel into the creepiness of night's peril with me. "I love you," she whispered.

How could I doubt her love ever again? "You really do love me?"

"I know you've always questioned my love, but I've got my insecurities, too. What if something happened to my looks? Would you still love me?"

"I guess we don't need to doubt. Never again. Not anymore." I handed her the bag. "Can you manage this? I'll toss Derwin over my shoulder. Fireman's lift."

"I'll hold your family treasure carefully," she promised.

I leaned down and lifted Derwin onto my shoulder. I was glad he had such a slim stature for his nine-years. Skinny as a rail. "Just relax, Pal. We'll get you outta this marshy mess."

Feeling his nod, I heard him pledge, "Vicky, I'm *never* gonna run away again. Not ever, ever again."

"Thanks, Pal. That would be the best gift you could give me. Stay. Please, just stay."

When I glanced back at Charlene, I noticed her eyes were damp, too. She blew a kiss. She knew from my expression that I'd caught that kiss and stored it in my heart.

The return walk wasn't any easier, but the rain had softened a little. Colorado rains are like that – their dispositions change. The sky was telling me the game wasn't over yet. It would probably rain all night.

It was still like walking on a muddy slipper-slide. It was well after midnight – probably around two in the morning. Both Charlene and I had turned off our cellphones. So if Momma was trying to contact us, it was of no value to us. We already knew where Derwin was. We also knew where the damned sundial was.

As we walked, Derwin's sagging body became heavier and heavier. But the poor kid had been petrified, and the least I could do was to give him a lift. From the look of terror in his eyes, I guessed he'd never want to run off again. Encountering this danger ensured that he would think twice about taking off. That was a fairly failsafe way of making certain he would always be safe and secure. He would honor his promise to me.

When we got to the car, I pulled two blankets out of the back and wrapped Derwin with one. Then the other went around the shoulders of my sweet woman. "I love you so much," I again whispered in her ear.

Derwin chuckled.

"Did you hear that?" I questioned.

"Yeah," he answered. "You'd be a fool not to love a hot woman like Charlene."

Chapter 33

We'd called Momma immediately before driving to her house. In front were parked Sully's car and a van with Tanovich Music Store creatively imprinted on the side panels.

"The gang is all here," I said. "Come on, Pal," I rousted Derwin from his sleep. "Let's go in and see Momma. Maybe your mom's there, too."

We walked in, and the entire Brent tribe plus add-ons were gathered at the large round table. "Where's his mother?" Charlene's brittle inquiry was a pre-stinger.

Char had just waded through weeds, mud, and whatever other misery might be lurking, to locate a child. This was not going to end without words.

Momma glanced up. "Why, she went home some after midnight. Mercy, it's nearly two AM. What happened to the three of you? You're wet and muddy."

With a fatigued voice, I answered, "Momma, we were searching for Derwin down by the gulch. It was raining and very, very muddy." I eased the canvas bag down on the table top. "Here's your precious treasure."

I could feel Charlene's heat building – and not in a good way. I'd only seen Charlene upset once before in the past dozen years. I didn't want to see it again. That time, she had caught an employee doing something deceptive. She wouldn't stand for fraud – and she hadn't! It was like, five, four, three, two – blasting the danged roof off.

She began by muzzling her thoughts. And went from there. I could see it. Finally, she asked. "Really?" she spoke while anger jabbed its way out of her throat. "Oh, we were out in the rain, risking life and limb, and Dottie got tired at midnight." Her hands went to her hips. "I just watched the woman I adore risk her very life. Call that bitch and tell her to get her ass over here *now* or I will go over there and drag that goddamned, lousy *mother* myself."

Momma's eyes were wide – in fact, big as saucers. "Pardon?" eased timidly from her mouth.

Grabbing my phone, I called. "Dottie, we need you to come over right *now!*" I listened to her barely coherent garbled excuse. "Get over here before all hell breaks loose." I commanded. By all hell breaking loose, I meant Charlene's rage boiling over.

Isabel quickly motioned, "We should put Derwin to bed." She stood.

"Yes," I agreed. "How about taking him to my old room." As she led him away, we said our goodnights.

Momma finally said, "Well, it's a fine thing that you found Derwin. And the family treasure."

"Yes," Lea concurred. The two men were speechless. They were smart. That quiet had provided the older man a life of nuptial peace. The younger man was learning by example. He wanted lasting time in the Brent family. He now knew how to play it. Quiet worked like a miracle.

When Isabel returned, she said, "He didn't even have time for prayers. He did say that Vicky went out into the water and saved the sundial. He said he still didn't know why she risked her life on something that didn't work."

"He thought we were going to throw it away, anyway," I offered, "since it didn't work."

"Vicky, you could have perished." Isabel said contritely, "I'm sorry about everything I did."

"You're my sister." I answered. "Aw, hell. I'll always love you both." We had a mini-group hug. Momma looked pleased. "And we love you, Momma."

I heard someone pounding on the back door. "Come in, Dottie," Momma called.

Once inside, Dottie nearly twisted her head off looking around at all the Brents and add-ons. "You found my boy?"

Momma answered, "He's safe. Vicky and Charlene found him. But he could have been drowned or snatched or lost. Don't you see it?"

"What?" she asked dumbfounded. A fringe of hair continued to slide across her face.

Charlene didn't bother to raise her hand to answer. She wasn't asking permission – she was in no mood to believe she needed it. She charged. "Listen, bitch. Your son could have died. You didn't know where he was, and you must not have given a flip because you needed your beauty sleep. What kind of mother does that? But then, we all know you are one of the most irresponsible mother's ever created."

Momma agreed quickly. "Dottie, you don't tend to that child. You never have. You can't deny that."

Charlene is such an excellent take-charge person. She pointed her finger at Dottie as if Dottie were about to go down for a major crime. "You don't deserve that child. I think we should call the police right now and have you arrested for neglect."

Dottie began to tremble. "You take that kid from me and my check gets cut in half."

"You're pathetic," my lover accused. "Here's the deal. Keep your damned check. But that little fella deserves better. If it takes this family to care for him – so be it. To me, it looks like they've been caring for him all along."

Dottie shook. I wasn't certain if it was booze or fear of the slammer. "You gonna take my kid offa me?"

Charlene continued, "The deal is – I think all of us should watch Derwin. He could stay some of the time here with Willa, the rest of the time with each of the sisters. What do you all say?"

I jumped in, "If I'm going to be working part-time, I could watch him when Momma isn't here. Well, we could. Char and me."

Momma added, "Of course, he's good company for me. He's welcome to stay here."

Lea grinned at Ari. She spoke tentatively at first. "It would be good parenting practice. Ari asked me to move in with him. I said yes, so we could watch him. If you want, Ari?" She said looking at Ari's face for encouragement.

"Sure, I'll teach him music," Ari said. "And he can hang out at the shop while we wait on customers. He loves hanging out there.

My Dad used to love when he came in. He'd tell me about how interested Derwin was in the musical instruments. Great!"

Sully glanced, presumably for permission. "I could teach him auto mechanics. Also tinkering with things – fixing things around the house."

"Well," Isabel added with a snooty tone, "it is the work of the Lord to care for children. Our house will soon be empty now. He could stay over with us, too."

Dottie disputed. "What you all doin' takin' my child away?"

Momma said, "We're giving you a choice, Dottie. We are taking charge of Derwin entirely. Until you get your life together – if you get your life together. Until you put up the bottle and your ways, and are able to prove to us that you're sober and sane. You will only see Derwin when the social workers drop by."

"But the money," she whined.

"Deal is," Momma continued, "as long as you're trying to get yourself sorted – you can keep the money. We keep Derwin. If you don't like that deal, just say so. I'll have the police here in five minutes – and you'll be carted off to jail. You'll never get him back."

I added, "Dottie, you need help. Once you're straightened out – you'll see what a wonderful kid Derwin is. He'll win your heart. Then you won't want to waste a minute being sauced. You'll want to be his mother. Prove yourself, and he'll be returned to you. If you don't, he stays with us. And you'll lose everything. You're approaching life in the gutter. Don't do that to yourself, and don't inflict that on your child."

"I got no choice." She crumpled onto the chair. Her head went down to the table and into her arms. "I got no choice."

Charlene answered, "Dottie, you've got a choice – clean up. That may not be your preference. We're not giving you another choice. That sweet child can't make his own choice." This time, her voice was soft as she continued, "One of my firm's clients is a rehab institution. They might be able to help you. I'll talk with them." Her eyes were filled with concern.

"My kid," Dottie's voice sputtered to a stop.

"He'll be cared for, one way or the other," Charlene said. Her hand rested compassionately on Dottie's shoulder. "Children deserve to be cared for and loved. One thing I know about this family. They may know how to fight – but they also know how to love one another."

She reached her other hand toward me. I felt us both squeeze. "Well, that went well," I quietly muttered into her ear.

She tipped her head. "Just draw up the contract. We've got signers. The deal is done. We all now know the boundaries. We know the rule of how it's going to be."

Chapter 34

Saturday morning, Charlene and I slept until noon. Momma's phone call awakened us. I pressed the message button. She wanted us to come to a late lunch at one o'clock. She billed it in as being a backyard picnic.

"Shall we give it a miss?" I asked my lover. We curled tightly together.

"Nope. We've got to be supportive. We're now co-foster-parenting with your family. Your mother will be orchestrating the rest of our lives. Until Derwin hits twenty-one."

"You did the deal," I reminded her.

She held me closely. "The kid needs us all. I saw the look on your face when we found him. You're right – maybe we *all* need the kid." With a hesitation, she closed her eyes a moment. "Vicky, I also saw you praying. I get that part of your life now. Your faith provides you with something special. I hadn't realized part of your strength emanates from that part of you. That's part of you I love."

"I do believe. Not all," I confessed with a grimace. "But I'm aware that faith must be personalized to work." I considered Momma's clandestine divorce. "Even Momma is a little cafeteria."

"Good. Because we've signed on for another decade of *us*. Family and all. No turning back." Her words were soft and comforting. "You'll go on a part-time schedule so you can write. Regardless of any treasure money. We'll deal with the finance."

Nodding my agreement, I said, "I'm not sure what you see in me. But I'm glad to know you see enough to extend my contract. I'm not gorgeous, wealthy, or exciting."

"Vicky, we went through this last night. And so many nights before. You just don't get it. No matter how many times and ways I say it. Has it occurred to you that I might worry about losing you? I might lose my looks – you might fall out of love with me. I'm older than you."

"I'd never fall out of love with you, Beautiful."

"But what if you couldn't call me beautiful?"

My lips curved. "There's not a moment I can ever imagine that I wouldn't be calling you beautiful. I fell in love with you. *You!*"

"Well, accept that I fell in love with *you*. You're irresistible. The way you express everything – that's part of your charm. That's why I want you to be free to do some writing. The first time we met, I noticed that you saw life differently. You explained what you saw in a different way. You make each corner of living new when you talk and when you write."

"You don't think I'm weird?"

"You may very well be weird. You don't think normally, Vics. You construct words differently. How you write isn't textbook writing or the way others approach words. Your approach is different. My job is creating – but it is more constructive marketing. So I appreciate the less traveled road, as Frost might say. I appreciate your creativity."

"Speaking of writing. I'd better post my blog."

"Relax. I did it earlier when I got up to go to the bathroom. I figured if you began tinkering with it, the day would be gone. So I pushed the 'publish' button."

I grimaced. "Plenty inventive." I would probably need to get used to her editing style. She already had been my encouragement and my Muse.

We bathed, dressed, and headed to Momma's for a picnic lunch.

For some reason, when we pulled up in front of Momma's there was a different feel to the home. I always wondered if there are spirits – like ghosts or angels or something, if they hang out and watch the people they loved when they were flesh, bones, and blood, etc. Maybe that's it. Grandma had hung out with us – then we pissed her off by being miserable. She wasn't in the mood for us acting out. Now, just maybe, she's returned. She's thrown Derwin into the mix, hoping the kid would keep us too busy to plot against one another.

Grandma's spirit might have given us a few shoves just to provide a little perspective. For that indelible night without time – we'd been complexly broken down. We were tearing one another apart and being torn apart by the behavior of everyone concerned.

On that same night, we could have lost Derwin – the same way we'd lost my father. But we didn't. Grandma must have been involved. It was to teach us a lesson.

The keynote speech Grandma was probably making would be a dilly. 'Okay, suckers – the money is out of range. Gone. But so is the kid. How do you like that, you ignorant, sinning, piss and moan, selfish earthlings?'

The thought of Derwin being harmed, hurt, and yes, the thought of him suffering enough to steal something – well, memories pressed me to my knees. I could see his smile – it always waggled before discharging. I could hear his voice saying something profoundly wise with its simplicity. His walk, his ways, his expressions, and most of all, the long trail of perfect love that he dispensed – it could have all been lost. We hadn't appreciated it. He told us the sundial was worthless. Without Derwin, the treasure was indeed worthless.

As we were getting out of the car, I commented, "So much has happened in the past week. This time last week, we were all making it from one pay day to the next. We've only had the possibility of being flush for a week. It nearly tore the family apart. We were all nearly ruined by suspicion and greed. For whatever reason, I've now been freed of something that's pained me for years. I was now wondering what the impact on the others really might be?"

Charlene shrugged. "Maybe your momma has made her mind up. That should show us if your sisters have softened."

"Conversion from avaricious snarkers isn't always easy. But just maybe they'll cure one another," was my conjecture.

Inside, we were told that Sully had his championship bowling match and couldn't be there. Ari was working, but Lea said he sent regrets. Charlene was there – that should have gotten her points with Momma.

Momma sat us down around the table. Her face was marked with serious wrinkles – all leaning into her question. She asked each of us what we'd do if we got a portion of the proceeds from the sale of the sundial.

She pointed to me first – probably since I'm the least contentious.

After thinking a moment, I explained it would help me do what I'd always wanted to do – write. Work part-time, and write, I'd stammered.

When she pointed to Lea, I hoped it wouldn't lead to a dispute. "Well, I thought it would go to fixing my face. But Ari likes me how I am. Before he knew about this windfall, he said he'd pay for the surgery if I wanted it. But one way or another, he loves me. So I'm not sure. I do know it will help give me a new start. A start with the man I love so much."

Momma's finger next pointed to Isabel. I gave a quick side-glance over at Char. We were both thinking that this might put an end to the niceties. Let the hostilities begin.

"Momma, I been thinking about it all. Tad doesn't want to go to college. I went into his room this morning. I asked him what he wanted. I'd never even asked before." Her eyes began to tear. "He wants a small van to travel all over the United States and take pictures. Then maybe he might want to go to a photography school to learn more. More than what he'd learned through his on-the-road experience." Isabel looked off to the side.

Momma stated, "Good parents listen."

"I asked him if he thought I was a good mother. He said I was, but I wasn't letting him go after the life he longed for. I apologized to him for being controlling. I need to stop being controlling and become more accepting. I couldn't even be that with my family and with my son. But now I'll try to be better."

"You've been a good mother," Momma complimented. "You always loved him."

"Yes, that I have. Loved him. So I'd take the money to buy him a van and pay for a photo school. Let him be what he wants." She glanced over at me. "I want to be done with my controlling ways." In her eyes, I saw the first genuine glimmer I'd ever recalled seeing. "So to fill up my house again, I'll have lots of time for taking care of Derwin. The life I've chosen should be for myself. But it can't be right for me unless I allow those around me to be what they need to be."

Momma sighed heavily. "Well, I decided what I'm gonna do. First off, anyone who disputes *any* part of my decision is going to be immediately cut out." She made a slice through the air with her hand. "Whoosh! Gone," she warned.

With a deep gulp of air, Momma began. "I talked to an auction house this morning. Those folks know their stuff. They'd had a representative at the Roadshow. I'd talked with him. They told me that the starting bid would be six-hundred thousand dollars. And it easily could top one million dollars. Since they'd had inquiries about it, as well as an offer, they figured it would be the higher figure. The offer came from a very interested large, prestigious museum. The auction house takes a percentage of the money – right off the bat. I did some calculating, and I figured if we split it five ways…"

"Five?" my sisters questioned.

"Five," Momma repeated. Her eyebrows lifted over a warning glare. "A share for me, a share for each of you, and a share put in a trust for Derwin when he's twenty-one. He'll need a start, regardless. We could each have a nice chunk of change after taxes and all."

There was silence. I finally spoke, "I think it's a great idea. I think Grandma would like it that each of the people she loved will have a gift that's of importance to us. She would also approve of it being in a museum where lots of people could see it and study it."

Remembering the admonition that they'd be cut out if they objected, my sisters quickly agreed. Momma was not going to take any pissing and moaning. I was glad to have a wise mother. Everyone seemed pleased with her decision. Char winked at me and I winked back. For whatever reason, things were now suddenly cohesive.

"Where is Derwin?" I asked.

"Outside. He figured you'd play baseball with him. But that might have to wait because lunch is almost ready. Lunch, then baseball," Momma instructed.

Lea asked, "Did you take the sundial back to the bank?"

"It's still outside," Momma said. "Derwin and I took it out to see if we could figure time."

Rapidly, we all rushed to the back yard. There on the round stand that lifted from the center of the birdbath was the sundial. It stood proudly, with elegance beaming from it. We gathered around laughing. Derwin giggled when we said it was an hour late. We set out the plates and glasses on the picnic table. As the food was being dispensed, eaten, and enjoyed, I listened to laughter and kindness. Amazing what good-will and buffalo-burgers with condiments slopping over the sides of homemade buns can do.

Plates were packed high with corn on the cob, lush salad, and baked potatoes with a spread of shredded cheese and a crumble of bacon bits. Momma mentioned that we might want to save room for silk chocolate pie.

Life was again dandy. The birds didn't crap all over the sundial. It didn't matter what time it said it was – it was a great time. Momma said they'd take it back to its vault after lunch. Until then, we'd let it get sun. Museums only simulate sunshine. So it may not get a chance for real sun for a long time.

We had our picnic, talked about our week of discord. And we laughed about our behavior.

One thing we all knew. Last night was indeed a night without time. But it was bright now, and we knew it's *always* time for sunshine and laughter. Lea, Isabel, Derwin, and Momma prepared for their Brent security-guarded trip to the bank in Momma's well-aged Honda.

I asked if she might want to get a new car. She said she'd decline until the wheels fall off her buggy. But she was thinking about a cruise somewhere exotic. She also mentioned she wouldn't mind having a vacation fling.

That shut us all up. In fact, I didn't say a word until Charlene and I were on our way home. Then I asked, "Think Momma really wants to get bonked on a cruise?"

"It would be fun for her. A shipboard romance! And why not? Everyone else will be doing what they want to do. I hope she does."

"Me, too." I thought a moment. "You're convinced I'll be able to write an entire book?"

"Sure. Write about your family. They'd make wonderful copy."

"Naw. Nobody cares about a family like mine." My face twisted into an objection. "Readers wouldn't care."

"Sure they would. I think it's a great idea. You can write about this *treasure* journey. That's what it seemed to be."

"Char, I'm telling you, no one would be interested in a family like mine. This sundial adventure might be considered dull. I can't see it being of interest."

"Don't rule it out."

I continued to drive. Thoughts were teeter-tottering their way through my brain. My sisters were characters, all right. And Momma was made of a sitcom.

Plot. What could the plot be? Just a lost sundial that changed our lives. And a kid? The main character was a small boy who was wanted and loved after all. Treasures aren't always as they seem.

I contemplated that perhaps they aren't seen clearly or appreciated adequately. When they are in your grasp – well, binding them to your heart is wisest.

With great satisfaction, Charlene spoke. "Vics, you must be considering it. You just passed our turnoff."

I captured a weak excuse and used it. "I was thinking that we forgot to bring the sack of vegetables Momma fixed for us."

"But I did remember to bring two slabs of pie," Charlene chimed.

I tipped my head toward her. "Okay, you're perfect. You didn't forget the pie. You're everything I want and need. Let's take the plunge and get married?"

Her index finger went to her ear, and she tipped her head. "I didn't hear you?"

"I was asking if you'd marry me. Will you marry me?"

"When?" she cautiously questioned.

"Whenever you want."

I was pretty sure she had a date in mind – and I knew we'd both be on time.

*

About the Author

Kieran York has written mainstream works including poetry and general fiction. She is the author of the lesbian mystery series featuring Royce Madison. *Timber City Masks* and *Crystal Mountain Veils* were written and published in the mid-1990s. She also wrote a collection of lesbian short stories entitled *Sugar With Spice.*

In 2012, York's book, *Appointment with a Smile,* was published and was a 2013 Lambda Literary Society Award Finalist in the romance category. Her next novel, *Careful Flowers,* was released in 2013. In 2014, Scarlet Clover Publishers released *Earthen Trinkets.*

York was also a contributor in *Sappho's Corner Poetry Series – Wet Violets, Volume 2; Roses Read, Volume 3;* and *Delectable Daisies, Volume 4.*

In 2014, her volume of poetry, *Blushing Aspen,* was published as the Sappho's Corner Solo Poets book of poetry.

Previously, during the seventies and eighties, Kieran worked as a reporter and reviewer for both newspapers and magazines and was a newspaper publisher for three years. She also wrote and performed songs with a woman's band. She has been guest lecturer and panel member at various events, including Rocky Mountain Book Exhibition, Colorado Musicians Series, Sisters in Crime Mystery Writers, and Mystery Writers of America, Inc. She is a member of Lambda Literary Society, and Golden Crown Literary Society.

She has written for *Journal of Mystery Readers International.* In addition, she has given numerous campus and coffeehouse poetry readings, as well as taught poetry and creative writing workshops.

She graduated from a Kansas University and attended Mexico's University of the Americas her junior year. She has done graduate work at the University of Colorado.

Kieran lives in the Rocky Mountain foothills of Colorado with her schnauzer, Clover. She enjoys gardening, music, literature, art, and theatre. She considers her valuables to include Clover and other family and friends, her library, her antique typewriter collection, her guitar, and her garden.

Additional information is available on her website. She has a blog – Embellish Your Smile at http://kieranyork.com.

www.ingramcontent.com/pod-product-compliance
Lightning Source LLC
Chambersburg PA
CBHW050524260626
47157CB00004B/1453